Novels by Annabelle Lewis

The Carrows Family Chronicles

Charlotte McGee, Book 1

Titan Takedown, Book 2

Carrows Justice, Book 3

The Bad Penny, Book 4

Fisher of Men, Book 5

Mr. Hyde, Book 6

The Boston Clairvoyants

Dead Cat, Run
Cut and Run

Short Story

Caliburnus

BOOK 7

THE
Carrows Family
CHRONICLES

ANNABELLE LEWIS

This book is a work of fiction. People, characters, places, events, and situations are the product of the author's imagination. Some historical names, celebrity names, and actual venues appear in the novel in order to place the story in a historic or modern cultural perspective, but these names are used in an imaginary context and do not suggest that any of the incidents ever happened, or the celebrities endorse the work, or participated in any way.

Contact Annabelle at annabellelewisauthor@gmail.com

All rights reserved.
ISBN-13: 978-1-7343757-7-0
First Edition

Publisher: PePe Press
Cover Design: JD&J Design LLC
Editor: Russ Rhode
Interior Design: Manon Lavoie

For my flower girls. Mommy has your back.

The Carrows Family Chronicles

Carrows Family

Henry Carrows - Patriarch, head of the clan. Henry's father was Hank.

Julia Carrows - Family matriarch.

Charles Carrows - Oldest child. Charles has hotels/casinos in Atlantic City, Las Vegas, and London. Father of fraternal twins, Velvet Carrows and Max Carrows, born in Book 6, *Mr. Hyde*.

Angelica Renner Carrows - Newly married to Charles. Pregnant in Book 5, *Fisher of Men*, with twins. Mother of fraternal twins, Velvet Carrows and Max Carrows, born in Book 6, *Mr. Hyde*.

Charlotte Carrows Macchi - Middle child. As a young girl she changed her name to Charlotte McGee, but then changed it back to Charlotte Sofia Carrows. After her marriage to Alex Macchi, she became Charlotte Sofia Carrows Macchi. Mother of Petunia and Lily.

Carey Carrows - Youngest child. Often works for Charles. A free spirit, flirt, and party girl. Often prickly and difficult to control. Dated Harley through several of the books. Married to Owen Kai in *Mr. Hyde*.

Petunia Carrows Macchi - Charlotte's child with David Torres Cordoza. Born in Book 1, *Charlotte McGee*. Adopted by Alex Macchi in Book 3, *Carrows Justice*.

Lily Carrows - Charlotte's child with Alex Macchi. Born in Book 3, *Carrows Justice*.

Velvet and Max Carrows - Charles and Angelica's fraternal twin babies, born in Book 6, *Mr. Hyde*

Whispering Cliffs - The ancestral family home in California.

Macchi Family

Anthony Macchi, Sr. - Patriarch. Deceased in Book 2, *Titan Takedown*.

Marie Macchi - Matriarch. Lives in Bay Ridge, NY (Brooklyn).

Alex Macchi - Private investigator hired by Julia in Book 1, *Charlotte McGee*. Married Charlotte Carrows in Book 2, *Titan Takedown*. Adopted Petunia Carrows in Book 3, *Carrows Justice*. Father of Lily with Charlotte.

Tony Macchi - Cop in 10th Precinct, NYC. Married to Abby. They have a boy named Riley.

Michael Macchi - Alex's partner in Macchi & Macchi. Married to Lauren. Michael and Lauren have two children, Leonor and Andria. The girls are cousins and good friends of Petunia Carrows Macchi.

Nick Macchi - Youngest boy. Lawyer. Runs Macchi & Macchi, London.

Isabella Macchi Laferty - Youngest and only daughter of the Macchi family. A good friend of Charlotte's. Isabella is a schoolteacher and married to Finn Laferty.

Finn Laferty - married to Isabella. Owns a farm outside Ithaca, NY. Prominently featured Book 2, *Titan Takedown*.

Renner Family

Angelica Renner Carrows - Charles Carrows' wife. She enters the series in Book 3, *Carrows Justice*, and uses an alias of Daizy Durand.

Dr. Patrick Renner - Angelica's father. Surgeon. The family lives in San Antonio, TX.

Natalie Renner - Angelica's mother.

Hailey and Diana Renner - Angelica's siblings.

Macchi & Macchi

Family-owned security and private investigations firm. The Carrows' go-to for all matters regarding personal security, hotel and casino security, muscle, and investigations—clandestine or otherwise. Branches in Manhattan, Los Angeles, and London. Anthony Macchi, Sr. began this firm, but passed away in Book 2, *Titan Takedown*. Oldest son, Alex, along with his brother Michael, now run it. Nick Macchi, the youngest, came on board in Book 4, *The Bad Penny* and now runs the London Branch.

Renzo Castrogiovanni - Bodyguard for Charlotte and her family. Single. Divorced.

Luco - Bodyguard for Charles and his family. Brooklyn-born friend of the Macchi family. Served in the military.

Sean Murray - Brother of Connor. Brought in for dirty deeds.

Connor Murray - Brother of Sean. Brought in for dirty deeds.

Santiago (Santa) - Brought in for dirty deeds.

Karla Fernandez - Crackerjack employee

Baach, McKenzie & Blake

Legal firm used by the Carrows with branches in LA, NYC, and London.

Oliver Baach - Founding partner of Baach, McKenzie & Blake. Close personal friend of the entire Carrows family.

Bruce McKenzie - Firm partner.

Allen Blake - Firm partner, criminal law specialty.

Recurring Characters

Owen Kai - Carey Carrows husband from Book 6, *Mr. Hyde*. Previous employee of Macchi & Machhi.

Bacon - The Carrows family's go-to hacker.

David Torres Cordoza - Petunia Carrows Macchi's biological father.

John and Rosita Gonzales - Factotum/staff at Whispering Cliffs. Have lived on the property since the Carrows children were young.

Cheryl Davis/Cherrie Corona/Paula Butler/Geneva Crawford - Friend of the Carrows family. Go-to for help on sting operations. She was born Cheryl Davis. Her stripper name was "Cherrie Corona" at an LA bar named Lacey's. Paula Butler was her alias used in Book 3, *Carrows Justice*. Geneva Crawford was the alias she used in Book 4, *The Bad Penny*. In Book 5, *Fisher of Men*, she returns with her birthname, Cheryl Davis, and is the manager of Angelos, a successful nightclub in Carrows London.

Jaqueline Dunn - Charles Carrows' primary personal assistant.

Tabitha Chapman - Henry Carrows' personal assistant.

Lloyd Greiner - IRS agent in Book 2, *Titan Takedown*. The family worked with him on a sting operation in Atlantic City.

Brandon Linnington - Son of Barford and Jane Linnington, Earl and Countess of Hambley. Brandon is an attorney in London who met Cheryl Davis in Book 4, *The Bad Penny*.

Linnington jewels - Reference to a parure of jewels originally owned by the Linnington family in Book 4, *The Bad Penny*.

Marcel Broussard - A personal friend of the Carrows family and go-to for sting operations. Based out of New

Orleans and introduced in Book 4, *The Bad Penny*. He owns the Broussard Gallery and has a dog named Steve.

Alana Whittaker - Head of Carrows public relations.

Summer Ash - Head of Carrows public relations in London.

Sir Hugh Brocklesby - New Scotland Yard investigator. Knighted by Queen Elizabeth for personal service.

Chapter 1

Clayton Krueger kicked hard at the dirt-packed parking lot outside his liquor store as the Bud truck unloaded. Having just fought with his wife, Penny, frustration overwhelmed him. Furious that she'd gone behind his back and met with a bankruptcy attorney, he felt out-maneuvered by such a gutsy, uncharacteristic move. They were a team; he was the captain, she was a player. He thought he had her under control, but Penny was no longer playing her part. It worried him.

They'd begun their relationship as high school sweethearts living near the small town of Crosslake, Minnesota. Neither one came from much, but together they'd been working the plan, building the dream life, one long day at a time.

Penny, always the achiever, had worked part time through school, squirreling away her money so she could make her own way. Immediately after high school graduation, she did just that. Landing a great job as an admin, practically running a body shop in Brainerd—the largest city in the area—she could finally afford her first apartment. About the same time, her mother and wild younger sister, who Penny had never gotten along with, abandoned Minnesota and moved to California to start over in a warmer climate. Penny chose to remain in Minnesota, and Penny's mom blamed the decision on Clayton.

The acrimony was no surprise. The two had never seen eye to eye, and anytime Clayton and Penny broke up—which was often—Penny's mom jumped at the chance to run down Clayton's character. Each time, her hope that they would stay apart backfired though, and Clayton and Penny had been together ever since.

Clayton's life growing up was a little different. The Krueger family lived in a small but nice home on the back lot of their family-owned business. The Backwoods Café & Bait was both a restaurant and convenience store. The café was a popular breakfast joint with the locals and the tourists, and the store offered the typical fare for last-minute needs. The Backwoods, as people called it, had been around for three generations and it kept the Krueger family alive, but not wealthy. During the brutal Minnesota winters, business dropped off, and even though deer hunters and locals kept the doors open, the Kruegers would take second jobs to stay afloat.

It was a hard life, but Clayton loved it. Or rather, he loved Minnesota. He was an up north guy. The lakes, the fishing, the hunting, the lifestyle, it was all he knew. The few times he'd visited the 'shitties'—the Twin Cities—confirmed home was where he should live. But it wasn't necessarily his plan to own and operate the Backwoods. In high school, he'd wanted to become a mechanic and took every tech class his high school offered. After graduation, he landed a good job in a garage working on cars, boats, tractors—practically anything with a combustion engine. He even managed to take some classes on electrical systems, which gave him a big bump in salary.

For a while, they did just fine. Clayton spent most of his evenings at Penny's apartment in Brainerd . . . when he wasn't with someone else. Which was a problem. Over the years he'd rationalized his deceitfulness with Penny and moralized that by keeping his private life a secret, he was doing her a favor. Why tell the truth? What she didn't know, couldn't hurt her.

Clayton reveled in the bar life, gleeful there were thousands scattered around the state to choose from. Especially small hole-in-the-wall places. The type you could find near every single one of the state's 10,000 lakes. And with hundreds of lakes in the Brainerd area alone, the options seemed endless. There was always someone new to meet or something happening in the area bars and Clayton loved to party. He was good at it, too, and knew he had a way with the ladies. Penny couldn't appreciate how difficult it was for him to remain faithful, but he did try . . . sort of. Anyway, he told himself he gave it a shot.

Because Clayton either stayed with his parents, Penny, or some other old or *new* friend, he lived rent free and could afford a fine Ford truck, perfect for his outdoor adventures. He spent all his available money on his varied recreational activities until the impossible happened and Penny got pregnant. Her doctor, who was clearly an idiot, had said Penny couldn't get pregnant. And while Penny's infertility had upset *her*, Clayton had been totally cool with it.

Instead, they were given a goddammed miracle. What could they do?

They decided to get married, and shortly after had a daughter, whom Penny named Violet. She was a cute baby, and Clayton loved her, but he didn't try very hard to develop a relationship and he certainly never spent much energy taking care of her. But he always put in just enough. Just enough time, just the right words, and just the right gesture to keep his home life together and Penny in line. And it worked. For a while.

And then life changed again.

When Clayton's parents decided to retire, decisions had to be made about what to do with the Backwoods. Clayton's older brother, serving a three-year prison sentence in Stillwater on a meth charge, was out. If they wanted to keep the Backwoods in the family, Clayton would have to step up and become the fourth generation to own it. *If* he wanted it. And he surely did.

Being a bar owner was Clayton's big dream. Hanging out with the customers, letting other people do the lion's share of the work, being a big shot owner, that was *it* for him.

The problem was, the Backwoods didn't have a bar. It had a small, thirty-seat restaurant that catered mostly to the breakfast crowd. The attached convenience store sold a lot of bait, chips, soda, and Minnesota's own 3.2 beer, but no liquor. The place needed a real bar, and Clayton knew he'd finally be the Krueger to make the Backwoods a really big success.

But he had to convince Penny.

Because by then, Clayton was a married man, with a kid. He schmoozed like hell to convince Penny to give up their apartment and move back to the country. His vision—*his dream*—was to move into the Krueger family home, expand the Backwoods, branch into the liquor and party business, and maybe update the house a little. But Penny was a hard sell. She'd watched the Krueger family struggle for years to keep the business and their lives afloat. At least in Brainerd, she'd argued, they both had good jobs and health insurance. And the roads were plowed regularly in the winter, and not by them.

Clayton, not dissuaded, went ahead and met with a couple of bankers to talk about loans for his dream. Oddly, they too were reluctant to embrace his big plan, but did agree to lend them *some* of the money, at which point Clayton realized he would need to modify the upgrades. He could only afford a small expansion of the Backwoods, which included a short bar nestled in an off-sale liquor store addition. The Backwoods would at last be able to sell beer and booze so people could have a Bloody Mary with their breakfast. But further expansion would be delayed.

Clayton thought it was a pretty good compromise. And with a hard campaign—a few nice dinners, declarations of undying love, some real elbow grease around the apartment, and a few tender moments with the kid solidifying the family scene—he sold Penny on the plan.

After Clayton's parents left for Florida, Clayton, Penny, and Violet uprooted their Brainerd lives and moved into the Backwoods.

And it all went to hell.

The first problem was they had to quit their day jobs, which meant no steady income and no health insurance. In addition, the loan for the remodel and new liquor inventory meant a huge debt load. Even though the bar doors were open, it took time for the world to catch on. Plus, it turned out most folks preferred to buy their beer and liquor from cheaper big box stores, especially the liquor. That just sat and sat. They moved the beer, but almost no one came in at night to sit in the small bar to shoot the shit with Clayton. There were better places to go.

Clayton and Penny worked long hours, neither having appreciated how hard it was for the elder Kruegers slogging through their day-to-day. The cinnamon rolls alone were enough to make them cry. The Backwoods was famous for them. They were by far their biggest selling item, their biggest draw. People expected them to taste the same as they had for years, and when Penny, who had always been an avid runner, tried to change the recipe to make them less fattening, the customers were unanimously upset. They complained so loudly she went back to the original recipe and rolled out the lard-laden dough each night, going through the time-intensive process to keep the rolls traditionally gooey. Decadent and delicious, but a product of drudging, time-consuming labor.

Clayton didn't help with the rolls, but he was good with the bacon and eggs, so he was the short-order cook. *When he felt like it.* Young Violet had been with them in the kitchen or restaurant from the start. From the age of eight, when they moved in, if she wasn't in school, she was working. Violet learned to cook and was a big help in the kitchen. She was a hell of a good waitress too. Capable, Clayton thought. So why shouldn't she help out?

But the years of arguments, living poor, and hard labor took their toll. The fighting and backstabbing became a part of their every day, particularly around their goals for raising Violet. Clayton saw the writing on the wall and knew something needed to change, but his idea of change and Penny's were wildly different.

Just that morning they'd had another of their ever-escalating arguments.

"It's. Not. Working. Clayton. What part of that sentence do you not understand?" Penny had gritted her teeth at him.

"You're just being short sighted! I told you, we've got to give this thing a few more years. At least! Mother of God, Penny! This is my parents' *legacy*. My *grandparents'* legacy. Doesn't that mean anything to you?"

"No. It doesn't. Not anymore. I want out. We're broke, and the debt is crushing us. We haven't had any real income since we came here four years ago and now you want to cut our health insurance too? I won't have it, Clayton! You, me—*one of us* has got to get a full-time job, with benefits, and pull in some real money if we want to make a go of this. I know *you* don't want to get up at four a.m. to get the rolls going, so *you* need to get a job. I'll hire a short-order cook to help in the kitchen. It's the only way."

"Just use Violet! She can do it. She's twelve now for God's sake! We were both working summer jobs when we was twelve—she can too."

"It's not what I want for her! It's one thing for her to help occasionally, but now you're telling me you think we should homeschool her and have her work here full time. That's bullshit, Clayton. You're not going to homeschool an eighth-grader and neither am I. We need to cut our losses and get the hell out of here. My mom said we could live with her rent free in California if we wanted, and I want Violet to be settled somewhere before she starts high school. She needs an opportunity for a *real* life, Clayton. She's not the adult, we are. She's not the one who got us in over our heads in debt—that would be you."

He stabbed his finger in her face. "Bullshit. You agreed with me every step of the way. You knew what we were signing up for. I told you this thing was a *long-term* investment. Not a *short-term* one. You agreed to it. Now we just need to make it work. Everyone needs to pitch in."

"I'm calling your bullshit, Clayton, because you haven't pulled your weight around here since the day we pulled into the lot. You know it and I know it. It's not working, Clayton. I want out. Do you hear me?"

"Shut the fuck up, Penny. We'll talk about this later." He turned to leave.

"I left the card for the bankruptcy attorney in the office. Call him. He said he'll speak with you separately at no charge. Do it, Clayton. I mean it. It's time."

He was halfway out the back door to meet the beer truck as she finished her last sentence. This was all bullshit. He knew they could make it. He knew it! They just needed to expand the place and turn the little bar into a big bar. Something to draw crowds at night. Something serving food at night too. Maybe pizza delivery. The place would take off if he hosted a few bands, contests, meat raffles, and some events. His lifestyle, his *life* was wrapped up in this place. Move to California and live with her stupid mother? What the hell kind of plan was that? No way. He was never leaving Minnesota.

The problem was Penny's signature was on everything. All the documents, all the loans, and he needed her to run the place. She was at least right about that.

If I do go back to being a mechanic . . . Dammit! No!

He'd need to work full time at a good garage to pull benefits and he did not want to get into greasy coveralls every morning and punch a clock. He would never sell his place; he just had to come up with a better plan.

Clayton gave a chin jut and wink to the Budweiser driver as the guy rolled shut the back of his truck and turned to leave. *I'm a bar owner. That's who I am. No one is going to take that away from me.* He spat in the dirt and glared back at the door to the Backwoods.

Luckily, he'd been thinking about a solution for quite a while. Penny might think he was short sighted and lazy, but by God, he was *proactive.* He'd been working on his insurance policy for the last *year.*

And her name was Ginger.

Chapter 2

A nd I don't want anyone to know who we are," Petunia beamed at her parents as she wrapped up her presentation to sell them on her vacation plans.

Charlotte held her smile in check as she glanced at Alex's face to gauge his reaction. Amused by his apparent bewilderment, she turned to their beautiful eleven-year old daughter, and breathed in, enormously grateful Petunia was a part of their lives. With her unruly mop of dark curly hair and freckles across her nose, she was growing tall and into a lovely young girl, glowing with health. Her daughter was also born with a strong personality, which she thankfully only wielded for good.

Petunia kept the family on their toes and was loved deeply by all, but she was born a Carrows, and that came with baggage. Both good and bad. Over the last couple of years, her face had been the target of paparazzi, her name shackled to the terrible custody scandal that landed her thief of a biological father in prison. Unoriginally, but effectively, dubbed "the poor little rich girl" in the press, Petunia sadly, but bravely, bore the brunt of her infamy. The Carrows family and her adopted father's family—the Macchis, did everything they could to protect her. Still, in public, people often stared at her and her family, and too many times, aggressively approached or even verbally assaulted all of them.

Delighted, though, with her daughter's zest for life and her ability to energize the troops to her bidding, Charlotte smiled knowingly at Alex as he patiently folded his hands and took charge. "I see. That was a very thoughtful and oddly detailed plan and itinerary you just laid out there, honey. Have you been working on this for a while?"

"Not long, at least on the details, but the idea has been percolating for a while, Dad. I think I need to see some of the country, and I think I need to see it from the vantage point that most people do and not from five-star hotels. *And*, I think we should go incognito."

Petunia paced in front of them, throwing out her hands for emphasis. "I know that won't be easy, but I was thinking if Mom left her jewelry behind, and maybe if none of us wore any cool designer clothes, you know, anything with a big label, and maybe if we shopped at big box stores for shorts, and goofy T-shirts, Keds, some regular hiking gear, you know, we could blend. And if we traveled by RV, it would be perfect! We could all fit in one vehicle and make regular stops all across the country. We could meet people we wouldn't normally meet, and I would feel more like a regular person. Not that I don't feel *regular*, you know, or *grateful*, it's just that I know there are people living life so differently from me, and I'd like to experience that this summer. My teacher said a road trip would also be a great summer story for our fall project, so I'd even be ahead in school if I kept a diary."

"My goodness," Charlotte grimaced. "How long did you say we'd be gone?"

"Well, I thought at least two weeks. I mean, driving time alone will eat up a lot of that, and we'll need to stop and see things." Petunia waved a hand through the air. "Listen, I've got it all mapped out. I think we should head west and zig zag around and eventually make it to Yellowstone and maybe Colorado. That could take a couple of weeks, and if we returned the RV out west and *flew* home, we wouldn't have to spend valuable time driving both ways. So, what do you say?" She bounced from side to side, exhibiting jazz hands and a large theatrical smile.

"I think it's a great idea," said Charlotte. "I do. There's a few details to work out, but I love it. What do you think, Alex?" she asked, knowing that outnumbered he wouldn't dream of throwing a damper on the plan.

He raised a practiced eyebrow. "Two weeks? Two weeks in an RV. And who is going to drive this thing?"

Petunia pushed her arms forward. "Dad! You can drive! I'm sure you can drive it. And what about Renzo? He'll help. I'm assuming he'll be coming with us." She threw her head back laughing. "Oh my gosh, maybe we can get him one of those fishing vests with a goofy hat! Oh, oh, oh—shorts and socks and sandals! That's what he'll wear!" She trailed off in a fit of giggling.

"Petunia," Charlotte scolded. "He's not a doll for you to dress, he's a man who happens to work for us. He protects us. We can't ask him to wear anything he's uncomfortable with."

"Mom! He will! I know he will! He loves us! I know I can convince him to have fun with this. Really. As long as he can pack his gun, he'll be cool."

"Yes, well, I don't really care to think about that," Charlotte said, uncomfortably reminded of their day-to-day security issues.

"Come on! Lily will love it too. You know she will. Think of the tents and camping we can do in the Badlands and Yellowstone. We can do some fishing and hiking! Now that she's potty trained, we can take her anywhere, right?"

"Were you thinking of inviting anyone else? A friend, maybe?" Charlotte asked.

Petunia shrugged, her face suddenly serious, as her head dropped. "I thought about it, but I think this should just be a family thing. You know, just us, and Renzo."

Charlotte nodded at her daughter's sudden downcast look. She knew without being told the reason Petunia might be uncomfortable asking a friend to come along. Her best friend, by far, was her Macchi cousin, Andria, who was the same age. Petunia had many wealthy friends from her school and dance academy whom she socialized with, but she'd told Charlotte and Alex that she was beginning to feel competition from some of them and it made her uncomfortable. And Andria—by any accounts living a comfortably wealthy life—was not in the nosebleed section of wealth that Petunia and her Carrows family were in.

Charlotte recognized Petunia's angst, caused by her plan to rub shoulders with "regular" people, which might make her sound like a reverse snob. Charlotte, Alex, and even Renzo had had conversations about Petunia's worry her words would be misunderstood and she might embarrass herself or hurt others. Petunia realized their wealth was a high-class burden, and it meant she sometimes felt differently than other people. Charlotte herself had struggled with the issue growing up. It was Charlotte's and the family's responsibility to teach, guide, and support Petunia in learning to fit in.

"Are you sure you won't be bored just hanging out with the adults and your little sister?" Alex crossed his arms, a look of skepticism on his face.

"You know the only friend I'd really want to go with is Andria, but I don't know if she'd want to go. And if I asked somebody else, you know, then Andria would get her feelings hurt and I don't want that to happen."

Understanding the unspoken words, Charlotte put on a bright face and looked at her husband. "Well, Alex, I'm in. What about you? Can you take off for a couple weeks and drive a recreational motor home across the country?"

He glanced between them. "Of course I can. I think." He frowned. "I've never driven one, but I suppose I could figure it out."

"Yes!" Petunia threw herself into his arms. "I love you, Daddy, thank you."

Next, Petunia launched herself on her mother. Charlotte soaked up the love and held her daughter tightly as she stared over her shoulder at her wonderful husband who, although dubious, looked as happy as she did.

Chapter 3

Alex walked down the hall toward his home office and did a double take at the latest side table Charlotte and the decorator must have added. He stopped in front of the antique French table, pulled open a drawer, and smiled, surprised to find a cache of Petunia's favorite Tootsie Pops already tucked inside. While wondering who put them there, he peered down the hall before grabbing a cherry one. He unwrapped it and walked into his designated private space—a very masculine office in their practically new, remodeled home in the West Village of Manhattan.

It had taken over a year, but their dream home was finally complete. The 14,000-square-foot architectural masterpiece was finished. Somehow the interior design group had made the generous proportions feel livable and welcoming. All the headaches had been worth it. Boasting six floors, including an outlandish private rooftop terrace, the space could accommodate guests with its seven bedrooms. On the sixth floor, away from the family rooms, were two staff bedrooms, each with a small private kitchen and bath. In addition to a basement garage and the rooftop terrace, there was a large, landscaped garden, five wood-burning fireplaces, a gym with a barre and mirrored walls for Petunia's ballet, an elevator which ran throughout the home, and, of course, a state-of-the-art security system.

Alex sucked on the candy and put his feet up on his desk, quite happy with the place. He picked up his phone and messaged Renzo to come to the office.

Renzo Castrogiovanni had become more than employee, more than a part of their protection team; he was family. That said, the transition to the new house hadn't been without hiccups and some grumbling, but Renzo had finally accepted the invitation to live with them full time. It was a practical decision as they needed someone around at a moment's notice for their active schedule, and the challenges of Renzo's commute were taxing on him.

Renzo took his security job seriously. As a twenty-year employee of Alex's security firm, Macchi & Macchi, he was working for the boss in all ways and had to carefully tread the line between his employment duties and their personal relationship. He'd only agreed to the live-in position on a trial basis. Now, Alex knew there was another twist for the big man that would need to be handled delicately.

"Yo," Renzo said, entering the room.

Renzo's large frame on his 6' 5" body somehow always surprised Alex. The guy was simply imposing. The effect he had on people, Alex included, was impressive.

He pulled his feet off the desk and waved the Tootsie Pop at a chair. "You got a minute?"

Renzo sat in large chair and stroked the leather, looking down the sides before giving the arms a hard pat. Renzo, too, was getting used to all the new home decorating items which seemed to appear on a daily basis.

"Nice chair," he pronounced, settling in.

Alex put the sucker down on a piece of paper and got right to business.

"I wanted to talk about the in-house staffing issue," he began.

Renzo held up his hands. "Boss, I don't want to blur the lines here. I get that this isn't like a forever situation. I don't want any confusion here about my job and a long-term tenancy."

Alex shook his head and smiled. "We appreciate that, Renzo. This is all new to me too, you know. At Whispering Cliffs—Rosita and John, they run that place and wear those duel hats of both staff and family. God knows I wasn't raised with live-in help, so it doesn't come naturally to me either, but I think we can figure it out."

Thinking of Charlotte's parents and their live-in staff, he wondered if maybe he should talk to Rosita and John and get a take on how they made it work? But he knew he was procrastinating.

Rubbing his hands together, he got back on point. "Speaking of in-house staff, I want you to know we've finally hired someone. Charlotte and I agreed it would be nice to have someone run the household, so we could focus on the girls and our lives. You've heard rumblings about a dog too. Now that we're finally settled, it'll be nice to have someone here to watch over things and the shaggy beast whenever we're away."

Renzo moved uncomfortably in his chair, straightening his jacket, his hand readjusting his ever-present holster and weapon resting on his side.

Wondering if Renzo was aware of his habit of touching his firearm whenever a wisp of uncertainty blew his way, Alex continued, "The gentleman's name is Havish Khan. We did a deep background check on him and his family, and he seems like a decent guy. Charlotte said he's going to be our majordomo—whatever that is—so he'll be in charge. He can bring in day staff to clean, or cook, or whatever. He'll wear a number of hats. Charlotte and he will work that part out."

"What do you know about this guy?" Renzo gave him a hooded look.

Alex cocked his head. "Quite a lot. He and his parents were born here. His parents have been doing the 'in service' thing for most of their lives, so he's familiar with the lifestyle. Havish is in his mid-thirties and has a background in the catering industry and he enjoys cooking. But he was ready to try something different.

"He'll have the bedroom next to yours, but of course, you'll each have your own bath and kitchenette. You'll need to include him on all our security systems because he'll obviously need full access to everything in the home, with the exception of the safes, of course."

Renzo harrumphed, skeptical, but Alex pushed on, selling the guy and the plan. "I think you'll like him, Renzo. He's had an impressive education, he seems interesting, and he's Hindu, which is pretty cool. You'll still keep an eye on things, of course, but I'm not worried about him. Maybe he can help during our own transition months, figuring out how we're all going to live together. Keep me in the loop if any problems come up and keep the communication lines open with Charlotte and we'll all take it a day at a time."

Renzo's doubtful look never left his face, but he promised to give the guy a shot.

With remodeling and household staffing issues aside, Petunia's proposed RV vacation was now the family focus. In his home office, Alex peered closely at images of yet another monstrous RV, knitting his brows with concern.

"My God, Charlotte, look at the size of some of these things. And trailing a car behind it? How am I ever going to turn into a tight spot or back up? And the sewer lines, and the water lines; those look like a dream to deal with, too," he said sarcastically.

"Honey," Charlotte laughed. "You'll do fine! All three of us can learn how to drive it. We'll take turns. As for hooking up the sewer and water systems, if you absolutely insist on managing that, I won't object." She began rubbing his back and stared intently at the monitor over his shoulder.

He turned his head and glared at her impish smile, then turned back to the screen. "Right. I can't wait. Renzo and I are going to Jersey to see the 'Salon Bunk' model this weekend. They said I could give it a test drive to see how it handles. They'll walk me through it, but I have a feeling it's going to be more complicated than it looks."

Charlotte kept up the shoulder rub as she gushed over the pictures. "It's gorgeous too. Just look at it! Televisions, a functional modern kitchen, a shower, enough room for all five of us to sleep—we won't even need hotels."

"Really," he said, fully turning in his chair, staring at his wife. "You're completely cool with everyone showering in that tiny closet, doing the laundry when we pull into RV parks every evening, cooking, cleaning, and maintaining all the facilities. You're sincerely ready for all of that?"

Her eyes wide, she blinked slowly at him. "Well, I think this is what they call family bonding, darling. Yes, we're going to be stuck together for lots of hours in the mobile home when we're not sightseeing, but I think you're looking forward to it as much as Petunia. Renzo's okay with the plan now. He's on board, don't you think?"

"I think he'll feel better once he sees the security systems on these luxury models, but I don't think this is quite what Petunia had in mind when she said we'd travel *incognito*. Some of these rigs are a couple million bucks, and other people—especially other owners of motor homes where we'll be forced to stay—they'll know the difference."

Alex turned back to the screen and scrolled through the options. "We'll just have to compromise once we see what each model has to offer. Find something middle of the road. The security setup is our primary concern. We're really going out on a limb here, all alone in the wilderness, especially if we run into someone who recognizes us and decides to act badly."

It put a damper on their enthusiasm. "It'll be okay, Alex. There might be some people out there who recognize us, but we'll be so out of place, I'm sure most people won't even give us a second glance."

"They're gonna look twice at our palace on wheels," he said, jabbing at the screen, but then he turned and saw the look of worry cross his wife's face. Swiveling his chair again, he pulled her into his lap. "And what happens when they get a look at you? The most beautiful woman on the planet. They'll be standing in line to catch a mere glimpse of your lovely face," he said, kissing her.

She placed her forehead against his. "Speak for yourself, honey. I suspect that once the women in the RV parks get a good look at you, all manly, wrangling those sewer lines, looking all hot and bothered, they'll stampede over to help."

Alex smiled and whispered, "Ah, but at night, we'll be

all alone, tucked into our bed, a stone's throw from Renzo's snoring with the baby between us. It'll be heaven."

Charlotte laughed and got up from his lap. She moved over to a sofa and pulled her knees up, tucking them under her chin. "My family supports this trip too, you know. Mom said she thought it was a wonderful idea to get out and stop being so afraid all the time. She thinks we all need to shake the cobwebs of constant espionage off and live a little. She said she didn't want us to live paranoid."

Alex rocked back in his chair. "As usual, I'm sure she's right. We've done about as much planning for this road trip as we do for one of our campaigns, but now that's its close, I've got to admit I'm excited."

"A trip to remember, that's for sure." Charlotte smiled.

"Your brother told Renzo he wants to see a video of me the first time I try to park it. I think your entire family is enjoying this."

"Maybe we'll start a tradition." Charlotte brightened, "Maybe once Velvet and Max are older, they'll want to join us for a trip across America."

Alex remembered a beautiful moment when the ever-cool Charles lost his stylish façade because his twin babies had taken turns throwing up on him. Charles and his babies in an RV? That, he'd love to see too.

"And Carey and Owen? Do you see them on this fantasy trip as well?" he smirked, referring to Charlotte's unpredictable sister and husband.

"Hmmm, maybe not. I think Owen would be game, but Carey might have a ways to go."

"They're spending time outdoors this summer," he joked.

Charlotte laughed. "On a bespoke African safari. Not exactly roughing it and wrangling sewer lines."

Alex gestured to the computer screen. "We won't exactly be roughing it either, dear, especially since we convinced Petunia to reconsider the tail end of the trip."

He watched as she pulled a throw pillow up and lay down, curling her lean and shapely body around it. She pushed her long, dark hair back from her face and cooed dreamily, "The Rustic Inn in Jackson Hole for the last two nights before we fly home. That will be nice too. Kayaking, horseback riding, and rafting, maybe even do a little spa-ing? Is that even a word?"

"Sì, il mio amore, it is. So, let's get this party started, lock down the rental vehicle, and try to get ahead of the mob attempting to secure reservations at Lenny's RV Park and Resort outside of Cleveland for our first night of vacation. I've been told it's important to secure a place which has the necessary hook ups, but on a flat piece of land so we won't be leaning."

Charlotte laughed. "That's a good tip! And then it's on to the Wisconsin Dells for the wonderful water parks."

"And along the way, seeing America, at its finest. Truck stops and diners. Only mom and pops. And by the way," he said opening a desk drawer and pulling out a ring box. "I picked this up for you today." Alex walked over to the couch and handed her the small box.

Charlotte opened it up and smiled at the plain gold band. She removed her large wedding ring and slipped the simple gold band onto her finger in its place.

"Thank you, darling. Legitimate at last," she said, reaching up to pull him down for a kiss.

He sat down beside her and gathered her into his arms, warming to the reception. "Thank *you*, my wife, and you're very welcome."

Chapter 4

Clayton knew Ginger Krueger, his second cousin, had the hots for him. Most women did. He'd known when they were kids that Ginger—the way she looked at him—had it bad. Ginger was a single gal about his age living in   a trailer on a small parcel of land about an hour away in McGregor. She cleaned cabins mostly, which earned a pretty decent living, and since she didn't do much more than work and watch TV, her expenses were pretty low. Well, she ate a lot too, but Clayton wasn't in it for the scenery.

Sitting on Ginger's raggedy sofa, he pulled back as her wide ass maneuvered past him to her recliner. She put a massive bowl of popcorn on the end table between her chair and the sofa, then popped the leg extension and lay back.

"You want to pick up where we left off?" she asked, her eyes blinking, excited. She grabbed a two-handful scoop of popcorn, put her head back, and began shoveling it into her mouth.

They had big things to talk about tonight, but he nodded, wanting her fully lubricated for the sell.

"Season Four is ever-y-thing," Ginger groaned through her food, her eyes rolling into the back of her head.

Breaking Bad. She lived for that shit.

He'd been hanging out with Ginger, grooming her as his backup, just in case the shit with Penny hit the fan. The situation with his wife was looking pretty bad. It was time to make his big move, and Penny had no one to blame but herself. She'd surprised him when she'd spoken to a bankruptcy attorney.

What would she do next? How could he predict it? His wife had turned into a sneaky bitch. What was next—a divorce attorney? Maybe she'd just leave him. Then what? No. Clayton was a *proactive* person with a *proactive* plan. He'd do whatever it took to retain his up north lifestyle. *Whatever it took!*

Thank goodness he had Ginger in the hopper. He'd been worried about his home situation for the last year and had been nurturing Ginger in case the day came when he needed her help. At first, he'd only a vague idea how Ginger would be useful. After hanging out with her, he realized he could count on her to do anything he asked. Then, she became really attractive.

Hanging out with Ginger at her trailer was a low-key social event because she only really liked to do two things— eat junk food and watch crime dramas on TV. Her primary line-up included *Criminal Minds*, any variation of the *Law and Order* franchise, *CSI*, *The Sopranos*, even *Columbo*. But her primary obsession was *Breaking Bad.*

Every time Clayton went to her place, she was watching one of her crime dramas. Clayton always displayed enthusiasm while they watched an episode or two of *Breaking Bad.* He actually enjoyed the show, but not to the extent she did.

Watching her view it was like watching Pavlov's dog, just completely absorbed, drooling, waiting for the next bell to ring. It was borderline weird.

On a couple of occasions over the last year, Clayton convinced her to leave the trailer and go to a local bar. Initially he did this because he couldn't bear another night in front of the TV, but afterwards, he realized the outings cemented her bond with him.

Ginger Krueger clearly loved being with him in public and he used it to keep her home fires burning. Because while Clayton knew he would never, *ever* be interested in her sexually, he knew Ginger felt differently. For the sake of the long-term plan, and as inappropriate as a relationship would obviously be, Clayton occasionally made offhand comments about what ifs, and he watched her gobble them up.

"I need a drink," Clayton said, rising from the sofa.

Ginger lunged for the remote, pausing it. "Sure. Make one for me too."

He watched her lean down and grab a large bowl filled with candy off the floor. "I got some Twizzlers in here; we can use them as straws."

In the kitchen, Clayton inhaled, trying to calm his nerves. Tonight was the big step. He mixed the drinks while thinking back to the moment roughly eight months ago when after another viciously unreasonable fight with Penny, the proverbial lightbulb had popped over his head. A plan began to form, and from that day forward he took *proactive* steps to cover his ass as he began to line it out.

Because his plan would require Ginger's assistance, Clayton had needed to feel out and probe the depths of her subservience. It turned out watching repeated episodes of *Breaking Bad* really helped. The story lines helped

Clayton introduce conversation about moral obligations, and damnation, and helped define how far either would be willing to go. Maybe there was something in their blood, some family DNA, but the thought of crossing boundaries, of doing whatever necessary to get them what they wanted was A-okay.

Until now, neither had ever seriously tested themselves by stepping too far over legal lines, yet they each held loosely defined morals. Clayton knew he lied daily to his wife and to others on any number of issues, but he was surprised when Ginger confessed that since she'd started watching *Breaking Bad*, she'd started to shoplift things.

Ginger now proudly diagnosed herself as a kleptomaniac. Clayton couldn't forget the night she'd told him this, whispering her sins, her face on fire, her eyes wild with excitement as she shared her secret with another human being. She'd practically wet her pants telling him about her shoplifting escapades. He'd endured it—partly out of sheer fascination, partly because of his budding plan. Those first confessions greased the path toward more voracious conversations about things they would be willing to do, and what lines they would not cross. Clayton surprised himself when he realized how far he'd be willing to go and was relieved when it became clear that Ginger was right in step with him.

Once those lines were established, he opened up and poured his heart out to her, explaining the details, most of which were fabricated, about the *sacrifices* he endured in his life. About his dreams—most of which were true— of being a successful bar owner, living his life without boundaries in the Up North Country. He wanted to enjoy his ride on the planet and not be slowed down by anyone, especially his wife Penny. During their TV dates, he kept Ginger up to date on his *setbacks* and *worries* and made sure she believed his troubles were her troubles—because, he explained, she was one of his best friends in the entire world.

Clayton walked back into the room and handed her the drink. He walked to the front door and reached down for a bag and then resumed his seat on the couch. He put the drink down on the coffee table.

"I got something for you," he said, reaching into the bag.

Ginger used the lever to pull herself up. "Yeah?" she said, her eyes bright.

He pulled out a couple of burner phones.

"It's time, Ginger. I need you."

Her mouth dropped open, her face reddened as she looked at the phones. He knew she understood.

"We need to move forward carefully. Just like in one of your shows. We gotta help each other now.

"No one can know we're talking," Clayton pressed, his voice lowered. He nodded purposefully at her, staring hard into her eyes, making sure she understood. Once she licked her lips and nodded, he handed her the phone.

And just like that, he knew he had her. She lovingly turned the phone over in her hands, stroking it. Inhaling deeply through her nostrils like she was taking a blood oath, she said, "I promise I'll do whatever I can to help you, Clayton. I'll be your Skyler White, only I'll never turn my back on you, no matter what comes our way."

"Okay, Ginger," he said getting the *Breaking Bad* reference that he was Walter White to her Skyler. "I appreciate that. You mean the world to me."

With that, the two of them got decidedly busy being *proactive*, laying out their plans to help Clayton realize his dreams and for Ginger to as well.

He'd given Ginger a gift. She was finally, actually living in her own, real, goddamned crime story and lovin' every minute of it.

She'd been well worth the investment.

Chapter 5

Violet Krueger peddled her bike fast, worried she was going to be too late to help her mom get the dough ready for the morning rolls. Violet had been out, lying on one of the nearby deserted private beaches. Over the years, she'd learned which ones were rarely used. It confused her that some people would own these lake homes on perfectly wonderful beaches but would only use them a few times over the summer months. Whenever Violet saw the owners' cars in the driveway, she'd pedal away, but today she'd been lucky. Her mom had given her the afternoon off, and she'd found her special beach gloriously empty. She'd put on her sunscreen before she left, so all she had with her that afternoon was a towel and one of her many beloved books. Lying on the white velvet sandy beach, lost in the world of J.K. Rowling's *Harry Potter*, time flew by and now she was pumping her legs as fast as she could to get back and help her mom at the restaurant.

She loved her mom and had watched her work hard every day, seven days a week, with almost no breaks. Her dad was rarely around to help them. Today though, he'd said he could handle it and she and her mom could take a few hours off. *Whatever*, Violet had thought. Like he was doing them some big favor.

Her fair skin was, as usual, sunburned despite the sunblock. She was hungry, tired, and thirsty as she pushed her bike up the weedy dirt path to their home. There were no customers in the parking lot of the Backwoods. She walked up to the house and felt her stomach drop as she heard the familiar sound of her mom and dad arguing.

"We're not going to declare bankruptcy, you hear me? At least not yet! Or *never* if you'd just give this place some more time. You're not seeing the big picture, Penny! You've never been good with math, you know nothing about numbers, but I'm telling you, this place has a real chance for success if we just hang in there!"

"Clayton! You're living in a dream world. This place has no chance for success. I might not be good at math, but I can see the writing on the wall and barring an unforeseen extraordinary miracle, we're wasting time until the inevitable happens and we'll be forced to close the doors. We're close to that every single month! Every single month we scrape by. *Barely scrape* by. It's too much and I'm not going to let Violet become enslaved to this place like we are. She already does more work around here than you."

Violet listened, torn and sick to her stomach. She wanted to help them so badly, but she didn't like working so much either. Maybe it was her fault this was happening. Her mom continued to berate her dad.

"And how does that make you feel, Clayton? Like a good dad? A good husband? Because you're neither! I don't know where the hell you go at night, but a part of me is relieved when you walk out the door. Relieved that I don't have to look at your face, or have another pointless argument with you. Attempting to get you to see the light of day, attempting to get through to you that you need to change, attempting to get through to you that you need to be a better father, a better husband, a fucking provider, or helpmate. None of which you apparently care about. Every spare dime that comes into this place goes out the door in the evenings and onto your bar bill, on our Visa card, and I can't take it anymore! Your damn DUI alone nearly killed us. Your constant drinking, your lifestyle. I'm telling you for the last time, please believe me when I say that if you won't change, then I will file for divorce, and then the Backwoods will close for good. Violet and I will leave and go to California and live with my mom and by God I will get a good job and I will support her with or without you."

"Don't you dare! Violet's my daughter too. You can't just take her away. What do you think the courts would say about that? You can't do that, Penny. I have rights too and I'm telling you we can work this out! Just listen to me!"

"Clayton, I can't keep this up! I can't keep doing this! I've busted my ass around here for years, and I can't—I *won't* do it anymore."

Violet had heard it all before and when she saw a customer pull up at the convenience store, she dragged herself away. Heavy with the load of all the pressure they were all under, she didn't know what was going to happen, but she knew she was scared all the time now, and worried. It sure didn't sound like things were getting better, but she couldn't imagine it any worse. She'd be extra helpful tonight to her mom. It was all she could think to do.

Chapter 6

The beautiful motor home was delivered to the Macchi's West Village doorstep as the sun rose. Ready for the drop-off, the family hurried out the door and loaded it with their supplies and luggage. Waving goodbye to Havish, the five, heading out on their great American adventure, hit the road.

It started with a challenge.

Alex gripped the large wheel and pumped the brakes with slow pressure, glancing in all the mirrors, feeling like a clown in some twisted Manhattan-based video game. From his perch, he looked down through the side window to see someone flipping him off. Another person had their head out the window screaming something at him.

Grinding his teeth, he caught himself short from cursing and tried to ignore it. Horns blared all around them as the EZ Pass allowed the RV entry into the Holland Tunnel toward Jersey.

"I told you we should have loaded the thing in Jersey and not had it delivered." Renzo gripped the arms of his own bucket seat in the front passenger bay next to him.

"Not helpful," Alex said, then inhaled.

"Havish said so too," Renzo muttered.

"Mickie said they delivered to Manhattan all the time." Alex felt a lump grow in his throat thinking back to the RV dealer, Mickie Micatrado, wondering for the first time if the guy knew what he was talking about, worrying that he did and was presently having a good laugh at Alex's expense. He swallowed hard as they moved slowly through the tight tunnel, the passenger side mirror practically scraping the concrete wall of the narrow tube.

"You got this," Renzo said as he lowered his window and looked outside.

Coming out the Jersey side, Alex hadn't driven far before he saw the flashing police lights.

"Oh my God!" Petunia yelled. "They're after us! You're being pulled over!"

"Shit," Alex said through his clenched teeth. "Where the hell am I going to do that?"

The intermittent sirens from the cop car sounded like something from *Star Wars*, but the eventual voice from a blaring speaker as they searched for a place to stop was all Jersey cop. "Pull Over. Pull Over! Now!"

"There's a Staples up ahead." Renzo pointed to the large retail store.

"This is so exciting!" Petunia bounced behind him.

"Get back there and buckle up or something," he raised his voice to his daughter as the RV came to a merciful stop. He glanced back at his family. Both Lily's and Charlotte's eyes were wide, but his wife had a hand covering her own mouth. He caught the glimmer in her expression … she was laughing.

The Jersey City cop eventually came to Alex, who rolled down his window.

"License and registration," the cop barked, one hand extended, his other on his gun.

"I'm sorry, Officer," Alex said, searching for the paperwork. "What did I do?"

"What did you do? You can't use the tunnel with this rig! You got more than three axels here. Whaddaya doin?"

"I thought the motorhome was three axels?" Alex gulped, confused as he handed him the paperwork.

The cop gestured to the back. "You got a trailer. It's an extended vehicle."

"How many axels do I have then?" Alex asked.

The cop jabbed a finger at Alex, his mouth in a hard line. "You wait there, smart ass. I'll be back."

The police officer walked away. Alex knew he was going to get a ticket.

"I'll just text Micatrado real quick and ask him," Renzo said.

"Yeah," Alex replied, thinking back to the sales guy's smug face. "I think we missed something there. He told us to take the tunnel, didn't he?"

Renzo nodded.

"I think we got played."

"It's the toad."

Alex shot Renzo a look. "The toad?"

"RV lingo," Renzo said, picking up a manual. "It's like a dingy—you know, like on a boat."

"I know what a dingy is. That's why we put it on a flatbed behind us so no one would have to drive it separately."

"How'd that work out?" Renzo mumbled into his phone.

"He *told* us . . ." Alex began. "Never mind."

Ticket in hand and the cops driving away, they pulled back into traffic and thankfully merged safely onto the interstate heading toward Amish country, Pennsylvania. Alex wiped his sweaty palms on his pants and sighed in relief. "Thank God I never have to do that again," he said, thinking ahead to Lenny's RV Park in Cleveland. With all the stops and drama, this trip was going to take forever.

"Pretty gruesome, Boss, but you did it."

"Okay. The next big city? It's your turn, big guy. Then we'll see who has the flop sweat." Alex focused intently on the road and raised a sweaty palm to be cooled by the air conditioning.

"Oh, stop complaining. You did great. Other than a run-in with the law. Really impressive. You want me to do anything with the video Charlotte took while you were screaming out the window at the cars below? How about the one Petunia has of you talking to the Jersey cops? TikTok, Facebook, Instagram?"

"No. I'll cue them up the next time Petunia has something she wants to complain about."

Joking aside, Alex was mightily relieved Renzo was with him. He'd been slightly irked when he'd discovered that Renzo and Havish had a habit of spending late evenings together on the rooftop terrace, drinking brandy. Glad Renzo had given Havish Khan his blessing, Alex realized the hurt feelings he had about never being invited to their shindigs were sophomoric, but he couldn't help it. It was another growing pain in trying to figure out the whole personal-professional thing.

Renzo glanced into the back of the motorhome as the sounds of giggling trickled forward. "Well, you're doing just fine now. Look at you! King of the Road. You got three ladies back there, all proud as peacocks, you got the sewer system tutorials all cued up for you here on a podcast, and the next six hours to listen to it. I'd say life was pretty good."

Alex couldn't disagree, but thoughts of the many hours between him and a well-earned cocktail was top of mind.

Renzo picked up a stack of flyers and continued. "You should know Petunia's jigging with the itinerary. She was telling me last night she thinks we should make a detour once we're in Illinois to see the Largest Bottle of Ketchup. I think she said it would only add an extra hour or two to the plan, but I've got to agree with her on this one, Boss. That'd be a sight to see!"

Shoving a few brochures into Alex's line of sight, Renzo said, "You got the Largest Turtle in Dunseith, North Dakota—we might think hard about seeing that one. Then you got the Largest Ball of Twine in Minnesota . . . maybe we should hit that one on our way to the cabin up north. Then of course, once we get to South Dakota, we for sure want to see the Dinosaur Park, and maybe the Corn Palace. That one—the Corn Palace, in Mitchell, South Dakota— that one looks spec-tac-u-lar."

Alex slid his friend and employee a cynical eye as he listened to him jabber on. Intermingled with the sounds of his family laughing hysterically about something in the back, Alex tried to relax, but worried about the tasks ahead.

"Why don't you make yourself useful," Alex barked, "and see if you can figure out how to use this NASA-designed dashboard and cue up that podcast. And don't even think about moving to the back. We're in this together."

———————————

For the rest of the traveling party, RV adventures began as soon as they boarded. Thrilled by the space, Charlotte and Petunia busied themselves organizing their gear. Lily, fascinated with the new onboard potty, tried it out several times, and to everyone's enormous relief, the facilities seemed to work perfectly. They had all kinds of snacks and food, but they'd planned to stop as many times as possible along the way to try local restaurants and cuisine.

Finally reaching Amish country, they made their first scheduled stop in Bird In Hand, Pennsylvania. They took their time and visited several shops and arranged for a number of quilts to be shipped back home. Second and third stops for sightseeing and lunch were pleasant too, but Alex felt surprisingly grateful when he saw the large, painted sign for Lenny's RV Park and Resort outside Cleveland.

The incredibly long first day of driving, sightseeing, and games came to an end as they drove past other RVs and campers and coasted onto their designated spot. They were happy to come to a rest and stretch their legs outdoors. Alex was less enthused because Lenny's promises of a flat surface and state-of-the-art facilities were not quite accurate. This led to trouble as an unfortunate sewage line hookup, pulled too tight to reach its port, broke loose. Alex spent some time outdoors cleaning himself with a hose but was reassured by Petunia that he'd love the video footage when they got home.

Those items aside, they all recognized the itinerary had to be adjusted, and not just because of the added sightseeing detours. They hadn't factored in the slowness of the RV along with the number of stops for gas. They decided to double the next travel leg from one to two days, which unexpectedly had them overnighting in Chicago. Winging a reservation at a KOA campsite outside of Chicago was hotly debated and rejected, so they booked a suburban Chicago Marriott with a big parking lot and a pool for night two.

Original itinerary out the window, day two planning complete, Alex fell into bed exhausted and had a hard but restless first night. His alarm woke him before dawn and he quietly hit the head. When he emerged, he tossed a pillow at the lower bunkbed and Renzo's head as he made his way to the cockpit to warm up the Frog. Petunia had named it the Frog because they were towing a Toad.

Firing up the rig, Alex felt his anxiety return, but he and Renzo navigated out of Lenny's RV Park in darkness and began the Cleveland to Chicago run.

"At least you got a real bed," Renzo grumbled.

The big guy's arms were crossed and eyes closed; his head rested against the back of the seat. Alex knew they both needed coffee. And while he shouldn't complain since he and Charlotte—with Lily predictably sandwiched between—had slept in the one and only big bed, it wasn't exactly luxury with Renzo's snoring ten feet away. Still, with Renzo's height, Alex was sorry to see that he'd been cramped.

"Marriot tonight, my friend."

"Yeah."

After the girls were awake, the crew spontaneously chose a diner, the decision based solely on the heavy advertising of billboard after billboard enticing them with the "best breakfast in Ohio." The excitement built as they edged off the interstate near Toledo toward Gramp's Pancake House.

"I'm telling you," Alex stretched as he emerged from the RV in a parking spot a good distance from the front door of Gramp's, "we need to park it as far away as possible. I can't maneuver into designated spots." He complained good naturedly, then broke into a run to grab Lily's hand. She'd jumped off the rig and begun running toward the restaurant. Although his daughter was not in any real danger, Alex felt his adrenaline pump as he caught up with her and swept her into his arms.

"Little muffin, you cannot run through parking lots! Even though there weren't any moving cars around, there might have been, and you need to be careful." He set her down. "Hold my hand from now on, please."

Lily agreed and skipped him toward the restaurant. Complying with her silly request to skip along, he looked back to see Charlotte and Petunia mimicking them. The family laughed their way into the restaurant. All Alex needed now was some strong coffee and breakfast. After that, the day could only get better.

And it might have, if they hadn't been recognized.

After ordering their pancakes and eggs from the harried and oblivious waitress, Alex experienced the familiar feeling they were being watched. Before turning around to see who was behind them, he glanced at Renzo who had a direct view. The man's eyes were hooded, his face suddenly serious.

The U-shaped booths had high backs that obscured the views of someone short, but the adults could see around the restaurant without difficulty.

"Renzo," Charlotte looked across the table and whispered, "is everything okay?"

Renzo stared openly across to a four-top table behind Alex's back. "Not sure, too soon to tell."

Alex finally turned his head and came eye to eye with a couple in their early fifties who were pointing at them.

He turned back and gave Renzo a level stare, but then picked up a crayon and helped Lily draw on her menu. Petunia, sensing the situation, picked her head up, straightened tall, and stretched. She looked across the back of the booth, directly at the woman. Alex watched the stranger's mouth fall open as soon as their eyes met. Petunia slumped down quickly, lowered her head, and went back to drawing on the menu.

Alex was annoyed for all of them, especially having to watch poor Petunia in her effort to shrug it off, but he didn't react until he heard the unmistakable sound of camera shutters whirling from the booth behind him. He peripherally glanced at the couple to confirm his suspicions and watched as they put their heads together whispering, phones still positioned up, at the ready. Trying again to ignore it, he sensed and heard movement. He turned his head and caught the woman's arm extending, phone held high over the back of their booth as she snapped more pictures of his family, and especially Petunia.

When she actually stood with camera phone in hand, apparently intending to come over to their table, it was time for decisions.

Sometimes on the streets of New York, and definitely at public events, the Carrows Macchi family would experience curious glances, some outright staring, some attempts at discreet picture taking, and some aggressive individuals who couldn't get enough pics and even addressed them personally. Depending on the level of aggression, Renzo's response would be different. Everybody felt the children, Petunia and Lily, should be off limits, but some people didn't see it that way. Renzo was there to remind them. Alex gave the big guy a chin jut. It was time for him to manage it.

Released of his restrictions behind the table, Renzo, all 6' 5" of solid wall, got up and approached the couple. He loudly dragged a chair out from their four-top and then sat at their table. The woman, too, sat down.

Alex listened in.

"Hi there," Renzo said in a sing-song voice. "You folks having a nice breakfast? Gramp's Pancake House any good? First time we've been here, and the kids are pretty excited to try the pancakes. You know how it is. They want to color on the menu, drink their milk, talk to their parents, spill syrup, take in the beautiful Ohio morning, and eat their pancakes in peace. Same as you, same as you."

Renzo lowered his voice, Alex turned to watch.

"They're just little kids over there, and I was wondering if you folks wouldn't mind putting your cameras away while we get them some breakfast. I know I'd appreciate it. I think you got all you need, right? So, let's settle down and introduce ourselves."

Renzo pushed his large torso aggressively forward and stuck his ham of a hand into the face of the man at the table. The man leaned back. "Hi there, my name's Renzo Castrogiovanni, from New York originally, but I get around. Ma'am," Renzo said, swinging his hand like a tennis racket over to the lady. "Nice to meet you. Where are you folks from?"

"Chicago. We're heading to Ph-philly," the man stammered, scooting his chair back. "For a family reunion."

"Well isn't that nice!" Renzo said, breaking out into a frighteningly large smile. "A family reunion! I'll bet there'll be lots of good food, lots to catch up on, lots of stories to tell. Family is really wonderful, ain't it? That over there, the ones you just took pictures of, that's a family too. A really nice little family. With small children. It looks like you took enough pictures, and now that you got yourself a story to tell at that family reunion, how about I ask a personal favor, and ask you to stop."

The woman pulled her cellphone to her chest, protecting it.

"You can have the pictures, ma'am," Renzo said. "I won't take them from you or anything. I'm not that kind of man, at least not in front of small children. No, in front of them, I think *manners* are very important, don't you? I don't want to do anything to spoil a perfectly good platter of chocolate chip pancakes. So, do we have a deal?"

The husband glanced at his wife. The woman sat up very straight, lifting her chin. "That's the Carrows right? The little girl is Petunia Carrows, right?"

Renzo leaned in, ever so slightly toward the both of them and whispered. "It is. And it's my job to protect her. All of them. Just so we're clear. I'm the man—I'm good at my job—and I take it very seriously. *Very* seriously, you see, 'cause you never know what people's intentions are. I'm sure you folks aren't over here cooking up some evil plan, but, like I said, it would be great if we can agree to keep our cameras nicely put away, and keep our voices down. Then I can go back over there and finish my coffee and you folks can get back to your eggs."

Renzo pulled back from the one-person huddle, picked a grape off the man's plate, and popped it into his mouth. "So, whaddaya say?" He chewed with his mouth open.

The man rumpled his napkin and licked his lips as he watched his wife, apparently waiting to see what she would do. Fortunately, she put her phone into her purse and smiled smugly at them.

Renzo relaxed his posture. "Thank you for that, ma'am. I appreciate it. You all enjoy your breakfast and have a nice day." He hovered his bulk over the table before standing to full height, then scraped his chair loudly again as he pushed it back in place.

After returning to his seat, Renzo picked up his coffee and gave the couple, who were still apparently gaping at them, a hard stare. He continued to do so for some time.

Alex focused on his family, confident that Renzo had done a good job. A moment later, their pancakes arrived, and were worth all the aggravation. Renzo spent the rest of the meal on high alert, but thankfully, nothing further happened.

Walking back to the motor home, Alex said to him, "Nice job back there. I appreciate it."

"No problem, Boss, but hey, next time we get out, how about we wear some of those hats."

Alex nodded. It was good idea.

Renzo lowered his voice. "We got another problem though."

"What's that?"

"I can't go through another session of 'this is the song that never ends.' I mean, I love those girls, but damn, man, that was rough."

Alex laughed. "I get it. I'll encourage RV Bingo today. You can start it out." He orated theatrically, gesturing toward the sky. "I spy with my little eye . . ."

He broke off laughing as Renzo did a face palm.

———

After that, they had little trouble maintaining their anonymity. Hats and sunglasses on, hair pulled into interesting configurations, they spent a quiet night outside

Chicago, up early and off to the Wisconsin Dells, where they had a ball at a water park—five anonymous people among the throngs of anxious or inebriated adults watching their children run wild through the water rides and floating down the lazy rivers. They had fun shopping and visiting some of the other attractions before heading back to the RV for another night of rest.

One full day and two nights in the Dells was determined to be definitely enough. Alex and Renzo again woke early to drive quietly through the darkness and get a jump on the next leg of the journey while the girls slept. Their next arranged stop was the much-anticipated lake house seven miles outside of Crosslake, Minnesota. There, for three nights, they would leave the confines of the motor home and stretch out at a beautiful lakeside property with white sandy beaches, a boat, canoe, and kayaks. They were all looking forward to fishing and grilling at the lake, which promised pristine water, no weeds, and a bottom so soft it felt like velvet. Playing games and making s'mores around a quiet bonfire in the middle of nowhere certainly sounded like heaven.

Chapter 7

Hell. I'm in hell, Penny thought as she cut the cinnamon rolls that morning at 6 am getting ready to open the restaurant. Once again, Clayton had not come home, and she was at the end of her rope. She had *nothing* left to give. Nothing to give the Backwoods, nothing for Clayton, and next to nothing for herself. Violet was the only person or thing she could muster the energy to care about anymore.

She loved her daughter and thought her a wonderful child. She knew Violet was one of the smartest kids around, although Penny watched her daughter painfully try to hide that from others. Last year, her teacher had laid out her impression of Violet at the year-end parent-teacher conference.

"She's smart, Mrs. Krueger. Really smart, but for some reason she doesn't want anyone to know it. Her schoolwork is good, above average, but it's the occasional flash of brilliance she shows, usually by accident. But once anyone notices, she shuts down. When that happens, I can almost predict her test scores will fall. I think she's doing it on purpose. That said, for whatever reason, she allowed herself to go for it on the MCAs and she scored in the 99 percent range in every category. She's naturally gifted, and I've spoken with her about entering our gifted program and taking advance placement courses for college credit, but she won't commit. I think her shyness is holding her back, but there's something else. I hope you can speak with her and get her to see she could have a tremendous academic future if she'd only choose to pursue it."

Penny herself on several occasions had witnessed her daughter demure to others who seemed less intelligent, but Penny assumed it would work itself out as Violet grew older and more confident in her abilities. But after that conference, things had changed.

Now that she knew Violet was purposely getting bad grades to downplay her intelligence, Penny was worried. She couldn't help but think it had something to do with their financial situation and Clayton's threats of homeschooling Violet so she could spend more time working in the restaurant. Penny realized Violet was trying to protect and help *them*, rather than the other way around. It was a pattern that needed to be broken, and *before* she entered high school where the advanced academic opportunities were given.

Flour up to her elbows, she beat down and rolled out more of the endless dough, knowing she didn't have a choice. She must leave Clayton, take Violet, and get away from it all. If she didn't, and Clayton had his way, Violet's future was in jeopardy. Penny was the only person in the world willing to stand with her daughter and protect her. As her mother, it was time she did. She'd already made too many mistakes, and her beautiful daughter was paying the price. *Enough*, she thought. *Enough.*

Chapter 8

Charlotte sat near the front of the RV behind Alex as he drove through Brainerd, Minnesota. She smiled as Petunia, from the passenger seat, smacked her lollipop and gave her father a hard time.

"Yes, indeed, the trip is going very well." Petunia smiled brightly at Alex. She plopped her feet on the dash and continued. "Dad, when we get there will we still have time to go fishing today?"

Alex glanced in the rearview to consult with Charlotte, who nodded. "I don't see why not. The boat is supposed to be gassed up and ready. We'll just need to make sure they have all the fishing rods and gear before we head out. The weather looks good, and as the water cools late this afternoon, the fish will come up from the bottom to eat, so we might get lucky."

"Mom said she's only been fishing once when she was little. Do you think I'll like it? Are we going to eat them?"

"Well, depends on what we catch. I've heard some fish are really good to eat, but some have a lot of bones, are difficult to clean, and have bad taste. We'll have to find out the Minnesota rules about keeping fish too. It might get tricky out there identifying them."

"Ding. Ding. Ding. Bonus alert!" said Petunia. "We're *learning* stuff. This road trip totally rocks." She smiled with all of her teeth at her dad.

"What kind of bait should we use?" Charlotte laughed, leaning forward.

Alex tore his eyes off Petunia's playful face and squirmed in his seat, then up straighter, intending to sell himself as a man-in-the-know. "I don't know. There are jigs, spinners, and other artificial lures. A spinner creates a visual flash that attracts fish and usually has some bright colored beads. Sometimes you use live bait: minnows, leeches, worms. Often you combine an artificial lure with live bait by attaching a leech or minnow to one of the hooks on the lure. It's a good idea to ask at the bait shop what's working."

"Did you go fishing a lot when you were younger?" Petunia queried him.

Alex rolled his head from side to side. "We rented a cabin a couple of times when we were kids on Chautauqua Lake and did some fishing with the family. I have some really nice memories from those trips."

"Do you think you'll have nice memories from this trip, Dad?"

Indulgently playing another round of the "thanks-for-thinking-of-this-trip game," he glanced again in the rearview and Charlotte chuckled, acknowledging the game.

"The best *ever*, honey. Thank you for thinking of it."

"Hey, no sweat," Petunia said, waving her lollipop around. "I wasn't sure if you and Mom would go for it, but I'm glad you did too. Do you think Havish misses us?"

Charlotte thought about the newest addition to their family, Havish Khan, and pondered the question. Havish had been with them now for over six months, and while the relationship had started out formally, it was warming up. They respected one another, and watching Havish tend to the girls, both she and Alex knew they could trust him. He was the fourth adult in the home the girls could go to for help and for love. When the girls tested him with their behavior or questions, he held a high moral ground and gave appropriate advice. They knew he would be honest, kind, and full of wisdom. They'd all learned to trust his instincts and now sought his advice.

"Maybe," Charlotte answered. "But I'm sure he's enjoying his time off too."

What she wasn't telling Petunia was that Havish had been given an assignment. The day before they were due to arrive home, he'd be accepting delivery of their newest family member—a purebred German Shepard pup. Havish would have to deal with the puppy for its first night in their home by himself. Petunia had wanted a dog for many years, and now that Lily was finally old enough to respect and appreciate an animal, it was the right time. The dog came from a long line of smart and beautiful service animals, and they'd been lucky to secure a male from the litter. The sire had been close to 120 pounds, so if the male puppy followed in his father's footsteps, they would have a huge animal roaming their home and hopefully not tearing it to shreds. It was going to be a labor of love to train the dog, and hopefully Havish would agree.

"I think he misses us," Petunia said with certainty. "I wish he could have come on the trip."

"You're right, he probably does miss us, but he needs some alone time too. We all need a little bit of that in our lives, don't you think?"

She watched Petunia nod her head as they all scanned the wooded landscape near their destination outside of Crosslake. Following the directions, they pulled into a private driveway next to a string of nice homes and cabins sharing a long stretch of beach.

Charlotte got out of the cramped RV and deeply breathed the pine scent and the clean, beautiful air. A cool breeze floated through the trees up to the cabin from the pristine-looking lake. As nice as their RV was, it felt good knowing they'd spend the next several days stretching out. The place looked marvelous. She followed the crew to the house, where Alex found the keys and they walked inside. Beautiful views of the lake surrounded them.

The realtor, expecting their arrival, had placed fresh flowers and what looked to be a homemade pie on the kitchen counter. Charlotte took a moment to poke around the kitchen, getting an idea of what was stocked. They'd prepared a grocery list and prearranged delivery of the items, so they wouldn't have to waste their time shopping for supplies.

"Let's go down to the lake," Petunia yelled, kicking off her shoes and grabbing Lily's hand.

Definitely the centerpiece of the property, the lake was spectacular. They went down to the dock and were happy to see the water was crystal clear. You could walk into it from the white sandy beach or jump off the dock. The boats, as promised, looked perfect. The lake was quiet and peaceful and glistened in the late afternoon light. They watched a small family of loons swim by.

Alex walked up and kissed her. "I think we can manage here."

Charlotte agreed. "It's perfect."

"Come on, hurry up," Petunia called to her mom before getting into the backseat of the Toad, Renzo at the wheel. She was anxious to get the errand done and go fishing.

Her mom ran up and got in the front. "I've got the list ready. Just a few things. I think we should head to that convenience store we passed on the way in and check that out first."

Renzo drove down the gravel driveway to the highway and took a right. They traveled only a mile before approaching the Backwoods Café & Bait.

"There!" Petunia pointed.

Pulling into the cracked concrete parking lot, she scanned the Backwoods setup, thinking the place fairly old looking. There was a long, green-painted wooden building with the paint chipping off the sides. *Bait, Food, Beer* in red neon lights overhung the front door, old gas pumps stood out front, and the small parking lot offered two entrances. One to the convenience store and restaurant, the other with more neon announcing *Bar* and *Off-Sale Liquor.*

Petunia pushed through the main door, and bells jingled as they entered. A fishy smell assaulted her nose, and the sight of huge tubs with live swimming minnows greeted her. Next to the minnow tanks was a glass-door refrigerator with a sign listing the price for worms and leeches. Petunia grimaced at the containers of swimming leeches in the fridge and turned to walk up a short flight of concrete stairs. From there she could either go straight past the checkout register and deeper into the narrow convenience store or turn right and go into what appeared to be a small restaurant.

The entire place seemed empty of customers, and a slight, blond girl about Petunia's age was sitting behind the register reading a book. The girl looked up and put down the book.

"Hi," Petunia said to the girl, watching Renzo do a fast walk into the restaurant, his head swiveling, checking the place out. Her mom, too, said hello to the girl before walking deeper into the convenience store aisle.

"Hi. Can I help you?" the blond girl said, sitting on her hands.

"Um, yeah, I think we're going to get a few groceries, and some gas, and we need fishing licenses. We just got here, and we don't know what kind of bait we'll need."

Renzo came up to them, and the girl tilted her head back and looked up at him as he spoke. "Do I pump gas out there and then pay, or do you need me to pay up front?"

"You can pay me when you're done." The blond girl responded.

"Okay, thanks." He nodded and said to Petunia, "I'm going outside to take care of that. I'll be right back."

She gave him a small smile and watched him leave. Pans rattled in the restaurant area, probably coming from the kitchen.

The girl asked, "How long are you staying? Do you have a place up here?"

"We're just staying a few days, at a place we rented down the road. We're going to do some fishing in a few hours, but my dad said the adults would need to have licenses."

The girl slid a pad and pen toward Petunia. "That's right. Children under the age of fifteen are free. How many did you need? You'll need to fill one of these forms for each license. There're all kinds of licenses depending on if you are a resident of Minnesota or not, and how long you'll need it."

"Oh, well, we're visitors, and I think we'll need them for three days."

"Then you'll want the non-resident twenty-four-hour, seventy-two-hour, or seven-day license. Where are you from?"

"New York," said Petunia.

"Wow, that's far. How did you end up in Minnesota?"

"I have an uncle who likes to fish. He's been here before with some friends and told us about it."

"And you like to fish?" the blond girl asked.

"I don't know, this will be my first time." Petunia smiled.

"Oh, well I hope you catch some. So how many adults are there?"

"Hi there." Her mom interjected as she reached them, placing a few items on the counter.

"We were just talking about the fishing licenses," explained Petunia.

"Yes, I think we'll need three. Just adults. Is that what you said?" her mom questioned.

"Yes, three adult, non-resident temporaries are $12 each. You may want the seventy-two-hour or the seven-day license, but they're more expensive. I'll need you to fill out these forms too. They require your name, driver's license number, date of birth, and last four digits of your social security number. The usual stuff."

Petunia watched her mom chew on her lip as she looked over the forms. "Do you mind if I fill these out outside?" The girl handed her mom three slips. She put a hand on Petunia's back and said, "Honey, I'll just be outside putting this together. I need to call your dad. I'll be right back."

Petunia nodded her okay and turned her attention back to the girl and noticed the book she'd been reading was *Harry Potter and the Half-Blood Prince.*

"Hey, are you reading that?" Petunia asked.

"I am. Have you read them?" The girl perked, smiling for the first time. She was really pretty.

"They were awesome. Have you seen the movies?"

"No, not all of them. I saw the first two."

Petunia waved her arms. "Oh my God, you have to see the movies. They did a really good job. They're almost exactly like the books, but I think the books were probably better."

The girl nodded her head. "I thought so too. At least the ones I've seen."

"Do you like to read?" Petunia asked.

"Um hmm," she said, glancing toward a banging sound in the restaurant.

"I like to read too," said Petunia. "What grade are you in?"

"I'm going into eighth grade."

"I'm going into seventh grade! I wonder if we've read a lot of the same books."

Just then they both startled to a crash from the kitchen area and the raised voice of a man shouting, "Goddamn it! It's none of your business, Penny! Get this done and we'll talk later."

The counter girl blinked rapidly and put a hand over her mouth.

Petunia tried to change the subject. "Do you travel? Gone anywhere fun?"

The girl again sat on her hands. "Not really. I wish. Anywhere but here. The winters are so cold. We might be moving to California soon, though," she shrugged.

A woman's voice from the kitchen called out, "Violet . . ." The voice trailed off as the speaker entered the store and realized there was a customer present.

Petunia perked up at the name Violet for obvious reasons but held back saying anything—also for obvious reasons. So far, the girl didn't seem to know who she was, and Petunia didn't want to change that.

"Oh, hello. Violet, do you have this out here? Do you need help?"

"No, I got it, Mom. We were just talking. About books," she said shyly, giving Petunia a quick look.

Petunia turned to the bells jingling at the front door as her mom and Renzo came back inside. They handed over the fishing licenses, which went uninspected by Violet into a lockbox. The two moms exchanged pleasantries, Charlotte letting on they'd be visiting for a few days. She continued the getting-to-know-you conversation with details about the trip and where they were staying.

"That's a beautiful property. It's such a small community. I think we know everything about everyone around here. Oh, let me show you the restaurant. I'm Penny Krueger," the lady said as she led the group into the other room and showed them the menu. "We're famous around here for our homemade cinnamon rolls, but really, we do serve a great breakfast. We open at six with breakfast until ten. You should come by and get your day kicked off right here."

As her mom and Penny talked some more, Petunia looked around the smallish place thinking cinnamon rolls sounded awesome. Leaving, she turned to say thanks and give a final wave of goodbye to the girl named Violet.

Petunia looked out the window at the Backwoods as they drove away. "That girl in there, her name is Violet. But I didn't tell her my name was Petunia. I didn't want to give her a clue or something. I don't think they recognized us, do you?"

"No, I don't either," said her mom.

"Do you think we can come back tomorrow morning for breakfast and maybe it would be okay if I told her my name? I mean, not my full name, but just my first name. She seemed really nice, and we're almost the same age and all."

Charlotte glanced back. "You can do that, but you need to be prepared for the consequences. How would you feel if she did put it together?"

Petunia looked away, slightly exhausted by the effort they put into hiding their identities. She didn't like it. But she also didn't like people going all ga-ga weird and treating her differently when they knew. "I don't know, Mom. I guess it would be nice to think it wouldn't matter. Maybe once in a while I could try it, you know? I mean, I'm just a regular kid when I'm standing in front of someone. They can see that. So maybe, if it's okay with you, tomorrow, I'll try it out."

Her mom glanced at Renzo but smiled. "Sure. She seemed nice. Her mom was very nice too. Go ahead, honey."

Petunia wondered about her mom's actions, going outside to fill out the licenses. She frowned thinking about the effort they always made to hide stuff. "Did you give them our real names on the fishing licenses?" she asked.

"No. I'm sorry to say we didn't. You may think that was wrong, and you're probably right, but it's only a fishing license, honey. I don't think we'll be in too much trouble if we get caught—which I think is highly unlikely anyway."

"But isn't it a government form?" Petunia pressed.

Her mom turned around to face her. "Yes, but not a very large part of the government and certainly not one interested in our well-being. We're not trying to take advantage of a system or a tax. We just want to fish privately. You let me worry about bad fishing karma coming our way and just enjoy yourself."

Petunia was silent the rest of the way home. At least her parents were always honest with her. They were dependable like that.

Chapter 9

Petunia stopped eating and slumped, placing her hand on her full stomach. What had been a massive plate of cinnamon rolls was nearly empty. She watched her mom pour water on a napkin then clean Lily's sticky fingers. The five tourists had returned to the Backwoods that morning for breakfast. Now, at what must be the tail end of the breakfast crowd, there was hardly anyone left in the place. Violet—the girl from the convenience store—and her mom had served them. Petunia could see into the kitchen, and there'd been a guy in there cooking, but he'd gone into the bar.

Violet walked up and laid down the check.

"I heard your mom say your name is Violet." Petunia perked up, ready for the introduction.

"Yes."

"That's so funny, because my sister and I are named after flowers too. My name is Petunia and my sister is Lily." She smiled warmly at Violet, who did not realize the gravity of the moment.

Violet tilted her head. "That's cool. My mom really likes names with flowers." She gestured shyly toward Charlotte. "I guess you do too."

"Violet," said her mom. "It's a beautiful name."

"Thanks. So hey, how was the fishing yesterday? Did you catch anything?" Violet asked.

"We did!" Lily exclaimed loudly. "We caught fish!"

Violet's face became more animated as she spoke with Lily. "Do you know what kind of fish?"

"Fish!" Lily said holding out her hands showing the size of their catch. "This big!" Lily's hands had started out small, but as she spoke, she moved them, by degrees, much farther apart.

"I see. Wow! That would be a big fish!"

"We didn't eat it." Lily shook her head solemnly. "We let it swim away."

"Well that's good. Did you catch any that you ate?"

"We did, or at least we will," Petunia said, taking over. "Dad cleaned them last night and we're going to cook them for lunch today. But first, we'll take the boat out and *try* to do some skiing. Do you water ski?"

"I have. I'm not very good at it, but I've gotten up a few times."

"I've never water skied, none of us have, but there are skis in the boathouse, so we thought we'd try it. Hey, would you want to come with us and show us how?" Petunia brightened at the idea of having a friend along for the day. Looking belatedly at her mom, she telepathed an unspoken please-say-it's-okay. Charlotte nodded and Petunia relaxed.

Violet tucked a stray lock from her ponytail behind her ear. "I'm not sure." She pointed to the liquor store, where the man who had been cooking could be seen behind the counter. "My dad just told me I have the afternoon off, but I think I should check with my mom first."

Petunia clapped her hands. "Please come with us. It'll be fun, it's a perfect day, and we could really use your help teaching us how to ski."

"Maybe I should check with my mom first." Violet reached out and gathered up the plates and debris on the table.

"I can speak with her too. Reassure her we'll take good care of you." Charlotte added.

"Okay, I'll be right back." Violet dashed off.

Alex put some money on the table and moved to get up. "How about Renzo, Lily, and I go over to the convenience side and check out the bait while you wait for Violet?"

Petunia stayed with her mom at the table and in short order the girl came back grinning from ear to ear. "She said it would be okay! She's still in the kitchen, but she said she'd be right out."

Penny Krueger came to the table wiping her hands on her apron and greeted them. She was a pretty lady who looked a lot like Violet, blond and slight. "Thank you for offering to take Violet boating. It looks like perfect conditions out there. You folks are staying down at the Madison's place, is that right?"

Charlotte stood up from the table. "Yes, about a mile down the road. They have a beautiful home, and the boat has lots of room. We have plenty of life vests, sunblock, towels . . . I think the girls would have a fun time. I'm Charlotte, by the way," she said, extending her hand.

"Sounds fine." Penny smiled, shaking it. She turned to her daughter. "Violet, did you want to ride your bike down there?"

"We can take her with us now," Charlotte offered. "And we're happy to bring her home whenever you say or whenever she's ready."

"Are you sure? I could pop down later and pick her up," Penny said.

"We can bring her back too." Her mom reached into her bag and pulled out a piece of paper and pen. "I'll give you my cell number and you call me if you need her."

Petunia and Violet beamed at each other, realizing the deal had been sealed.

"Mom," said Violet. "Can I leave now with them? I need to go put on my suit."

Penny looked around the place, toward the bar area and to the few lingering breakfast diners. "Sure. Go grab your stuff and you can go with them."

"Okay," Violet said to Petunia, "I'll be right back."

Petunia stayed at the table and watched the moms walk into the convenience area of the store. They jumped into discussion with the rest of the family, shaking hands and making small talk.

Happy about an unexpected friend to hang out with, she grabbed the last gooey piece of cinnamon roll off the plate and popped it in her mouth. Realizing there weren't any napkins left, she looked around and spied a stack of clean ones folded neatly on a table near the interior doorway entrance to the bar and liquor store. Retrieving a napkin, she spied the back of Violet's dad standing behind the bar.

Petunia wandered over to the nearby jukebox further down the wall and began looking at the selections. She heard voices and looked up to listen to a conversation taking place in the liquor store between Violet's dad and a woman. She eavesdropped, hearing Violet's dad say:

"Just get rid of it this afternoon. I'll make sure she sticks to the schedule. Violet's got the afternoon off. You be ready. Don't call me, I'll call you. When you're finished, get to the bar fast."

"I'm worried," said the woman.

"It'll be fine. It's all ready. Just be cool," said Violet's dad.

"I'm cool. I'm cool. The cancer won't come back."

Petunia's brow knit with confusion by what she'd overheard, especially the word 'cancer.' She left the restaurant quickly and joined her family assembled in the parking lot loading ice into a cooler.

Once outside, she looked toward the separate bar entrance and saw Violet's dad walk outside trailed by a heavyset woman with dark hair. He was doing something on his cell phone, and the woman put her head down and turned away, lighting a cigarette, her back to Petunia. Violet emerged from the store, hugged her mom, and then walked toward her.

Petunia didn't look back at Violet's dad and the woman again. She and Violet hopped into the car and they left the Backwoods. A beautiful day and loads of fun on the water awaited them. Excited she was going to have a normal day with a normal person who wouldn't treat her like someone who should be stared at, Petunia was happy Violet didn't know who they were. She wondered if her mom had given Mrs. Krueger their real last names. Probably, since they were taking her *kid.* But so far, Petunia hadn't noticed any difference in anyone's behavior. She supposed not everyone knew their name and story. That was a good thing.

Chapter 10

Penny waved at Violet as she left with the Macchi family then went back inside the restaurant to finish cleaning up after the last breakfast customers. She had to get the kitchen in order so she could begin preparing the dough for the next day's morning rolls.

Tourists rarely asked Violet to join them, but it had been known to happen. Penny didn't have any concerns about her daughter's safety. The Macchi family seemed quite courteous and kind. For some reason, she had the nagging feeling she'd met them before. To some, allowing her daughter to go with strangers might seem like an odd idea. But she had a good feeling about Petunia and the parents. She knew Violet would be safe a mile down the road at the Madison place.

Her daughter had a good head on her shoulders, and the Macchis had invited Penny to join them too. Penny felt a familiar lump in her throat thinking her daughter didn't have many friends. Since Violet was perpetually busy at the Backwoods, her friends were beginning to forget to ask her to do things. Skiing, in particular, was another something Violet was probably good at, but her kind-hearted daughter said she was always nervous about hogging time on the skis.

Penny sighed deeply, glad that at least today, on this beautiful summer day, her daughter was finally getting a chance for some normal, healthy activity outside their dismal business. She realized how good it felt to see Violet smiling. It reinforced her belief that they had to get the hell out of this place and start again.

Charlotte said she'd bring Violet back whenever she called, but Penny had no intention of doing that until suppertime. She was definitely not calling Violet home to work in the dank and depressing store. She also didn't want to intrude on Violet's time and didn't think she'd accept the invitation to join them. Not that she'd have time anyway.

Later, as she was working in the kitchen, Clayton walked in. Steeling herself for another round of arguments, she looked up and was surprised to see him calmly staring at her.

"Penny," he said softly. "Listen, I feel really bad about everything and it's so nice outside, why don't you kick off and let me handle everything here today. Violet's got a nice thing going, and you deserve a day off too."

Almost astonished, she recognized the tone of his voice as the one he used when he wanted to make up and draw her back into his net of charm. That it no longer worked was lost on him, but she was relieved that for the moment, they could take a breath and not argue. It was emotionally exhausting living as enemies, and she really didn't want it to end that way.

"Really. It's gorgeous outside," he prompted. "Why don't you take advantage of it. Get out of here, go for a run. I know it's been awhile since you've had the chance to do that and I know you miss it. Hey, you should run down Horseshoe!"

Horseshoe was a road not far from the Backwoods, which was a super woody and secluded private dead-end leading to their neighbors, the Petersons. Their cabin lay empty most of the year, but being so close, the Krueger family had inevitably formed a relationship with the Petersons. They sometimes did favors for the Petersons—tending to maintenance, or letting a repairman in, or just checking on the cabin—while they were gone. People looked after each other like that up north, and the Petersons were always generous in one way or another when they were around to compensate for the neighborly help.

Clayton continued. "Kevin called yesterday and asked me to check if a package had been left on their stoop. He said he thought UPS was scheduled to drop something off. Anyway, I went over there, and down the road, on the bend, there was an eagle's nest. I couldn't believe how low to the ground the eagles made it. I mean, usually, they nest in the top of the trees, but I looked over, and there was the nest. The bird looked right at me! She had a couple of babies with her too. It was amazing. You should take a look. It's right past the bend, on the right side of the drive. You can't miss it."

Penny was interested. Despite any ulterior motives Clayton might have, going for a run on a day like today sounded like a great way to relax. She wasn't going to wait to be offered this opportunity again. She'd deal with Clayton's quid pro quo later.

"That sounds good. I'll finish putting up the dough and then kick off for the day."

"Hey," he said, extending his arms. "I got this. In fact, why don't you go now? Do you want to take your headset?"

"No," she said, untying her apron, ready to leave now that she knew that she could.

"Are you going for a run?"

"Yeah, that sounds good, actually."

"Head right down Horseshoe to see those birds. It's amazing, but I'm worried about them. That low? Why did the birds build the nest so low? We might need to call someone to see if something should be done about it."

"Well how low is it?" Penny questioned, interested now in this odd phenomenon.

"About chest high," he said indicating a line across his torso.

"That is strange," she said.

"Head down now. You gotta see it to believe it. I'm telling you, those birds are in danger. Gonna be taken out by a badger or a bear or something."

"Huh, that is odd."

"Take off, Penny. Enjoy your run."

Penny looked at Clayton, surprised she thought she saw real compassion in his eyes. She didn't know what to think but nodded and left.

———————

Five minutes later, Clayton watched his wife stretch, then begin jogging toward Horseshoe Road, out of his sight—hopefully out of his life forever.

Chapter 11

"Violet said to keep your knees together," Petunia cupped her hands around her mouth and hollered at Renzo, who was currently bobbing in the water in the middle of the quiet lake. The big man lay on his back, his skis askew as he struggled to swim toward the tow rope.

She giggled and turned to Violet, who was smiling too. "He's never going to get up."

"He might. But it's tiring," Violet said.

Renzo was on his fourth attempt. Despite perfectly calm water conditions and the advice given by Violet, Renzo hadn't managed to get up on the skis.

Petunia and Violet leaned over the side as the boat neared him. "It's the driver's fault," Renzo grumbled. "He doesn't know what the heck he's doing."

"He punched it as hard as he could, I watched him," Petunia said. She covered her mouth to stop laughing. On the last run, Renzo had done a hard face plant into the water. He drifted away as the large speedboat with the two huge outboard engines idled past him.

"Don't jerk me out of the water so fast," Renzo yelled at the boat.

Alex, at the wheel, shouted back, "Oh come on. Show a little backbone."

Petunia knew her father was playing with Renzo, making it difficult for him and purposely driving the boat full out. Violet had said the boat was super-fast compared to any she'd been on before, and had politely coached Alex how to gently pull them out of the water when it had been Violet's and Petunia's turns.

"Did you want something to drink?" Petunia offered her new friend. She came forward and ducked under the canopy to where her mom, dad, and Lily were seated.

Violet called, "No thanks."

She dug in the cooler for a Dr. Pepper and grabbed a couple bags of Chex Mix. Returning her mom's warm smile, she turned and walked back to Violet and handed her a bag. So far, they'd had a fun time and Violet was beginning to come out of her shell and joke with them. Petunia thought she was smart, and funny too, and even though Violet was a year older, Petunia felt like she needed to protect her.

Violet opened the bag of snacks and grabbed a handful before turning to look back at Renzo. He had a firm grip on the handle, the line was tight, and the boat was slowly dragging him through the water, ski tips up. Violet called, "Are you ready?"

"Hit it!" Renzo yelled.

Petunia threw her head back laughing as she watched Renzo squat on the skis above the water, his body jerking back, forth, and sideways as he wobbled around trying to get his balance. He nearly made it before doing another wild fall, both skis coming off, his feet flying away in opposite directions.

"Aww," Violet smiled at Petunia. Their laughing eyes met, each in sync with the moment, and each other. They'd been together now for several hours and there'd been no judgments, no bad attitudes or manners, no catty or snarky moments, no one-upmanship about who had what or oh-my-Gods about this or that. They were relaxed around one another and life was good.

Her dad drove the boat back to Renzo, who was swimming to fetch his wayward skis.

"Did you want to try tubing with Lily?" Violet called to Renzo.

Petunia smiled. It was nice to have a real friend.

Chapter 12

The next day, after a wonderfully fun-filled stay at their cabin, the Macchi family prepared to leave Minnesota and head to the Black Hills of South Dakota. But the final stop in Minnesota that Sunday morning was the Backwoods—to refuel and say goodbye to their new friends.

The door chimes jingled as Petunia entered. She waited until she saw Violet come out of the kitchen. Her new friend had a worried look on her face and seemed startled to see Petunia.

"Hi," Petunia smiled as she extended a piece of paper. "We're leaving, but I wanted to come over and say goodbye. That's my phone number if you want to call or text."

"Okay," Violet said, distractedly taking the paper. Petunia thought Violet's manner seemed odd. She thought they'd had a load of fun yesterday and might really be friends.

"Hey, are you okay?" she asked with concern.

"Yeah, I'm okay," Violet said licking her lips. She glanced behind her to the kitchen. "It's just my mom isn't here and I'm not sure where she is."

"Oh. Maybe she had errands to run or something? I'm sure she'll be back soon," Petunia said, hoping to help.

"I know," Violet shot back, seeming embarrassed. But she frowned, pulled her lips tight and a small tear escaped the corner of her eye.

Not sure what to say, but knowing her family was waiting, Petunia, clearly flustered, could only manage, "Well, text me, okay? Let's stay in touch."

"We don't have a big data plan and I don't have a smart phone, so I don't know if I can." Violet swiped the back of her hand angrily across her face.

"Oh," Petunia said, sorry that this obstacle hadn't been considered. She now worried she'd offended her new friend. "I'm sorry, Violet. Hey, listen, I had a really fun time yesterday, we all did, and I just wanted to say it was really nice to meet you."

Violet waved. "Okay. Thanks. Well, goodbye. Have a nice vacation."

Petunia hesitated. Not quite knowing what was wrong and uncertain how to mend things, she reached out, gave Violet a hug, and turned around to leave. "See ya, Violet," she said after jingling the door and taking a last look back.

But Violet was gone.

Chapter 13

The Macchis left Minnesota and headed west to the beautiful North Dakota Badlands and then south to the Black Hills of South Dakota. They had reservations at an RV park not far from Hot Springs. Along the way, they made several side trips. First, driving through the gorgeous Spearfish Canyon and hiking to Bridal Veil Falls. In the town of Deadwood and Lead, they got a huge kick out of a staged old-west gunfight. The next day, they checked out the Ice Age fossils at The Mammoth Site and spent some time hiking the Hills.

When they left the Black Hills, they angled northwest to I-90, skirting the western edge of the Hills heading to Gillette, Wyoming. They visited Devil's Tower, an 867-foot-tall rock pillar near Gillette, and then it was on into Yellowstone. They were staying in a rented cabin with spectacular views. At times, Charlotte stayed behind in the cabin so Lily could nap. The rest would head out in the Toad investigating the park. But they all found the park and its inhabitants, both the people and animals, captivating.

Pulling themselves away from Yellowstone, they traveled to their final destination in Jackson Hole and to their last stop—the Rustic Inn. It would be a luxurious end to their vacation, but Petunia would miss the road. She knew they all would, even her dad.

It was with mixed emotions that they unloaded their belongings from the RV and watched it get picked up by a local company. One last group picture around the rig and their temporary home took off.

"Come on, Pinky baby." Her mom smiled, giving her a hug as they waved goodbye to the RV. "There's days more fun ahead of us before we fly home."

Petunia thought the entire trip wonderfully memorable, and in all ways, it had been super different than normal life. It had definitely been quieter. For the most part, they'd rarely turned on the television. They'd spent most of the time doing stuff outdoors or cooking. In Yellowstone— where the Wi-Fi connections were spotty—they didn't have any television or streaming options, but they got used to the silence and nature.

Late Saturday morning, walking with Renzo into the main lobby of the hotel to speak with the concierge about horseback riding, Petunia stopped. A television news report was talking about the search for a missing woman. They watched, curious, and when a picture of the missing woman appeared on screen, Petunia's jaw dropped.

"Renzo." She pointed at the screen. "That's Penny Krueger. That's Violet's mom!"

"I know. I remember her," Renzo said, edging closer to the television.

"What's happening? What's it saying?" Petunia said.

They stood frozen, listening to the reporter detail the search for a beautiful missing mom from Crosslake, Minnesota, including the date she was last seen.

Trying to make sense of it, Petunia felt her throat tighten when the reporter claimed Penny Krueger disappeared six days ago Sunday. She put her hand over her mouth. "But that means she disappeared the day we left! How can that be? That's the day we were with Violet, on the boat!"

She recalled her awkward goodbye with Violet, remembering Violet mentioning her mom not being home, but the thought that something really bad had happened never occurred to Petunia. She hadn't understood.

Now though, she began to cry, scared for her friend, scared for Violet's mom, and shocked someone she had just met was missing, maybe kidnapped or worse.

"Petunia," said Renzo, putting his arm around her and guiding her outside. "Let's get out of here and talk to your folks. Come on. Let's go," he said gently as he guided her back to the car.

They drove up to the bungalow and she saw her parents sitting on the front porch drinking coffee. Renzo came to a fast stop, and Petunia jumped out and ran to them, trying to hold back her tears.

"What happened?" Her mom stood, grabbing a post.

"It's Violet! Her mom! We saw it on the TV in the lobby. She's missing! The police are looking for her, but they can't find her."

Petunia let the tears fall as Renzo stood on the porch behind her.

He nodded. "It looks like Mrs. Krueger went missing the day we had Violet with us—on Sunday. Apparently, she never came home that night and there's a search for her."

She choked back a sob, trying to control her crying while her mom held her. Just then, Lily, inside, began crying too.

"It's okay, honey." Her mom led Petunia inside as her dad went past them to get Lily.

"Should I text Violet?" she asked, pulling her phone out of her pocket. "The last time I saw her, she said her mom wasn't home, but I didn't get that she was really missing."

Her mom shook her head, while Lily wailed in the background. "I don't know. We'll talk about it. Hang on."

Petunia sat at the table trembling, thinking hard, as her mom and dad bustled around calming Lily. Renzo brought her a blanket.

"We have to go back." Petunia controlled her snuffles and huddled in the blanket. She tried to think straight, her thoughts traveling backward as they gathered at the table.

"Sweetheart," her dad said softly, "I don't know what we can do to help. I'm sure the local people and the sheriff are handling it, and we might be in the way."

Petunia shook her head and put a trembling hand on the table. "But, but I think I might have heard something."

There was dead silence in the room. Her dad gave her a sidelong look. "I don't understand. What did you hear?"

Petunia let the blanket drop and gripped her fists on the table in front of her. "If her mom went missing while we had Violet, if it was that day, then, then I think I heard something before we left. Violet's dad was talking to someone and it was weird."

Her mom reached out to hold her hand. "Okay, take it slow. Back up, try to remember. Take us back to where you were."

The three adults stared at her. Lily too, while chewing on the end of a sippy cup. They all focused fully on Petunia's next sentence.

"Okay, well, you know after we asked Violet if she could come with us, and we met with her mom?"

The adults nodded and Petunia looked at her mom and continued, "And then you left and went out into the parking lot with Dad, and Renzo, and Lily?"

"Yes," said her mom.

"Well, I stayed inside alone, waiting for Violet. I was eating the last of the cinnamon rolls and I couldn't find a napkin, so I saw some by the bar, over by the juke box machine, and I was just looking at the songs, waiting for Violet to get ready, and I heard her dad in the bar, the store that sells beer. He was talking to someone, a woman, and it was strange."

"What was strange about it?" her mom asked.

"Well, at one point the woman mentioned something about the cancer not coming back, but that was right at the end when I saw Violet, and then I left."

Her dad pulled his head back, a quizzical look on his face. "Cancer? How do you know it was Violet's dad? Did you meet him?"

"I heard him the day before, and I saw him, we all did, and I recognized his voice. The day before he was in the kitchen and he was having a fight with Violet's mom."

"Okay, honey." Her dad nodded. "So let's focus on what you heard the day Penny went missing first. You're sure it was the dad speaking?"

"It was. I'm positive of that. Later I saw him in the parking lot with the lady too. She was smoking."

Her dad nodded. "So back to the jukebox. You were standing by it. What do you remember?"

She squeezed her eyes closed bringing the picture back to life, then opened her eyes. "He was saying to get rid of it that afternoon, and he would make sure she sticks to the schedule, and that Violet had the afternoon off. Oh, and the woman said that she was worried, and he said not to call him, that he would call her and she should get to the bar fast. She said she was cool. Like, 'I'm cool, I'm cool,' and then she said something about the cancer not coming back."

Her dad sat back, his brow furrowed in confusion. Her mom said, "All right, and the day before, when you heard them arguing, what did you hear?"

Petunia blinked. Biting her lip, she closed her eyes again and thought back. Opening them, she said, "Okay. While you were out in the parking lot talking to Renzo about the fishing licenses, I was talking to Violet, and we heard something slam and the dad yelled at the mom about it not being her 'Gosh Darn business,' but he used other words. He yelled something like 'do it,' or 'get it done,' or something. I remember Violet looked really embarrassed. Oh my God, do you think something really bad happened to her?"

"I don't know." Her dad frowned at Renzo, who was nodding. "But they're looking for her."

"Dad! What about what I heard? Do you think it has something to do with her disappearing? Shouldn't we go back and tell someone?"

"I think we should find out who the sheriff is and give them a call," her dad said to her mom. "I think at the very least, he'll appreciate hearing the story of those hours, the day Penny Krueger went missing. Whether it helps or not, I don't know."

Petunia sagged with relief that her parents valued her word and would do the right thing. She realized they could have steered clear of the entire situation, said it was nothing important, or not their business, or not to worry about it, but she was glad they didn't.

Renzo said, "I'll find out who we need to call." He left the cabin.

She picked up the blanket and pulled it tight around her. "Mom, do you think what I heard was important?"

Her mom's eyes got sad. "Yes. Unfortunately, I do. I'm sorry your friend's in trouble, Honey, I really am, and I'm sorry you're going through this."

"What do you think it means? Do you think Violet's dad knows what happened?"

Her mom put her elbows on the table and covered her mouth with her fists as she looked at Alex to answer.

"I do," he said. "The timing is too perfect. He and the woman were talking about doing something which would require them to not contact one another and they were worried. I think what you heard means something fishy, but I hope they didn't do something to her."

"You mean you think they might have killed her." Petunia sat rigid, upset at the enormity of that possibility, and began to cry again.

"Don't cry," her mom reached out.

"Don't cry, Tunia," Lily said, mimicking her mom.

It made her heart glad, but sad at the same time.

Her dad shook his head. "I don't know what to think. In situations like this, you hear that the police always look to the family first. Anything is possible. Who knows, maybe we'll get good news and she may already have turned up."

Petunia cried, thinking of Violet's sad face the day they said goodbye. "Mrs. Krueger wouldn't have left Violet behind. She wouldn't have just run off without her. She wouldn't have."

Her mom got some tissues and handed them to her. "I don't think so either, which must be one of the reasons they're out there searching. Which is why it's gotten coverage—even out here in Wyoming."

Renzo returned. "There's a tip line that goes to the Crow Wing County Sheriff. I've got the number."

"All right," her dad said sadly. "Let's make the call."

Chapter 14

Sheriff Tate Becker sat behind his cluttered desk at the Crow Wing County's sheriff's office, his stomach growling. Trying hard not to give in to the temptation of grabbing another complimentary pastry from the small kitchen, he turned his attention to the ache in his shoulders. He was as tired as he was hungry. The assistance he and his staff were giving to the small Crosslake Police Department on the Penny Krueger disappearance was draining him and their resources. The longer the search went on, the more intense it got. And the longer it went, the more the chances of the woman being found alive went down.

The police tip line was being manned by the sheriff's office because they had more staff. The phone lines were busy, but the leads led nowhere.

"Sheriff," an officer said, poking his head in the door. "I've someone you're going to want to speak with." He pointed with his thumb over his shoulder. "Can I transfer it to you?"

Tate nodded. "Who is it?"

"Guy named Alex Macchi. Claims he saw Penny on Sunday before his family took Violet Krueger water-skiing for the day."

Tate's eyes popped wide, his fatigue vanishing. He'd been wondering when the mysterious family Violet had spoken about would care to check in. She'd given him the names of the people, but he hadn't yet contacted the Madison's realtor to get their contact information. The manpower issue had made it a loose end on his to-do list.

He searched his desk for the note with the family's name. Macchi. Something about it had been nagging him but he couldn't put a finger on it. "Yeah. Punch it over."

He flipped through the reports on Sunday's timeline as his phone rang. "Sheriff Tate Becker. Who am I speaking with?"

"Sheriff Becker, my name is Alex Macchi. I have you on speaker with my family around me. We're calling from Jackson Hole, Wyoming. We were recently vacationing in the Crosslake area and just heard the report on the news that Penny Krueger was missing. We have some information which you may or may not find helpful."

"Where were you staying when you were here?" Tate made some notes.

"At a cabin on the east side of Highway 3, south of Crosslake. A real estate agent in the area got us the lake house, but I heard it belongs to a Steven Madison, if that's any help."

Tate check-marked that information. "And when were you in the area?"

"My family and I arrived in Crosslake last Saturday and left on Monday. We spent two nights in the Madison's home, which is about a mile from the Backwoods Café & Bait."

Alex went through some other details about the visit, and Violet, and about them leaving town unaware Penny Krueger was missing. Tate was nodding; it lined up. "Violet told us she'd spent the day with a vacationing family, so I'm glad you finally called. It helps to form a timeline and confirm the events. Is there anything else you can tell me?"

Alex related the events of the morning before they left the Backwoods with Violet, and the details Petunia had given them about Clayton Krueger and a woman.

Tate felt a tingle on the back of his neck as Alex continued, especially over the identity of the unknown lady Clayton had been speaking with. He wished Petunia had gotten a good look at the woman's face, but that hadn't happened. "What exactly did Petunia hear them saying?"

"Sheriff Becker, for this part, I think it best if my daughter tells you. It's her memory of events, and I don't want to paraphrase or say something inaccurate."

"Okay." Tate nodded.

"Her name is Petunia. Petunia, go ahead and tell Sheriff Becker what you heard."

A young but strong voice came on the line. "Hello, Sheriff. Okay, so I was standing there, by the jukebox, and I heard a man saying—Mr. Krueger—saying something about getting rid of something that afternoon, and Violet had the afternoon off, and he would make sure someone sticks to the schedule. And the woman, she said she was *worried*, and he said not to call him, that he would call her, and I remember she said, 'I'm cool, I'm cool,' and then it was weird. She said something about the cancer not coming back."

Sheriff Tate Becker listened, not making notes, but knew in that moment he'd heard something vital. Working with the small Crosslake police force, he'd learned many facts. One being that longtime local resident Clayton Krueger was a ladies' man and probably not faithful to his wife.

He was also certain the Backwoods Café & Bait wasn't making much money, as was obvious to anyone who saw the place. The family home and business, where generations of Kruegers had spent their time, was run down. According to both the husband, Clayton, and the daughter, Violet, the last time either had seen Penny was on Sunday morning. Now the Macchi family's report confirmed that Violet had been away from home all day, from approximately ten a.m. until eight p.m. Clayton didn't report his wife missing until Monday evening. He told the police he didn't think they'd do anything until after twenty-four hours anyway—which in essence was true, but a normal husband might have been worried sooner and at least reached out. It smelled bad.

Initially interviewed by the Crosslake police, who had gotten a bad vibe, Clayton hadn't come across as someone all that shook up. They'd immediately notified the sheriff's office that a missing local woman—a young mother—had apparently vanished on a beautiful Sunday, leaving behind her identification and valuables as well as her husband and child.

Once in the loop, Sheriff Becker's office had acted quickly and search parties were organized, including a K-9 unit. Then the local news got wind of it, and somehow the case was plucked out of obscurity and became a national story. Probably, and sadly, because Penny Krueger was a very pretty, petite, blond mother whose disappearance stunned those who knew her. Bad shit in beautiful lake country during a slow summer. It was news.

Sherriff Becker scanned his notes, and his previously nagging thought finally bit him. His head popped up. "Did you say your names are Alex Macchi and Petunia Macchi?"

"Yes." Alex's voice sounded clipped.

"*The* Petunia Macchi Carrows? Of the Carrows family? The one the books were written about?" Tate squinted at the phone.

"Yes, Sheriff Becker. My wife, Charlotte Carrows Macchi, is here with us as well. We were hoping, since Petunia is a minor, only eleven years old, and the fact there is some notoriety attached to her name and our family, that you would keep her name and our statements anonymous. Any chance of that happening, sir?"

Shit, Tate mouthed. This case just took another weird turn. Now he had a notorious billionaire's kid to worry about? He jumped up from his desk and closed his office door.

"Ah, yes. I think it's extremely important we keep your name out of this. First of all, it would distract from the search and the focus of the case and what the family is dealing with, and second, because Petunia is a minor. I agree, we need to keep her name out of the press."

He took his seat behind his desk. "Look, I appreciate you coming forward with this information. I think it has value. Is there any chance you'd would be willing to let us interview you in person? I'd like the county attorney and another investigator to have a chance to speak with you too. Also, we're going to need a formal statement from all of you concerning the timeline, and specifically, what Petunia overheard at the Backwoods."

Tate listened to what must be the mom—Charlotte Carrows herself—speak. "Do you think there's any chance Penny might just turn up?" she asked.

"I won't put a never on that, but no, I don't think so. She's either dead, or she's been abducted—but either way, we believe something is preventing her from returning home."

Tate thought he heard a very young child in the background say, "Don't cry."

"All right," Alex Macchi said. "We were preparing to leave Jackson Hole in two days. We have a chartered flight home to New York, but we could arrange a stopover in Brainerd. I believe they have an airport?"

"We do. What time can we expect you?" he said, imagining being able to ask his own pilot to make a pit stop as if it was no big deal.

"We have a plane standing by to leave at eight a.m. on Monday. We should arrive in Brainerd, I don't know, I'm guessing around one p.m.? How about we give you call when we land, and we'll meet you at the sheriff's office. I'm assuming that's in Brainerd as well?"

"It is. Do you need one of my officers to pick you up?" Tate scratched out some notes.

"No. Thank you. We'll arrange for transportation and meet with you probably no later than one-thirty or two p.m. How long do you think you'll need?"

Tate frowned at the phone, not liking to deal with a harried billionaire's travel schedule. "Shouldn't take more than an hour. I appreciate you going to all this trouble, and I'm sure Mrs. Krueger would as well."

"We're very sad this happened and want to help if we can. She seemed like an awfully nice woman, and her daughter, Violet, is very sweet. We enjoyed our day with her," said Alex.

"I look forward to meeting with you on Monday afternoon."

Shoot! thought Sheriff Becker as he disconnected. *Holy hell.* This just got big. He put his hand back on the phone and punched out the number for his friend and County Attorney, Gavin Stewart.

"Gavin, you're not going to believe the latest in the Krueger case."

After filling him in, Tate continued. "I told them we would keep their names out of it. Do you think we can do that?"

"I know I can, and I know *you* can, but what about your other officers? I mean, the family will come traipsing through the squad room and all eyes will be on them. Someone's going to recognize them, but we need that interview."

Tate wondered about the officer who took the call from Alex Macchi. Had he put the name and the family together? If he had, he better not have spread the word. He'd talk to him as soon as he got off the phone.

"I can't believe they were up here vacationing and we didn't know anything about it," Gavin said. "And the Kruegers must not have recognized them because neither Clayton nor Violet mentioned them being big shots or famous. Maybe they don't look like their pictures?"

It was a thought. Sheriff Becker punched the Carrows Macchi name into the search engine of his desktop and waited for the images to appear. "Maybe. We'll find out on Monday. As to my officers keeping their mouths shut, I'll put my professional resentment aside and assure you that they won't say anything. You know what though? I'll call Alex Macchi back and tell him we'll just meet them at the airport."

"It's a good idea. Petunia Carrows Macchi may be a witness for the prosecution if it turns out Clayton killed his wife."

Sheriff Becker stared at the most famous picture of Petunia, looking sad as she walked through some ski resort in Switzerland surrounded by bodyguards. He pulled his eyes away from the screen and sat back, focusing on the ceiling. "Assuming Penny Krueger is dead . . ."

"She's dead. We both know it," said Gavin.

From everything they'd learned about Penny and Clayton Krueger since the disappearance, his instincts and experience told him that too. "Yeah. So someone killed her. But Clayton was at the Backwoods all day and night on Sunday—the day Penny went missing. There are too many witnesses to support him being gone for any length of time."

"I won't be convinced of that until I interview all the so-called alibi witnesses myself," said Gavin.

Tate nodded. "I suppose he could have stashed his wife while Violet was away, and then gone off to kill Penny later after Violet was home safe in bed, but I think he had an accomplice. I think he made sure he was at the Backwoods to establish an alibi, and I think he had someone else do the job."

"Clayton Krueger is the only one with a motive," said Gavin. "If Penny dies, he gets the insurance money, which by all accounts he desperately needs. It would set him up. Since Penny went missing, the Backwoods is a hot spot— he's got volunteers in his kitchen and bar and working the store."

Tate shook his head. "Petunia Carrows Macchi heard Clayton and Penny arguing the day before she went missing. *Petunia Carrows Macchi*, for God's sake—she'd have *no* motive to involve herself. She'll have credibility. And more importantly, what about what she heard Clayton and some woman talking about in the bar. They didn't know she was back there listening, and it sure sounds like they were up to no good. What was that shit about cancer, though?"

"No idea," said Gavin. "I agree it looks bad, but I'm anxious to hear it from her in her own words. I want to see if it holds up to what she told you and if she looks like the type of person a jury might believe."

Tate glanced at his computer screen. "Have you seen her? Freckled face, sad brown eyes, and curly brown hair. Really cute?"

"I know who you're talking about. My wife read the books her father wrote when they were having that custody battle. Didn't he end up in jail?"

"I think so," Tate scratched his head. "In Europe somewhere. Maybe we should brush up on them before we meet?"

"I think I'll wait until after. I want to judge their credibility as best as I can on my first impression. How is the search going?"

"Not well. At least, we haven't found anything yet. There are so many lakes and woods around, I suppose she could be just about anywhere or right next to her home. The search is organized, and they'll be going out in grid formation tomorrow about four miles from the Backwoods. Each day we're widening the search area."

"How's Clayton holding up?" Gavin asked.

"Seems a little shaken, but not as much as he should be. We've got more witnesses coming forward letting us know they've seen him out at various bars this week. He's been around these parts long enough, and his face is on the news, so people know him. Clayton likes to party, but since he has a DUI, we already knew that.

"He willingly let us interview him and told us their marriage was fine. They were struggling with the bills, but said he was thinking about going back to work at a garage to help, and once they had some loans paid off, in about five years, they'd be in much better shape. He admitted his wife did the lion's share of the work around the restaurant, but insists he pulled his weight in a million ways too. It's a hard life apparently, lots of hours."

"What about Violet? What does she know?" Gavin asked. So far he'd had little involvement and hadn't been privy to all the details of the investigation.

"She's the one I really feel for. She's a mess. You can tell she's trying to be brave and hold it together, but she just doesn't know where to look right now. She doesn't have much family. Clayton's parents are in Florida, retired, and he has a brother in Stillwater for a meth thing. The sister-in-law is MIA, and we're checking into her, but we think she just took off after the brother got sent up. Then there's Penny's family. Not much there either. Penny's dad is long gone, and her mom and sister live in California. So far, they haven't traveled this way, but I spoke with the sister, and I'm getting the impression that she might be unstable and the mother a bit fragile right now. They might show up, but I don't know when. Violet's leaning on her dad right now, but I don't know if that's a good thing or a bad thing for her. If the sky falls and Clayton goes down for this, then I don't know, there may be foster care for her."

"Jesus."

Chapter 15

Ginger Krueger sat on her sofa, eating chips at a clip, and watching her new favorite show. The news. The news about her poor missing relative, Penny. *My God.* She had never felt so alive. This must be what people felt like on coke or meth. She was wired, but loving every minute of it.

She shoveled up a handful of Sour Cream and Onion Lays, her eyes wide, fixed on the television. *Look at them!* The volunteers, searching for Penny, searching in grids with their whistles and maps and reflective vests, searching in the fucking *Wrong Place*, she wanted to scream at the television. She knew where Penny was located because she had killed her. So far, it had been the highlight of her life.

Jesus H. Christ, I can't believe I've spent all my life watching these shows on TV when I could have been living them! Who knew it would feel this great? The high of it was like nothing, *nothing* she'd ever experienced. Even Skyler White from *Breaking Bad* hadn't murdered anyone, but Ginger Krueger had! She giggled at the thought, some of the chips falling out of her mouth and onto the front of her shirt. She picked it up and licked the crumbs and felt over-the-effing-moon that she had one over on Skyler White. Although if she were honest, this didn't take away anything from Skyler. She still worshipped her.

Ginger froze as she reached into her bag of chips, her hand wrapped around another large handful of Lays, as she had another epiphany. *Hey?* What if she looked like Skyler White? How cool would that be? She would be an actual murderer *and* a hot blond bombshell. Clayton would pee himself every time he looked at her!

It wasn't as if she never thought about losing weight and getting into shape. The problem, she suddenly realized, was she'd never had the *proper motivation*! Well, whacking another human sure worked. Bet they don't have that in the Jenny Craig brochures!

Ginger threw down the bag of chips and ran to her car. She knew losing the weight would take some time, but by God, there was one thing she could change right away, and that was the color of her hair. She'd go beautiful blond, just like Skyler, and every day she looked in the mirror as she slimmed down, she'd be closer than ever to her.

As she drove to the drugstore, she plugged in her new favorite mental video—replaying over and over, *The Murder of Penny Krueger.*

Everything had gone perfectly. Colombo himself wouldn't be able to find fault with their plan. Clayton had not been thrilled to see her that morning at the Backwoods, but she'd been nervous and knew it would help to see him before it went down. Of course, that was before she'd been reborn as Skyler White. Now, she'd never be nervous again. She licked her lips and stole a quick glance at herself in the mirror as she drove into town. She knew she'd kick it as a blond.

Back to the show . . .

After speaking with Clayton, she'd left the Backwoods and gone to O'Toole's, a large bar and restaurant with a back patio big enough to accommodate an outdoor band, though it was used primarily as a place for smokers to light up. On a beautiful summer day up north, there were typically few people hanging out indoors, day drinking, but there were always some. Ginger had planted herself at the bar, regularly going outside to smoke. While she waited for the appointed time, she nursed her drink and used the bar Wi-Fi to scan her Twitter account and catch up on the actors she regularly followed. Munching slowly through her basket of delicious cheese curds, it calmed her to know that her favorite celebrities were out there in the real world doing some of the same stuff as everyone else. But unless they were on a movie set, she'd take bets they wouldn't be up to the same shit she was this afternoon!

Ginger, always a heavy smoker, had no trouble leaving the bar several times to step outside onto the back patio and smoke. Each time she stayed longer and longer, and by the time she was due to leave O'Toole's, she figured no one would notice when she disappeared out back nor clock how long she was gone. Leaving at the exact moment Clayton was convincing Penny to check out the eagles on Horseshoe Road, Ginger drove the roughly two miles from O'Toole's to the secluded spot on Horseshoe to wait for Penny to appear. She got out of the car and pulled off her jeans, revealing a pair of black running shorts, which she wore with her casual camouflage T-shirt. She was ready for action and waited patiently in the heat until she saw Penny running down the road, miraculously right on schedule.

According to the plan, Ginger would bend over and pretend to be sick by the side of her car, and predictably, Penny would stop to assist her. Stupid Penny.

In the car, lost in the fantasy, Ginger tingled as she remembered her favorite part . . .

"Ginger," Penny said, coming to a halt, apparently surprised to see Clayton's cousin throwing up on the side of the road in the middle of nowhere. "Are you okay?"

"Penny, oh, God, I'm so sick! I came down here to see if I could get a few pictures of those eagles I heard about and thought I would do some running, but the heat, and I had some jalapenos last night God, I'm so sick!" She screamed and grabbed the back of her shorts and said, "Oh, Shit! I'm coming out of my pants!" She ran into the woods.

Penny stood there, unsure what she should do until she heard Ginger scream from the woods. "Penny! Help! Would you bring me some toilet paper? I have some in the backseat! Oh my God!"

Ginger heard Penny do as instructed and enter the dense woods. Ginger had moved deeper in until she found the shovel she and Clayton had left behind an enormous oak tree. Hiding behind the tree, she waited until Penny, calling her, walked past. Ginger moved around the oak, coming up behind Penny, raised the shovel over her head, swung with all her might, and slammed the shovel into the back of Penny's head. She went down. And no blood! Ginger bent over and saw her lights were out. Moving quickly, she threw the shovel down, dragged Penny about twenty feet, and pushed her into a seven-foot hole she and Clayton had spent hours digging. She ran back, grabbed the shovel, returned to the hole, and pushed at the dirt and debris pile, covering Penny, but leaving the hole about three feet deep. Then, an almost harder effort, and certainly smellier, she dragged a small deer carcass they'd left near the hole the night before and threw it into the hole over Penny's dirt-covered body. Finally, she completely filled the hole with the remaining dirt and used her hands and the shovel to spread natural debris over the site. She back-tracked through the woods, covering their footprints with leaves and grass.

Emerging slowly from the woods, scanning the area and verifying she was still alone, she jogged back to her car, threw the shovel into the trunk, grabbed a water bottle out of the back, and washed her hands thoroughly. She pulled a mirror out, checked her face and hair for any debris, washed her face, grabbed her jeans out of the car and pulled them over her jogging shorts, got back into the car, and drove back to O'Toole's. She'd been gone nearly forty-five minutes. Materializing like a ghost from the back patio, she sat back down at her table, casually grabbed some delicious curds, pulled out her phone, did a quick, clandestine-like look around, and thought she was in the clear. No one seemed to have clocked her movements or noticed she'd been gone. She spent the next several hours in the restaurant, in and out of the patio area, smoking, and munching on a basket of delicious curly fries. They were the best-tasting meal of her life. Later, she switched to beer and made sure to mingle with the dinner crowd, even winning a pot roast at the evening's meat raffle!

Now in her car, sitting in the parking lot of the drugstore, she came out of her trance and realized she'd been sitting in the parking lot for ten minutes, lost in thought. Looking wildly around to see if anyone noticed her trance-like state, she had another epiphany. *Diet pills!* Maybe she'd see what kind of diet pills they had and take some of them too.

With her new outlook on life and some medical assistance, the weight would come pouring off. If they didn't have any ephedrine, she'd get something like it. Getting out of the car, she stopped to look at the sky and thought the colors were more vivid than she had ever noticed. *What a great world.*

Chapter 16

On Monday afternoon, Sheriff Tate Becker and Crow Wing County Attorney Gavin Stewart watched while the private airplane carrying the Carrows Macchi family touched down at the Brainerd airport and began taxiing toward them. There wasn't a lot of activity at the airport, and the plane was the only large Gulfstream making a landing near the private terminal. Besides, Alex had texted they were about to touch down.

"They're not the first billionaires we've probably met. Not up here. People don't flash their money around is all," Gavin said. He ran his hands through his hair as the wind gripped it and fussed, styling his hair back into place.

"Then why are you excited," Tate said, catching onto his friend's mood.

Gavin smiled. "I Googled them. Charlotte Carrows Macchi. There's this one picture of her, she's got on this backless dress . . ."

The door to the plane opened and the stairs automatically extended. Gavin and Tate walked toward the plane as the family emerged and came down the steps.

Hand shaking and quick introductions aside, Tate led everyone to a private hangar where a small conference space had been made available. Walking toward the building with the famous family following, his excitement level ticked up. He was a little in awe that he was meeting them. The evening before he'd spent some time looking at their pictures from various charity events, parties, and paparazzi. When the family was dressed up and posing for the cameras, Tate was amazed by how dripping rich and good-looking the entire clan was. Petunia had a vulnerability around her eyes which made her appear sad sometimes in pictures, but maybe that was because they were being taken by paparazzi and it upset her.

He certainly appreciated their phone call detailing the information they had on the missing Krueger woman, and in hindsight realized that they could have blown it off and not gotten involved, but instead they made an inconvenient—and no doubt expensive—detour in their vacation plans to make this interview. Of course, it was the right thing to do, but he was well aware not everyone did the right thing.

As they got settled into the room, Tate locked eyes with a huge bodyguard named Renzo Castrogiovanni and glanced at the Macchi's three-year old daughter, Lily. It surprised him they didn't stay on the plane until Charlotte filled in the blanks. "Renzo was with us, of course, the day we met the Kruegers, and the day we had Violet with us, so he's a witness as well. And we couldn't leave Lily alone on the plane."

Tate nodded in the glaring man's direction as everyone settled around the table. "Of course." He wondered what life must be like to need a bodyguard to take on vacation. Other than that large exception, the family seemed like any other family. They wore no special glamour or jewelry to give away they were one of the richest families in America, but then, Tate wondered if that was planned. The fact they'd gotten in and out of the Crosslake area during the high season without a reported sighting slipping out reinforced his belief they'd wanted to keep a low profile.

Petunia Carrows Macchi, in person, was one of the cutest kids he'd seen. There was definitely something about her that made you want to protect her, so the camera didn't lie when it picked that up. But there was also a strength it didn't capture. She sat straight and confident, clear eyed, and focused, and he had the uneasy feeling she was sizing him up too.

"Mr. Macchi, Mrs. Macchi, Petunia, Mr. Castrogiovanni, thank you for coming so far out of your way," Tate began. "We appreciate you coming forward with the information we spoke about over the phone, and I need to make you aware we are being recorded."

Alex Macchi laid his own phone on the table before him and tapped it a few times. "We understand. And just so you know, I'll be recording this too."

Tate glanced at Gavin, who shrugged, before turning back to Alex and continuing. "Fine. So, to get to the heart of the information, Petunia, I would like you to take Mr. Stewart through the conversation you overheard in the restaurant the day Mrs. Krueger went missing."

Petunia nodded and began, talking about the invitation for Violet to join them, and leaving Petunia behind in the restaurant while Violet got ready.

She adjusted her seat and glanced at her little sister, who had wandered over to Renzo and crawled on his lap. Renzo pulled a package of gummy bears out of his pocket and offered the little girl one.

Petunia continued. "So I was finishing off this big cinnamon roll, and my fingers were sticky and my napkin was gone, so I went over to this stack I saw on a table by a doorway which led into the bar. The doorway was next to the jukebox, and I was looking at the songs on it when I heard a man and a woman talking. I'm trying hard to remember the words exactly like they said it, and I think he said to 'get rid of it this afternoon' and to 'stick to the schedule.'"

Tate watched Petunia make air quotes around the exact words. He stole a glance at Gavin and saw he was taking it all in.

The young girl continued. "So then he said, 'Violet has the afternoon off' and to 'be ready.' He said 'don't call me, I'll call you' and 'when you're finished, you should get to the bar fast.' And then the lady's voice said, 'I'm worried,' and he said, 'It'll be fine, it's all ready and be cool,' and she said, 'I'm cool, I'm cool.' And then she said the weird part, 'The cancer won't come back.'"

Realizing the young witness was done, Tate looked over at Gavin, who smoothed his tie. The county attorney then took Petunia Macchi back through the events and went through the exact words she could remember again. He did some paraphrasing, which Petunia corrected, and Tate realized the more he did that, the more solid a witness she became. Gavin then interviewed each of the others on the timeline and events. At the end, Tate felt very comfortable that what they were saying was the truth.

Concluding the interview and understanding that the Macchis wanted to visit with Violet Krueger, Gavin and Tate released them. The visit would give Gavin time to prepare the forms and type up their statements. The documents would be ready for the family's review and signatures before they reboarded their plane. They agreed to return and left.

"Well," Tate asked Gavin. "What do you think?"

"I think she'll make a reliable and believable witness when Clayton Krueger is brought up on murder charges. I think she overheard the two conspirators, probably only hours before Penny Krueger disappeared. It was their last conversation before they abducted her or killed her. Has to be. I don't understand the cancer not coming back piece though, and that troubles me. A defense attorney could say the entire conversation was about cancer if you look at it that way, but I don't think they were talking about cancer. It's just too random a topic at the end of the conversation."

Tate frowned at that bit too, wondering if he should check for witnesses, suspects, or family members with cancer. But then again, he didn't want word to get back to Clayton that they knew anything about the overheard conversation. He'd have to give that angle some further thought. "So you definitely believe that Clayton was involved in his wife's disappearance?"

Gavin nodded. "I do. It lines up. Petunia recognized his voice from the day before, and when she left, she saw him in the parking lot speaking with a woman. You've got to find that woman, Tate. She's probably your killer since Clayton has the so-called alibi. They were working together, and if you find Penny Krueger, most likely dead, then I'm comfortable I can get a judge to issue search warrants for his home and property. If you can't find the woman who did this, we might still be able to get an indictment against Clayton and arrest him, and we might be able to convince him to take a deal if he gives us his partner."

"We're looking at everyone," Tate said, shaking his head. "We're searching the woods, but we've either been incredibly unlucky, or they had a pretty good plan. Petunia said the woman in the parking lot was a brunette, a little heavy she initially said, but after you pressed her, it seemed her manners kept her from saying she was someone 'very heavy.' Unfortunately, she only saw the woman's back. Also, it doesn't help narrow down the possible partners since Clayton has so many lady friends scattered around the lakes area. The call centers have had a number of women come forward to let us know he'd been with them. Amazing really, none of them seemed ashamed given that the man was married. Everyone wants their fifteen minutes nowadays—doesn't matter if it's for the right reasons. Famous is good, even if it's bad. We're interviewing all of them, but nothing's shaken out from it. They got alibis."

Gavin plucked away at his laptop, pulling up forms. "Keep looking. The killer's out there, but I doubt she'll be calling it in."

"How do you feel about the Macchis going to the volunteer center to see Violet before they head out of town?" He'd been a bit disconcerted when Charlotte announced they'd arranged for a family van Uber to pick them up for a trip into town after the interview. So much for keeping their stopover private.

Gavin shrugged. "I think it's okay. We told them to keep their information confidential and not tell anyone what they saw or heard. They know not to tell anyone we spoke with them, and I think they understood why it's important.

They appear pretty sharp—I think we can trust them. Nice family, all in all. Don't you think?"

"Very nice, but I wonder how they'll feel if we need them again? They live in New York City. Do you think they'll cooperate?"

Gavin stood up. "I do. I got a sense from them that they really want to help, and that they're in it for the right reasons. They certainly aren't interested in the publicity, especially for their daughter, but I think they want to do the right thing. I don't think they were intimidated by the process. It can be a lot for some people to handle."

Tate smiled at his friend. "I don't think they're regular people, Gavin. I don't think much intimidates them."

Chapter 17

"You did great, honey," her mom said as they drove through Brainerd. They'd been discussing the interview, and while Petunia had been pretty nervous meeting the police, she felt good about it herself. The sheriff and county attorney weren't mean at all, and besides, she knew she was telling the truth. She wasn't making any of it up. And if it helped find Mrs. Krueger, then that was all that mattered.

Volunteer search headquarters were at the Country Suites hotel in Brainerd. They parked and went inside, and this time, Renzo stayed in the lobby with Lily as Petunia and her parents found the conference room where the volunteers gathered.

Once inside the big room, the reality of the tragedy struck Petunia as she saw stacks of Penny Krueger posters with the words 'Missing' and 'Reward for Information'. Next to a volunteer sign-in desk, there was a stack of neon green high-visibility vests, whistles, maps, and another table with beverages and plates of picked-over donuts.

There were people talking with one another, sitting in chairs scattered about the room, and clustered around Violet, a small group of young girls, most with their heads in their phones.

Petunia took a deep breath, bit her bottom lip, and not quite believing the entire production, heard her mom whisper. "There she is." They made their way to Violet, who looked up from her chair, clearly surprised.

Violet's friends moved over to make room for the newcomers. "Hi," Violet stood and waved feebly.

Petunia hugged her. She whispered, "I'm so sorry your mom is missing. I can't imagine how worried you must be." They held for some time, and the intensity of her friend's pain hit her.

When Violet pulled away, tears were streaming down her face. Starting to sob, she covered her face with her hands.

Holding her again, Petunia saw a couple of girls offer their seats to her parents. Her mom encouraged Violet and Petunia to sit down. Reaching to Violet for her own hug, Charlotte asked, "Violet, are you okay? Honey, is there anything you need? Anything we can do?"

Shaking her head, Violet pulled some tissues from her pocket, mumbling, "I don't know. I don't think so. Everyone's looking for her."

"They'll find her," Alex said.

Petunia looked into her father's concerned eyes, knowing he was trying to be supportive, but everyone knew he was speaking words which might not be true.

"Violet," said Petunia, handing her a bag. "I got you this. It's a smartphone. You said you didn't have one, and I knew you could use it." Violet opened her mouth to speak, but her face reddened. Petunia placed the bag on the floor near her feet. Sensing Violet was worried, she rushed to continue. "It's paid for, and we purchased an unlimited data and messaging plan. It's yours as long as you need it."

Petunia pointed to the bag. "I wrote down the passwords I set up for you, which you can change, and there are some accessories, chargers and stuff. The phone has a credit card attached. The password's in there, too. You can use it to buy apps and stuff. We put $1,000 on the card, and if you need more, just ask. I hope it helps."

Petunia felt her face turn red. She knew all Violet really wanted was her mom. Stuff didn't matter, but it was all they could do at the moment.

"Thanks," Violet said, looking down. "That was really nice of you."

"I put my name and number in it, you know, your first contact. I hope you know we're friends and you can call or text me anytime you want."

Violet nodded, "Are you staying at the Madison place again?"

"No. We're on our way back to New York, but when we heard about your mom, we had to stop on the way home to see if there was anything we could do. And I wanted to give you a hug, you know, to let you know I . . . we . . . were thinking about you, and that we care."

Violet reached over and hugged Petunia again and cried some more, thanking her for coming. Eventually, it was time to say goodbye. Petunia felt worn out and sick when she left the room. She took her parents' hands, beyond grateful for so much, and they walked to the lobby to collect Renzo and Lily to fly home.

She knew there was more to come, but, for now, there was nothing else to do.

Violet watched the Macchis leave and was once more circled by her gaggle of friends. If at times over the week she had wondered at the nature of some of those friendships and the high drama of the events drawing kids she hardly knew to flock around her, she didn't have time to dwell on it. That the Macchis had made a special trip to see her was very kind. The phone and money was too. She'd call Petunia to thank her better later.

"Violet," one whispered. "Oh my God! I can't believe you *know* them?"

"What are you talking about?" Violet sat on her hands.

"That girl! That's Petunia Macchi!"

"I know," she said, confused why that required such a big pronouncement.

Her friend dropped her jaw and rolled her eyes. "That's Petunia *Carrows Macchi*, Violet. One of the richest kids in the world! From the *Carrows* family?"

Violet looked at the door where she'd last seen them. "What?"

"Oh my God, I can't believe you didn't know that." Her friend leaned over to whisper, "How do you even know them?"

Violet looked back at the popular girl with the super wide eyes and the others huddled near her, knowing that the entire group was really the popular girl's circle of friends. Violet suddenly wanted to protect Petunia and didn't want her treated like a celebrity sighting. She shrugged and said, "I met her this summer."

Violet grabbed the Verizon bag and walked away. She didn't know what to think about any of it.

Newly blond Ginger had been lingering near Violet's encounter, fascinated beyond belief for a variety of reasons. She realized she'd just seen the out-of-town strangers Violet had been hanging with the day Ginger murdered Penny. And they weren't just any family; they were the freaking Carrows.

Sensing the information was vitally important to the operation, she waited patiently at the volunteer center all day until Clayton finally showed up that evening. He'd made it a habit to thank the volunteers at the end of each day before he collected Violet and went home. After that, he usually went out, but never to Ginger's place. At least not for now.

Dying to speak privately, Ginger inclined her head, asking him to follow her out of the others' earshot.

She put her hands in her back pockets and her head down as she dished the dirt. "So, earlier today, Violet had some visitors. You know that family that was staying at the Madison place? You know . . . the one Violet hung out with that *daaaayyyy*?" she whispered at the end.

Ginger looked up just in time to see Clayton eyeing her cleavage. "What about it?" he asked, backing up.

She flushed. "Well, they came by this afternoon and gave Violet an iPhone."

"Wow, that was nice of them." He looked over toward the exit and at Violet.

"That's not the big part, Clayton. The big part is their name. The little girl, Violet's buddy, her name is Petunia Carrows Macchi. Does that ring any bells?"

"Sounds familiar," he said, looking directly into her eyes.

Ginger was delighted she would be the one to tell him. "Carrows, Clayton. *The Carrows family.* One of the richest families in the world? Ring any bells now? They have that big palace in California. Petunia's father was in a custody battle with her mom, and he wrote some stupid books about it? Hello?"

Clayton's jaw dropped. "What the hell? They were having breakfast at the Backwoods? And they invited my Violet to spend the day with them?"

Ginger nodded, began to smile, but then frowned and placed what she was certain would look like a comforting hand on Clayton's arm. She tingled from head to foot at the touch. "Now you're getting it. And they came back from vacation today to give your daughter a smartphone. Awful nice of them, wasn't it? Apparently, they live in New York, and they were on the way back. Violet's not talking much about them, and I didn't want to press it. Poor kid."

Clayton moved two steps away and pulled out his phone as if looking at something. "Yeah, hey, I gotta go. I can't be seen hanging with you, you know?"

Ginger sulked as she watched him walk away. He hadn't even commented on her new hair.

Chapter 18

____

The search continued, dragging on for another frustrating two weeks. As time passed, volunteers began to drop off. Those who continued searching were losing hope that Penny might still be found alive.

Buster Finlayson, who had a small cabin in the area, had returned home from a hunting trip and wanted to help. He knew he had one of the best damn tracking dogs in the state—hell, probably the country—and was confident his dog could find anything. He'd been training his young Black and Tan Coonhound and only recently realized the dog's exceptional talent.

Everyone knew dogs had an extraordinary sense of smell, but Buster knew for sure not all of them were as smart as his Ripley. He'd been lucky to get one of the pups from the leading Wisconsin breeder, and he and Ripley spent most of their time working together. Buster tirelessly trained the pup to be his nose when they went hunting. Ripley wasn't formally trained to be a cadaver dog, and he didn't have any specific K-9 search training, but Buster had a lot of faith in him.

He'd read the reports of Penny's disappearance with interest after he'd returned from their latest trip. He contacted a friend who he figured had been a part of the search.

"They haven't found anything nearby? No scent of Penny?" Buster asked. He'd met Penny many times at the Backwoods, and like everyone else, liked her and wondered what she saw in Clayton.

"A few loose threads, trails. Penny Krueger was a runner, so she left her mark here and there, but it hasn't led us to her."

"And the police, did they have K-9 units out, cadaver dogs?" Buster questioned.

"They did, but they didn't find anything. Found some dead shit, but no woman."

"Too bad."

"They thought they had something once, not too far from the Backwoods, down Horseshoe. There was a grave one of the dogs found, but someone had buried a deer, so that was a dead end."

"Why would someone bury a deer?" Buster puzzled.

"Who knows? People are crazy."

"Huh. You still have something with her scent on it? I'd like to take Ripley out, see what she can do."

"Nah, you'd have to contact the sheriff. He'll have something. They send the dogs out searching at the same time each day, but different directions, different grids. Not sure where they're looking now. I tell ya', it don't look too good for her. She sure as shit isn't just lying around hurt somewhere, not nearby at any rate."

"Maybe I'll try the sheriff," Buster decided.

"Couldn't hurt."

The next day, Buster Finlayson, after convincing a sheriff's deputy that he had a very special dog and that they'd been away over the last few weeks and wanted to help, met with a deputy who had one of Penny Krueger's garments.

Buster thought it a good idea to start at the Backwoods. Once Ripley got a nose full, the dog pulled him at a quick pace right to Horseshoe Road. Eventually, Ripley stopped at a curve and tugged Buster off the road and into the trees. Following his dog, Buster was led about thirty feet into the woods where Ripley suddenly sat down and howled. Clearly, there had been some digging at the spot and it looked like there was a grave. Buster figured it must be the deer his friend had told him about and was sincerely disappointed that his Ripley would get confused by a dead deer carcass buried in the ground.

Even after he let Ripley off the leash, the dog just ran around the grave, howling, and began digging at the ground. Buster Finlayson had confidence in his dog and a brain in his head. He told Ripley to knock it off and called the sheriff. After some back and forth, he finally convinced the man to get a shovel and meet him on Horseshoe Road. He wanted to see what Ripley would do when he saw the deer. Maybe then he'd stop barking.

But that didn't happen. After the sheriff and Buster reluctantly pulled and shoveled out the rotting remains of the dead deer carcass, Ripley ignored the deer, jumped into the hole and began clawing the dirt.

"Well ain't that interesting," said Buster. They pulled the dog out and called for help.

It didn't take them long. Another four feet of digging later, they found poor Penny Krueger. Ripley finally stopped howling, and instead lay down beside the grave and began to whimper.

Chapter 19

Ten days later, Clayton Krueger circulated among the throng of guests at the reception after his wife's funeral. Quite upset Penny's body had been discovered, he realized he might be in trouble. If they'd never found her stupid body, he would have been in the clear. Bodies were important. But now that the cops knew Penny had been murdered, he could feel the wagons circling. Indeed, he could feel appraising eyes watching him now. He dropped his head and put his hands in his pockets.

His concern over his own fate actually helped his ability to feign the expected grief over his wife's death. He'd watched some Hallmark show about another dead wife and paid close attention to how the actor—whom the viewing audience knew was the actual killer—behaved during the funeral. The man had done a first-rate job of fooling everyone and done a lot of frowning and throat clearing. Clayton copied those tactics today.

Another helpful item was the continuing support he'd been receiving at the Backwoods. Volunteer shifts running the joint had freed up all of his time to play the devoted husband, to participate in the search, and to see to Violet's needs. Not that Violet was sharing much other than her relentless tears. He looked across the room and spied her using a tissue to wipe her face as some woman Clayton had never even met stroked his daughter's arm, offering some kind of weird, stranger sympathy.

Given he was the one who'd had her mom murdered, he didn't really know what to say to Violet. He held her sometimes though.

He refocused on the conversation around him, trying really hard to listen closely as people stumbled around condolences. Intense *listening*, he had long known, whether you were interested or not—people liked that. They took it as a compliment or believed you cared. So he *listened* hard when they shared their stories about Penny, and everyone discussed the possibilities about who could have done this horrible crime.

It was annoying Penny had become such a saint. Since the discovery of her body, people looked at him differently. He found if he kept Violet close and played the doting father, they would still keep an open mind. He knew the minute he started behaving like anything other than a wrecked, heartbroken man, that would stop. People followed Clayton's gaze as he forced a worried glance in Violet's direction. For the moment, he felt the on-lookers relax, pulled back to his side.

But he didn't know how much longer he could keep up the act. He worried the mask would slip and was desperate for some lighthearted fun.

And there was Ginger to worry about too. Sensing she was looking at him, he made eye contact with her. What a fucking sight. Her over-peroxided hair combined with a dress two sizes too small made her stick out like a sore thumb. In his eyes, she looked a little wacky, and he hoped that others didn't notice it as well. But it was natural that the two of them speak at his wife's funeral, so he softly excused himself from the people around him and made his way to her.

Ginger gave him a hug, which lingered a little long for his comfort. When she released him, she said, "How you holding up, Clayton?"

"I'm okay. How are you, Ginger?"

"Good. Real good. I mean, okay, okay." She hung her head. "So, Clayton, you hear anything about them calling a grand jury?"

"No," he said trying to remain calm, trying to keep his eyes from widening, sweat breaking out on his back under his jacket.

"I heard it, Clayton. In the restroom right here at the funeral home. Don't know who was talking, but they said they heard it was comin'."

"Gossip. Probably just gossip." He felt his jaw muscles working but then forced his face into a frown.

"That's not all I heard," she said. She bit her bottom lip and looked away like she forgot where she was.

"Well what," he said with impatience.

"They have a witness. Maybe a witness, someone who heard or saw something."

Clayton felt his bowels loosen a bit. "Bullshit. When?"

"I don't know." Ginger began to whisper. "All I can think of was that morning at the bar. Maybe someone heard us there? I didn't say nothing to anybody, and I know you didn't, so, when? Who?"

Clayton let his eyes wander the room as he considered this, but they flew back to the crazy bitch when he heard her say, "You wouldn't turn on me, would you, Clayton?"

"No. Stop talking crazy. Look, I can't be seen spending too much time with you," he said, wanting to get away from her.

"Clayton." She put a hand on his arm. "It's natural that we're speaking at your wife's funeral. We're cousins."

But he could feel her fingers moving on his sleeve in a weird, circular way and pulled his arm back. Reconsidering the public move, he pulled Ginger into what he hoped was a goodbye hug and whispered, "If there's no witness, they got nothing. You understand what I'm saying, Ginger, my love? Stay on it. I appreciate it."

He moved away, but not before he witnessed Ginger blush, look down, and coyly smile.

Shit.

Chapter 20

Tate Becker and Gavin Stewart were elated when the Crow Wing County grand jury returned an indictment against Clayton Krueger. The case had been difficult to prove, but they'd arrested him, and begun a deeper search into his home, his life, his girlfriends, and his property.

After finding Penny Krueger in a seven-foot grave, they went back to the obvious question of who benefited from her death. Only one person. Clayton. He would get the life insurance, be able to pay off his loans at the bank, and for the first time, turn a profit at the Backwoods.

Once Penny's body was discovered, a local bankruptcy attorney had come forward with the facts regarding Penny's visit and her intention of filing for bankruptcy and closing the doors on the Backwoods. The attorney said he'd been anxious to help but couldn't divulge what he knew because of attorney client privilege—but once she was found dead, he was legally free to do so.

The lawyer's testimony, along with a friend of Penny's who confirmed she'd been talking about her concerns about the business, her concerns her husband cheated on her, and her concerns her daughter wasn't being given a chance to live to her full potential, had helped sway the grand jury. There was also testimony from women with whom Clayton had had affairs, and Gavin Stewart punched some holes in Clayton's alibi and opportunities for involvement.

The final straw, however, was Petunia Carrows Macchi's testimony on what she heard Clayton and a woman talking about the day Penny went missing. While enough to persuade a grand jury, now they would have to get a conviction in court, a much more challenging proposition.

Unless Clayton confessed or took the plea deal they offered in exchange for giving up his accomplice. The plan was to hold Clayton behind bars and sweat him. Gavin Stewart had filed first-degree murder charges, and Clayton was just beginning to experience what being locked up for the rest of his life might feel like. They'd delay the date of the trial for as long as possible.

The investigators continued their search for the accomplice and re-interviewed all the women who had come forward with information about Clayton. They noted that after his arrest, his cousin, Ginger Krueger had moved into the home to take care of Violet and run the family business.

After Clayton named Ginger Krueger as his daughter's legal guardian, Sheriff Becker brought her in for an interview. She was an interesting lady. Both shy and nervous at the same time. She claimed she was overwhelmed by the responsibility being placed on her and asked several times to smoke during the interview. That request denied, she took Starbursts out of her purse and ate them like a squirrel, nibbling at corners before laying them back on the wrapper, only to pick them up and nibble some more.

Weirdness aside, she claimed to have an alibi on the day Penny disappeared, and Sheriff Becker had personally gone to O'Toole's to check it out. He knew Ginger had no criminal record, and the picture on her driver's license showed her as a brunette, which was extremely different from how she looked now.

Sheriff Becker thought she could fit the profile Petunia gave them but was disappointed when Ginger's alibi at O'Toole's stood up. The owner said he definitely remembered her, and she'd even won the grand prize that evening at the meat raffle. He remembered she'd been in the place all day, shooting pool, playing darts, and ordering food. He didn't track her every movement, but she'd been there.

He'd keep an eye on her, but she didn't seem like an obvious candidate. Ginger just didn't seem sharp enough and was easily distracted. For the life of him, he couldn't think of a motivating reason for her to kill Penny Krueger. They'd need to keep investigating, and hope Clayton would crack.

So far, that plan wasn't working.

———————————

Clayton Krueger lay on the thin, lumpy plastic mattress on the top bunk in his dark cell. He rubbed a hand over his chest and belly as his body worked to digest the brown sludge and meat patty he'd been served for dinner. His chest tightened, but he breathed slowly through his mouth and closed his eyes, trying to think of better times. The effort proved elusive. Behind bars, being held in the Crow Wing County Jail, he'd been told multiple times it was a palace compared to his future potential home in Stillwater Penitentiary.

He couldn't believe he'd been arrested. His court-appointed attorney couldn't believe it either. According to his lawyer, the case against Clayton was entirely circumstantial. They had no physical evidence. Nothing. And Clayton had an alibi! Yet here he sat, bail revoked, in jail, awaiting trial.

He and his lawyer had been presented a deal by the fuckwad county attorney, Gavin Stewart, who told them he would reduce his sentence if Clayton pled guilty and named his accomplice. Like that was going to happen. If he did that, he'd be admitting to murder.

Placing his hand over his mouth, hoping to silence what he knew would be a world-class belch, he felt relief when the foul-smelling event released some of the pressure on his stomach. He ripped the nearly pointless, deflated pillow out from under his head and beat at it, trying to get it to form some support before rolling onto his side and placing the pillow back under his head.

I'm an innocent man.

Practice it. Believe it. He wanted people to think of him as a wrongly accused. If he confessed, yeah, he'd get some years taken off his sentence, but so what? By the time he got out he'd be twenty years older and a convicted murderer. Fat chance at a good life after that.

But, if he kept screaming his innocence, if he was acquitted at a bullshit circumstantial trial, then he would still have a chance to live his dreams. And from what he'd heard, the Backwoods was busier than ever. If he was found innocent, he would collect Penny's life insurance, and he'd use the money to make the Backwoods the place he'd dreamed about. He'd even be a celebrity.

Already since his arrest, women had been writing him. He had an actual fan club! Why in the world did Gavin Stewart think he would throw away his chances for personal happiness and plead guilty? Plus, his lawyer kept telling him he had a real good case.

Tucking an itchy sheet reeking of bleach under his chin, he thought about the case and the witnesses who wanted to hurt him. First was the goddammed bankruptcy attorney Penny had dragged in. The guy had testified. *Look what you did, Penny! I told you not to do that! See where that got us?* What a stupid twat his wife had been.

He supposed it was okay for people to know they'd been struggling. He told his lawyer their financial problems were fixable, and he was about to get another job to help them out of their hole. It was *fixable*. He told the guy to really use that word. Penny didn't need to be murdered for *fixable*.

A couple of his other casual flings had testified too. But being unfaithful didn't make him a murderer either.

Then there was Penny's girlfriend, Patsy Baker. He'd never liked that woman. It went all the way back to high school. He was sure that Patsy had had the hots for him, and she was just bitter because he'd never looked her way. Women gossiped. Women liked to complain to their girlfriends about their husbands. That was a fact of life, and his lawyer didn't see Patsy as the circumstantial witness who could seal his fate.

It was the anonymous witness who was going to try. The one who overheard Clayton and Ginger talking the day Penny went missing. Clayton could not, as many times as he tried, remember what he and Ginger actually said that day. He remembered he was pissed that the nitwit showed up at the Backwoods—but she'd claimed nerves, and they'd only spoken for a few minutes. That, he did remember. So who was the mysterious witness? And more importantly, what precisely, had they heard?

He figured it had to be a customer who was in the restaurant, who for some God-only-knows-why reason had their ear close enough to the bar door to hear them talking. The only thing by the bar door was the jukebox, so who would have been looking at that?

That morning, he'd done a little cooking in the kitchen, but had gotten a late start since he intended to give his family the afternoon off. He'd needed the extra sleep because he knew Penny would be dead and unable to help, and he'd have to work until 8 p.m. when they closed. He hadn't paid attention to the customers in the restaurant, so he didn't know who'd been in that morning, specifically when Ginger came in. But, he had seen Violet walk out of the Backwoods while he was in the parking lot with Ginger, and he'd watched her leave with the family that was vacationing down at the Madison place. He'd seen the girl, about the same age as Violet, look at him as they were leaving. Now, of course, he knew she was the poor little rich girl herself, Petunia Carrows Macchi. What were the odds of that?

His eyes squeezed tight as he froze on the image of that little girl's face. He could place her at the scene and realized she could have been the one in the restaurant. For sure. Petunia's parents, or the rest of her group, were already outside when Violet came out, so Petunia was looking like the best bet to be the witness who could fry him.

He wondered if Ginger was smart enough to figure this out too. They both knew that all conversations between them would be recorded, so he communicated with her through normal channels. He thought he gave her a clue when he met her along with his attorney, but he wasn't sure if she caught it. How could he tell her about his suspicions? More importantly, how could he get a message to Ginger to take the little bitch out? And shit! How would Ginger do it without getting caught?

It would be another long night.

———

"Aaaaahhh!" Ginger Krueger screamed as the long, metal pan crashed to the kitchen floor. Her heart beat hard from the shock of the noise, and she knew she was way too jittery. Not from fear, but from the damn diet pills. They were literally changing her personality. She picked up the industrial-size pan and decided not to rewash it before loading it with the next batch of dough. Ginger was alone in the Backwoods kitchen before sunrise. No one would ever know that she took shortcuts with the stinking cleanliness protocol.

Damn she was edgy. All the time. Nervous, sweaty, jumpy. The pills were making her feel lousy, and she wasn't sleeping well either. People around her had commented on her mood, and she'd sometimes break down sobbing, blaming stress. Fact was, the diet pills made her want to cry all the time too.

Worse yet, she was still eating! Her nerves were so shot she was either chewing gum or smoking or chewing on food to keep in step with the extra energy. She'd lost about ten pounds, but it wasn't even noticeable. After she bleached her hair and started taking the pills, she went out and spent a small fortune on cool clothes a couple of sizes too small, knowing, *convinced* the weight loss would happen quickly. But it didn't. And it pissed her off. And made her tearful. And pissed off some more. It was a vicious cycle, and while it might be good cover, it was driving her nuts.

She took a swig of her morning coffee, freaking decaf now, but it tasted pretty good with a teensy tiny squirt of whipped cream. There was only so much she was willing to sacrifice. Her whole life now felt like one big sacrifice.

The pressure had really built after they'd found stupid Penny. And then again after Clayton was arrested. Now she was living with Violet so the social workers wouldn't ship the kid off to foster care. She smiled thinking of Clayton's face the day he'd *pleaded* with his puppy dog eyes and *begged her* to take care of his little girl. He'd been so cute when he'd asked, and Ginger always felt puddly when he looked at her like that, but she also recognized her jealous feelings that Clayton's main concern seemed only for Violet. Why didn't people consider her needs too?

She'd counseled herself that it was she that Clayton was leaning on and knew the intimacy between them would continue to build if she took good care of Violet and kept the Backwoods up and running. But damn, it was a lot of work. Even with the volunteers still coming round, the hours were brutal.

The cinnamon rolls were making her crazy. She'd give Penny credit for that one. Ginger had to get up at 5 a.m. each day to get the damn things ready.

She grabbed a huge container of cream cheese from the fridge as well as whole milk to blend with the butter to make more of the delicious frosting. Violet had walked her through the entire process, and between the two of them they kept the restaurant going, but now that the Backwoods was busier than ever, they'd had to double the roll production. People thought by stopping over regularly to buy the rolls, they were helping the family business—but it was killing Ginger. She also discovered, to her horror, that the dough, dipped in a little cinnamon and sugar was damn good, even before it was cooked. Now she had a dough monkey on her back too. *Stupid Penny. It's all your fault!*

After Clayton was arrested, she'd visited with him and his lawyer to discuss the legal arrangements and power of attorney that Clayton signed so she could continue to run the business. It was at that meeting that she'd learned from Clayton about the witnesses who had testified before the grand jury securing the indictment. His lawyer insisted it was a purely circumstantial case, but here they all were! Clayton was in jail, and Ginger Krueger, aka, Skyler White, was working at the Albuquerque carwash, supporting the family, just like in *Breaking Bad.*

Except she couldn't recall Skyler making cinnamon rolls. *Whatever,* she thought as she yanked the beaters out of the blending bowl. She liked to lick them thoroughly clean; the action really helped her focus on their legal dilemma and next steps. "What to do, what to do," she said between long licks.

Even though the lawyer had thought it a bad idea for Clayton to share the prosecution information with his relative, Clayton had overruled him and gone into detail with Ginger about the witnesses who'd testified against him. When he got to the witness who had supposedly overheard him talking to someone that morning, he said it was unbelievable a tourist had overheard something and totally misconstrued the content and intent. That he emphasized *tourist* had not been lost on her.

Ginger had been thinking about the anonymous witness night and day. She knew Clayton was counting on her, and she needed to cover her own ass.

Moving into Clayton's home and getting to know Violet had been interesting. She'd known the kid since she was born, but really hadn't given much thought about her as a human being. She was *peripheral* to Clayton and to Ginger. But now she was Ginger's responsibility. Ginger didn't know if she liked being a mom, but Skyler White had kids, so she thought she would give it a try. She could play maternal.

She tossed the beaters into a sink filled with dirty water and dishes. Today, she'd leave that mess for Violet to clean. The kid needed something to do on a Saturday morning. Maternal tough love. That was the ticket.

During quiet times, Ginger did her best to cozy up to Violet, to hold her hand when she let her, to give her hugs, to talk to her and check in on her feelings. Although it was obvious how the kid was feeling, and it was bad. Violet was supposed to attend school, but most mornings she wouldn't get out of bed and missed the country bus. Sometimes Ginger drove her in late.

Ginger even got a call from the principal at the school, who was concerned and offered counseling sessions for Violet after school. Ginger thought it was a good idea, but Violet refused to go. The school's social worker stopped by the house to speak with Violet, and although the kid made promises to start attending school more regularly, she didn't follow up, and Ginger honestly wasn't sure she cared all that much about the school thing either.

The Krueger house didn't have Wi-Fi, and Ginger's data plan was limited—something she'd intended to change but had yet to do. Because of this, sometimes at night she asked Violet if she could borrow her phone to do some research. Violet had been initially reluctant, but Ginger guilted her that it was business stuff for the restaurant. In reality, she was looking into terms like PTSD and websites on signs of depression and suicide in teens. She was worried Violet might do some self-harm and then Clayton would feel let down. That would only complicate their lives and plans further. In the end, she didn't really have a clue what to do for Violet, so she focused instead on her own problems.

Walking out of the kitchen into the restaurant, she patted her apron and pulled out a package of cigarettes. Opening the pack, she placed a smoke between her lips and lit it as she used her shoulder to push her way out the door. Standing outside on the cracked concrete, the sun rising, the morning brisk and damp, she smoked, the nicotine coursing through her, offering her a bit of relief as she played out her games of *What If?*

What if A happened? What if A and B happened? How would life look? She inhaled deeply and started with her favorite What If—what if Clayton was found innocent and returned home to her. He would be so grateful to her, and she was sure this time their relationship would go further. Clayton was no longer married, and they were only second cousins, not *first* cousins, and people married their cousins all the time! Scenario A—her dream outcome.

Scenario B was if Clayton was convicted. What would happen then? She supposed Violet would get Penny's insurance money and she and Ginger would continue to live and work at the Backwoods at least until Violet turned eighteen. But then what would Violet do? If the Backwoods was legally Violet's, would she sell it and move on? Would

Violet leave Ginger in the dust after all she'd done for her? That would be terribly ungrateful of Violet.

Scenario C was the nightmare where Clayton decided to cut a deal with the county attorney and give her to the authorities. She didn't want to spend *any time* thinking about Scenario C. She needed to do whatever she could to get *Scenario A* to happen. If Clayton was found innocent and came home, they could play happy family. It all came down to the witness. If she could eliminate the witness, then they could live happily ever after.

Ginger thought hard about the morning she murdered Penny, and not always about the good parts. Who could the witness be?

Everyone knew the movements at the Backwoods that day. Penny had been working, Clayton moved from the kitchen into the bar, Violet was waiting tables, and then left late that morning with the people who were staying at the Madison place. The Carrows family. Violet drove off with the Carrows while Ginger was in the parking lot with Clayton. If Violet intended to go swimming that day, she would need her swimsuit, so there must have been a moment when she went and changed. Or packed. Which meant the Carrows girl would have been waiting for her. Waiting where? In the restaurant? Probably. It was logical. And Clayton had emphatically highlighted the word *tourist* when he'd talked about the witness, so he was telling her to look in that direction. Not a local. A tourist. Someone vacationing in the area. Like at the Madison's. Like the Carrows Macchi family. Like Petunia Carrows Macchi, waiting in the restaurant for her new friend Violet to get ready so they could have a luxurious day of boating and swimming.

Did Petunia Carrows come back to Brainerd and testify before the grand jury? *Jesus!* Didn't she have anything better to do? *She's just a kid!* Why didn't her stupid parents spare her from that? They probably couldn't be bothered with all their piles of money. Petunia probably had nannies raising her since the day she was born. The girl was a little snot—thinking all that money made her powerful, and that she could stick her nose in where it didn't belong.

Ginger realized she needed a plan to take care of Petunia Carrows. A permanent solution. She needed to find out everything she could about the family, and she needed to do it quietly. Not from her phone, and definitely not on Violet's.

And this is where Ginger's cat-like instincts and luck paid off. By not having an unlimited data plan and no access to Wi-Fi in the house, she was *forced* to use Violet's phone. Her continued cry of poverty was working wonderfully, for it allowed Ginger to glean information about Petunia from reading Violet's text messages. Borrowing the phone was a habit Ginger did every day, so it never seemed unusual.

Violet sent many texts to Petunia, and the rich kid always responded. Ginger *encouraged* this relationship. And because of this, Ginger was able to learn a lot about the Carrows' movements and how they ran their life.

Walking back inside the restaurant, she flipped on the lights, advertising the Backwoods, was open. Smiling now, she realized that later tonight when she hit the hay after another grueling day in the restaurant, she would once again have something big to dream about. She had *another crime* to plan. It felt good to be back in business.

Chapter 21

Charlotte was proud of Petunia and thought she'd handled the initial interview in Brainerd very well. On the plane ride home to Manhattan, they'd talked about how it was important to feel no guilt over being happy while someone else was in trouble. A person should care, should help whenever possible, but she counseled her children that another's pain shouldn't take away your own ability to feel joy.

Despite the awful circumstances in Minnesota and what it potentially meant, the adults knew there was a surprise—a good surprise—waiting at home. They were terrifically grateful for the timing, and as the transport van pulled up to their home, Charlotte couldn't wait to get inside.

Walking in the front door, Charlotte dropped one of their last bags next to the pile in the foyer.

"Where's Havish?" Petunia said.

"I don't know. I'll call him," Alex frowned as he and Renzo entered and closed the front door. He pulled out his phone and tapped it.

They heard the door to the basement open and Havish walked in with a puppy in his arms.

"Havish!" Petunia screamed seeing him.

"Vish!" Lily screamed, imitating her sister. Lily jumped up and down, a priceless look on her face as Alex recorded the moment on his phone.

Charlotte grinned, thrilled as Havish put the puppy on the floor and it loped over to her girls.

Just like that, a love affair started for them all.

"Is he ours?" Petunia squealed.

"He is," said Charlotte. "Surprise!"

"Oh my God, I can't believe it!" Petunia said as she and her sister hugged the ten-week-old puppy.

"Oh my God is right." Alex reached down to pet the scampering pup and smiled, stepping out of the way as Charlotte dropped to the floor. "Havish." Alex shook his hand, then held up his phone, videotaping him. "My dear man, so good to see you. How has it been going?"

Charlotte exchanged smiles with her handsome majordomo. A clean-shaven man with a broad, easy smile, even when Havish wore casual clothes, he always looked sharp.

Havish put his hands behind his back and spoke formally to the camera. "It has been going well. The pup seems quite sure of himself, but I'll not lie. There were a few tears last night. He slept in the kennel next to my bed, and we got through it. I didn't have a dog growing up, so training is new to me, but he's got a way about him. A rascal, I'd say. But quite sweet."

Alex laughed and turned as the puppy began yapping. "Thanks for holding down the fort and taking care of him. I think we'll move the kennel into our room."

"What do you think, Renzo?" Havish smiled.

"A good guard dog is an asset." Renzo replied.

"Yes. In my culture," said Havish, "dogs are revered as the guardian of the house. I feel this one may believe he is the master."

Renzo's frown made Charlotte laugh.

"Girls," called Alex over an outbreak of squealing. "You need to give him a name."

"Can we call him Dora?" Lily froze, wide-eyed with excitement.

"Dora? He's a boy," said Petunia.

Lily pulled her hand back from the puppy when it nipped at her. She stopped short of swatting him.

"Lily," said Charlotte. "He's a German Shepherd. He's going to grow into a very big dog. You need to remember to treat him with respect and to be gentle with him too."

"He chewed my fingers!" Lily complained. But she smiled, extending her hand carefully, allowing the puppy to gnaw it with a soft mouth. But still, puppy teeth are sharp. She pulled her hand back, but again extended it for more.

"Dogs, especially puppies, like to chew," Charlotte said, looking around as if for the first time at their beautiful new moldings and hardwoods. "Oh, Alex, we're going to need to train him quickly."

"We'll make sure he has lots of toys to chew, but we'll gate him off and introduce him slowly to the rest of the house. That's how we did it when I was a kid. The dog trainer will be here tomorrow, to train all of us. If we raise him to have good manners, then he can go wherever he wants."

"Even on my bed!" said Petunia.

"On my bed!" protested Lily.

"No, he can sleep in my room!"

"My room!" Lily pounded her hand on the floor.

"Okay, girls," Charlotte said, laughing. "We'll work it out. He's a part of the family now. And he's going to be everywhere. I suggest you name him before we decide where he's going to sleep."

"Thank you so much for the puppy," Petunia said, holding him in her arms and kissing him. "I just love him."

Lily leaned over and kissed the dog on the nose too.

Charlotte rose from the floor and hugged Alex. The adults watched the girls and knew this was a special moment, perhaps one of the best, and a very welcome one at the end of their curious road trip.

That evening, after exhausting poor Havish with tales of their adventures, the girls insisted on sleeping on the floor next to the kennel. They laid sleeping bags next to the crate and the three camped at the foot of Charlotte and Alex's bed.

"It's so good to be home." Charlotte smiled, holding Alex.

"It's nice to be in our own bed too, but tonight I thought we might be alone. You know, no Renzo snoring nearby, no girls. Now look at us. I think we've taken the nesting thing a bit too far."

She squeezed him. "It's perfect, Alex, and you know it." She snuggled in his arms, considering all they'd been through. "Other than the obvious, we have a lot of good memories from the trip, don't we?"

"We do. And now we'll make some more with that little guy over there."

"Do you think he's going to be as big as his father? I mean his paws are huge for his age."

"I don't know. Either way, I'll be glad to know there's a dog in the house protecting my family. They're an extremely loyal breed. Once he knows we're his pack, he'll protect us with his life."

Charlotte fully sat up and looked through the steel bars of the kennel. The puppy looked back and gave her a precious yawn, then fell onto his blanket and closed his eyes. She whispered, "Blue Carrows Macchi, goodnight. And welcome to the family."

On the rooftop terrace of the quiet and opulent house in the West Village, Renzo and Havish, at long last, resumed their ritual brandy under the stars.

Filling Havish in on the details of the sad situation in Minnesota and Petunia's involvement as a potential witness, Renzo scowled. "It's a sorry circumstance for Violet now without her mom, but in situations like this, it's usually someone in the family that did it. It sure looks like that son of bitch Clayton had his wife killed. If they ever find the body, they'll probably want Petunia to testify. Alex doesn't like it, neither does Charlotte—but I know them, and they'll do the right thing."

"Such a senseless tragedy," Havish said, swirling his brandy. He lay back on the chaise. "Such a shame Petunia and the rest of you are involved in this. I'm sorry for the girl. Thank you for preparing me for conversations I'm sure I will be having with Petunia. She's a strong young lady, but I hate to see her brought into this. You really think they'll make her testify in front of a jury? She's a minor."

Renzo shrugged. "I don't think that will matter to any of them. I mean, it's not something they want her to do, but what's the alternative? Petunia doesn't testify and Clayton Krueger gets away with murder? They'd probably subpoena her to testify. At any rate, it's one step at a time."

"Let me know if there is anything I can do to help, Renzo. I feel protective toward them."

"I'm glad to hear that," Renzo said, giving him the stink eye. "I wouldn't want a showdown with you."

Havish smiled and said in a lighthearted tone, "Ah, but I have a secret weapon. I was the *first* person in this house to spend the night with Blue. We bonded, even before the girls named him. All I need to do is snap my fingers and he will attack."

Renzo didn't immediately take the bait. Instead he said, "No kidding. I hope you never have to do that."

Still, the thought of violence against their family was sobering to both of them. They spent the rest of the evening in companionable silence, trying to ignore the problems of the world and instead, looked at the stars through a fine brandy.

Chapter 22

In the end, and as predicted, the entire family was sickened when Petunia was asked to testify before a grand jury. Alex and Charlotte traveled alone with Petunia and arrived in Minnesota late at night. They checked into the Country Suites in Brainerd using false names. The next morning, they snuck into a Minnesota courthouse and Petunia bravely gave her testimony. They flew back that evening and were in New York less than thirty-six hours after they'd left.

The day after they arrived home, Alex was back at work, but walked out of a meeting to take a call from Sheriff Becker.

"We got the indictment. Clayton Krueger has been arrested and charged with first-degree murder."

Alex closed his eyes, glad for the arrest, but disturbed Petunia would have to testify again if it went to trial. They all knew Clayton had a pretty good alibi. The county attorney would try poking holes in it, but most likely a first-degree murder charge wouldn't stick. It might—stranger things had happened—but Alex understood the folks in

Minnesota were playing a game. "You're going to pressure the bastard to take a plea, right? I'm not just talking for my daughter's sake, but for Violet. She could be spared some trauma if Clayton just pled to a lesser charge and went away."

Sheriff Becker cleared his throat. "Yeah, well, we'll see. In the meantime, and in preparation for the trial, I've been asked to tell you . . ."

"What?" Alex practically barked. What more could they want?

"Gavin Stewart told me to ask you to limit Petunia's social contact with Violet Krueger. The defense could make something of that."

Alex glared at his phone. "Just what do you want me to tell Petunia, Sheriff? They've found Violet's mother's body, arrested her father for murder, but she should ignore Violet if she reaches out now?"

"Well, maybe not exactly that way, but if she could, maybe limit the contact. And, of course, under no circum- stances can Petunia let Violet or anyone else know she is a witness for the prosecution."

Asking Petunia to lie to her friend was a heavy burden. They'd had the discussion before their first interview with the sheriff, and it hadn't gone well. Alex mouthed an expletive before tersely replying, "I suggest you do your job and gather more evidence, Sheriff. If your case lives or dies on the testimony of what my daughter heard that morning, then you're probably in trouble."

"We're doing everything we can here, Mr. Macchi. Believe me. We're stretched thin, but we're looking for evidence. We won't stop until Clayton swings for this."

"They don't have the death penalty in Minnesota."

"I can dream, can't I?"

"Keep me posted," said Alex.

"Will do. Thanks for doing the right thing, Mr. Macchi. We appreciate it."

Alex thought about that and wondered if it *was* the right thing to involve his eleven-year-old daughter so deeply in a murder trial. Conflicted, he grudgingly said, "You're welcome."

Chapter 23

Petunia felt her relationship with Violet growing, but it was fraught with difficulties, secrets, and pain. Not long after Petunia dropped off the phone and left Brainerd, she'd received her first text from her miserable friend.

Thanks again for the phone. BTW, one of my friends said you were famous and rich. Why didn't you tell me who you were?

I didn't want anyone to treat me differently. It tends to happen when people find out who my family is. R U mad?

No. I guess I understand. People are looking at me now like I'm a freak or something. It must be hard to have people taking your picture all the time

It is. Thanks for understanding. And you're not a freak!
Don't let people shake you

I know

Any news on your mom?

No

I'm sorry Violet. I wish there was something I could do to help

Thanks

Call me if you need to, promise?

Sure

Can I call you sometime?

Sure. Great

Take care of yourself

Petunia didn't hear from Violet much after that, but she had reached out when Penny Krueger's body was found.

I'm so sorry Violet. I'm so sad for you and for your mom. I wish I could give you a hug. I don't know what to say! I heard the news and its so sad

You didn't know her. She was the best mom in the world! I'm going to miss her forever. I can't believe this happened

I'm so so sorry! I can't imagine what you're going thru. Do you have family there to help? Is your mom's family there?

They're maybe coming for the funeral. I don't really know them. My dad's here and he's helping me

That's good. R you going to school?

They r making me go. I hate it

I was going to say I can imagine, but I guess I can't know how you feel. I guess you should do what you can. Your mom was proud of you. You told me she liked it when you read and got good grades. Maybe you should go for her?

Again, Petunia worried when she didn't hear back, but she didn't want to pester her. Petunia and her family sent flowers to the funeral. It was all they could think to do.

Of course, Petunia was called to testify before the grand jury. That day she'd been more nervous than any other time in her life. It had been super hard not to tell Violet she was in Brainerd. But while she definitely understood why it was important to testify, part of her was glad she was told to keep it a secret. She didn't want to hurt her friend.

When her dad broke the news that Clayton Krueger was arrested for murder, the adults in the house went into overdrive, checking in on her mental health. And while the concern was nice, it was Violet's pain that weighed on her mind. She was worried and spent more and more time texting with her friend. That was how Petunia learned a cousin named Ginger Krueger had moved in with Violet. Ginger was to act as her temporary guardian and was keeping the Backwoods open for business—the volunteers had mostly drifted off after Clayton was arrested.

Sitting in her bedroom one night, Petunia decided to call Violet.

"How's it going?" she asked in what she hoped was not a too-upbeat tone.

Petunia heard Violet choke back a sob, but she responded weakly, "Okay."

She felt a lump build in her throat knowing her sweet friend had been crying. Petunia was glad she called. "I'm so sorry. I don't know what to say. I hope it's okay I called, it's just we haven't talked in a while, and I wanted to hear your voice. I know you've probably got a lot going on."

"Not really. They're all leaving me alone. Most of the time."

"Are your friends there?" Petunia asked, chewing on the side of her thumb.

"Not now—since my dad was arrested, they've completely stopped dropping by."

"Oh. That's not good."

"I think their parents don't want them to have anything to do with me anymore."

"Oh, wow, that's terrible. You need your friends right now." Petunia sat on her bed and lay the phone next to her. She squeezed her hands with worry and stared at the walls, not knowing what to say.

Violet was crying but managed, "They're not my friends! Real friends wouldn't abandon me like that! They don't even text me back!"

"I'm so sorry."

"They're such hypocrites. I hate them. All of them. I hate everyone!"

"Violet, please, I'm so sorry. Please hang in there. It's going to be okay."

"It's not! It's never going to be okay again!"

"Well, I'm here. I'm here for you, Violet." Petunia felt tears well in her own eyes and her bottom lip begin to tremble.

"Yeah, until your parents find out you called me and they tell you to stop."

"They won't do that. I tell them everything, and they know I'm calling you."

There was a noise, another voice speaking, then Violet, said, "What?"

Petunia picked up her phone and took it off speaker. She put the phone next to her ear, listening intently as she heard Violet speaking with someone else. Someone who had come into the room. She heard a woman's voice but couldn't make out what she was saying.

Violet's voice: "I'm okay, Ginger. I'm just talking on the phone with a friend."

Petunia heard Ginger's voice grow closer and louder. "All right, well I heard you yelling, and I thought I'd check on you."

"I'm just fine."

Ginger was apparently still lingering because Violet said with some irritation in her voice, "Is there something else you need? Can I help you with something?"

"No. I'm cool, I'm cool. I was just checking on you. I'll let you get back to it."

The hair on the back of Petunia's neck rose. Tingles developed everywhere as her eyes grew wide and her body began to tremble.

"Sorry about that," Violet said, returning to Petunia. "That was my dad's cousin, Ginger. She's the one living with me so they won't put me in a foster home. They were going to do that if none of my *friends* or family would take care of me. What a joke. All those people who helped in the search and at the volunteer center? None of them wanted me. Even my mom's mom won't take care of me. Well, she *could*, but after my dad got arrested, she hasn't been calling Social Services and begging for me. It's like she doesn't care about me either."

Petunia was barely listening. She'd recognized Ginger's voice. It was the voice of the woman from the day Violet's mom went missing. It was the voice of the woman talking with Violet's dad. It was probably the voice of the woman who killed Mrs. Krueger. Violet was living with a murderer.

Shaking, realizing Violet was in danger, conflicted about what to do, her eyes filled with tears. Urgently needing to speak with her parents, Petunia wanted to get off the phone.

Snapping back to the conversation, she managed, "Oh, I'm sure she cares, Violet! Lots of people care about you!

Really! Lots of people! I care. My family cares. Really, just hang in there and you'll see. I'll bet your friends will come around."

"I doubt it."

Petunia yanked open her bedroom door and left her room, running down the upstairs hall. "Well, listen. Violet, I'm so sorry, but I've got to go. Can I call you back later? I promise."

"Sure," Violet said shortly.

She reached the top of the stairs and went down them two at a time. "It's just I have something I need to do right away, but I *promise*, I'll call you back later. Is that okay?"

"Whatever."

"How about tonight? Can I call tonight? How late do you stay up?" Her voice trembled.

"Whenever."

"Okay, I'll call you tonight. We'll talk. Okay?"

"Right. I gotta go too."

"Okay. I'll call you back!"

Violet disconnected. Petunia hit the landing of the main floor and ran down the hall.

"Mom! Dad! Where are you!" she yelled as she ran through rooms. "MOM! MOM!"

Her mom appeared from the kitchen and headed down the hall, followed by her dad, Lily, and Havish.

"What's wrong?" her mom said.

"Oh my God! Violet's in danger!" Her heart was in her throat as the tears streamed down her face.

"What are you talking about? What's happened?" Her mom held her by the arm.

Crying full out now, Petunia slipped to the floor. "I heard her. I heard the voice, *the woman's voice*. The woman from that day! The one who killed Mrs. Krueger. She's living with Violet! She's there! Right now! Her name is Ginger and she's living there, taking care of her and she killed her mom!"

The rest of the family circled around her. Her dad knelt and grabbed her shoulders. "Petunia, are you sure? What did she say?"

Staring up at her dad with hot tears streaming down her face she said, "It was her, Dad. I recognized her voice. I was talking to Violet and this woman came into the room and I *heard her voice.*"

"Stay calm, what did she say?" Alex said.

How could she stay calm? Her eyes grew huge. "Dad! It was her! It was her!"

"Okay, Honey, I believe you. Just take a breath and let's talk about it."

Petunia blew out some air. "She came into the room started talking with Violet and I was listening, and I heard her voice, and I heard her say those same words! She said, 'I'm cool, I'm cool!'"

Her dad sat back on his heels and put a hand on his face. "Okay. We hear you. Are you sure it was the same voice and not just the *words* that made you think that?"

Petunia threw her arms in the air, then pounded her hands on the floor. "Dad! No! Why won't you believe me? It was her! And we've got to help Violet! You have to call the police and tell them she's in danger! She's in danger! We have to help her!"

"She's shaking, Alex," her mom said, holding her. "Calm down, Petunia. Calm down. We believe you. Just give us a minute."

Petunia collapsed, totally sobbing in her mom's arms.

"Honey," she heard her dad say. "Come on now. We're going to take care of this. We're going to call Sheriff Becker and tell him what you heard, okay. Calm down, I'm sure this person isn't going to hurt Violet. She wouldn't do that because she's trying to hide."

Petunia caught her breath and looked at him. "But when they find out, they'll arrest her, right?"

Her dad's face screwed up with uncertainty. "I don't know. I don't know, but we'll find out."

"Then what's going to happen to Violet? She has no one! She'll go to foster care! All her friends have abandoned her. Her family is stupid. They won't take care of her. We have to help her. Can she come live with us?"

Her mom wiped at the tears. "You need to slow down. We need to take this one step at a time. Now, when you're ready, we'll get Sheriff Becker on the phone, and you can tell him what you heard, okay?"

"I told her I'd call her back. I didn't know what to do! She's mad at me 'cause I just got off the phone so quick and she needed to talk to someone. Her friends abandoned her, Mom. Their parents don't want them around her. She's all alone, and sad, and now . . ."

"Shhhhh," her mom held her, rubbing her back.

Petunia got control of herself as Lily, holding her blanket, squeezed onto their laps. She put a soft, tiny hand on Petunia's head and kissed her cheek.

Charlotte said, "It's okay, Lily. Your sister just got some bad news, and she's upset, but she'll be okay. Everything's going to be all right."

Petunia held her baby sister. She loved her so much. She didn't want to scare her too.

Alex fumed as he looked down at his crying puddle of a family, traumatized on the floor. *This is so effed up.* He wanted to kill Clayton Krueger himself.

"It sounds like terrible trouble," Havish said. "Renzo and Blue will be home from their walk soon. He's not going to like it."

Alex nodded. "Can you take Lily? We need to make a call."

Charlotte, Alex, and Petunia walked down the hall into his office. Petunia, calmer now, but still quite upset, scrunched into a corner of his sofa. Charlotte put a blanket around her, pulling it tight.

It was bullshit his daughter had to live with such continuing trauma, but he couldn't fault her tender heart. He paced nearby and then took a seat behind his desk.

"I agree we should help her," said Alex. "I do. And I think's it's time we really lend a hand and work with Sheriff Becker to get this resolved."

"What do you have in mind?" Charlotte asked, taking a seat near their daughter.

"I think we need to get eyes and ears on this woman, Ginger, and I think we need to do the same for Violet to make sure she stays safe."

"Send someone in?" Charlotte asked.

"Yes. Someone none of them know. Someone they won't suspect is there to spy on them."

Petunia stared at him with her big brown eyes. She was quiet now and alert. His eleven-year-old daughter had obviously never been involved in the aspects of a Carrows campaign, but she was smart enough to realize some of the things that went on were contrived for a purpose.

"Do you think Sheriff Becker will allow us to get involved? I mean, it's his territory, his case, his jurisdiction." Charlotte asked.

"I think he will. By now, he's got to have an idea about who we are and the fact I'm in the security business. He's a smart guy. I don't think he'll turn down the professional help. Not after we explain it to him."

"Do you have someone in mind? How soon can they be there?" Charlotte questioned as she glanced at Petunia.

Alex thought about that, and one particular face came to mind. "I do. After we clear it with the sheriff and make some arrangements, I think we could have him there in the next day or two."

"That fast?"

"Yes. I can pull him from what he's doing and get him up to speed tonight. All he'll need to do is pack and we'll put him on a plane to Brainerd. We'll get that real estate agent we worked with on the phone tonight—she seemed pretty capable. There's a ton of properties in the area we could rent. He could say he was checking the area out, thinking about staying, looking for work. He could get a job at the Backwoods. Become an asset. And he could report back to us and Sheriff Becker and keep an eye on Violet."

"You don't think the sheriff will arrest Ginger based on what Petunia heard?" Charlotte asked.

Petunia's eyes grew large in anticipation.

"I don't know, maybe, but it's doubtful. He might jump at the chance to find out more about her, though. It's an opportunity to lock down some evidence before she knows they're onto her."

"Petunia," said Charlotte. "How do you feel about this? Would it make you feel better knowing we had someone watching over Violet?"

Alex already knew that the act of doing something was helping his daughter calm down. He could see it on her face.

"I guess. You don't think Ginger will hurt her?" she asked.

Alex shook his head. "Let's see what the sheriff has to say, but I don't think so. There's no reason for her to hurt Violet."

"But she's a murderer! She killed Violet's mom."

"I know. Alex, call him," Charlotte said, turning to Petunia, "One step at a time, honey."

Petunia closed her eyes and lowered her head as Alex tapped the sheriff's number into his phone.

Damn you, Clayton.

Chapter 24

Sheriff Tate Becker was sitting in his office looking over reports when his phone rang. He glanced at it. Alex Macchi. *Now what?* He answered the call.

"Mr. Macchi. What can I do for you?"

"Sheriff. We just discovered something unsettling. I've got Charlotte and Petunia with me. About an hour ago, Petunia was on the phone, speaking with Violet Krueger. I'll let her take it from here. Petunia, tell the sheriff what happened."

My God, it's like a repeat of their first performance. He got up and closed his door as he heard a big intake of breath before the young girl's voice came on. "I was talking to Violet. She was upset because everyone, all her friends have ditched her. While we were talking, a woman, the woman who is living with her, Ginger, came into the room and they were talking and I heard her voice, and it was the same voice I heard that day at the Backwoods. The woman who was talking to Violet's dad. It's her. Ginger. It's her."

Sheriff Becker stopped, frozen. He heard the sincerity in Petunia's voice, but he needed more to be convinced. He leaned closer to the speakerphone. "Just her voice? You recognized her voice? Over the phone?"

"It was her voice, but it was also what she said. She said those same words, 'I'm cool, I'm cool,' and it was totally her. I'm positive."

Sheriff Becker knew it was true. It felt right; it had to be. It made perfect sense. He'd had a bad feeling about the woman, knew something was off, but he couldn't prove anything, and she'd been such a flake during the interview. Unfortunately, he didn't have any evidence against her other than she fit the general description of the *back end* of the woman Petunia saw that day in the parking lot. Clayton's phone records and text messages had produced nothing to implicate Ginger Krueger, or anyone else, for that matter. All of Clayton's technology had been a dead end. They'd been hoping Clayton would make a deal and name his accomplice. But so far, that hadn't happened. They were waiting for something else to break. *This might be it.*

He tapped his fist against his mouth. He needed to get Gavin Stewart on the horn and decide what they should do next.

"I see," he replied cautiously.

"You believe me, don't you?" said Petunia.

He could hear desperation in her voice. "I do. I want to, but you weren't in the same room with her. You heard the conversation from a distance, not even directly into the phone. She was speaking to Violet. Is that right?"

"Yes! I heard her come into Violet's room and they were talking, and she said it—twice! Exactly like I heard her say it before."

"Okay. Good, good." Tate nodded.

"Sheriff," said Alex. "I understand why you might be hesitant, but I think this is a legitimate confirmation. I believe my daughter because it stopped her cold. Not just because of the words, but because of the words combined with the voice. Is that right, Petunia?"

Petunia's voice: "It is. Sheriff, you've got to believe me. I think Violet might be in danger. You've got to help her!"

Tate rubbed his temple. "Yeah, okay. I'm going to give Gavin Stewart a call and see how he wants to proceed."

"Sheriff," said Alex. "Before you do, I'd like to make a proposal."

Oh hell, what now?

Alex continued. "I think you know I own a company, Macchi & Macchi, which is a security and private investigations firm. We've been in business for many years and run a very successful, very discreet business primarily from New York, but we have offices in several cities. I'd like to extend an offer to help with the investigation, and assuming you agree, I'd like to send an agent to the Brainerd Lakes area to keep an eye on things. I've got a guy who could be on a plane tomorrow or the next day."

Tate was listening hard, but wildly unsure about involving anyone but the local police.

"My guy could rent a place and get a job at the Backwoods. He could be our eyes and ears there, keep a protective eye on Violet, and see what he can find out about Ginger Krueger. He'll blend in, and you can count on him to be very professional. He's not going to go rogue or leave you out of it. He'll work with you, and very, very quietly, feed you what he finds and hopefully help you build a case. If Ginger is the killer, then something needs to be done.

Fast. But my advice is to move cautiously. I'm not trying to tell you how to do your job, but I think this could help."

Tate thought Alex was most *definitely* telling him how to do his job, but ego aside, it was an interesting idea. Extremely frustrated with the lack of evidence they'd found against Clayton and the killer, he had to admit they'd covered their tracks. They'd planned carefully and had the luxury of time to dispose of their incriminating evidence— including the murder weapon. Tate knew they had an uphill battle in court.

Penny Krueger had been violently killed and buried in a deep hole. They took away her life and her daughter's mental health. For what? For a few bucks.

Now Tate had something to go on. Now he knew where he needed to look for proof, but he had to do it carefully. Alex Macchi, his daughter, and wife had shown themselves to be dependable, generous, and ethical people. Once again, they were helping him solve his case and were offering tangible help. He really didn't want to say no.

Feeling a tingle of relief for the momentum, he said, "All right. Let me speak with Gavin. In the meantime, I guess I need to say thanks, again, for your help. I'll let you know."

Chapter 25

When Alex thought of Gilbert Gorsky, capable was the first word that came to mind. Now in his late twenties, Gilbert hadn't gone to college after high school, but had worked various trades in several different industries in the state of New York. He was what you'd call a handy sort of guy.

Eventually living on a small property in upstate New York near Ithaca, Gilbert became friendly with Isabella and Finn Laferty—Alex's sister and her husband. Isabella and Finn lived near Gilbert and ran a successful, mid-sized, organic poultry farm. While they employed people year-round, Gilbert worked for them part time between his primary occupations—hunting and fishing. He was an easy guy to like, and Isabella insisted they include him at social events—especially when she could pair him with one of her single friends.

Alex and Charlotte had finally met him at one such gathering. Usually, people became uncomfortable when they learned Alex was married to a member of the Carrows family, but Gilbert had taken it in stride. That had impressed Alex.

He liked the unflappable, steady kind of person who wasn't awed by the size of a person's wallet.

Always searching for good employees at Macchi & Macchi, Alex had offered Gilbert a contract by assignment retainer. A job which suited Gilbert Gorsky's lifestyle perfectly. Brought into the fold, Gilbert was a proven asset and had become a trusted member of their team.

And Gilbert was between assignments when Alex rang.

"Gilbert. How are you?" Alex said in a congenial tone.

"Real good, Alex. I saw your sister yesterday. She and Finn had me out for Taco Tuesday, or at least that was the lure. Interestingly enough, she'd also invited a friend, a teacher who works with her and happens to be single. What do you think the odds are she'll be around again for Fish Friday?"

Alex's youngest and only sister, Isabella, was a tender-hearted woman. Raised with four brothers, she wanted to mother them all. He adored her.

"She just might be sending you a message there. Any interest?"

"In the teacher or the fish?"

"Both?" Alex smiled.

"Too soon to tell. I find these women easy to catch and hard to release. If I don't dangle my line in the water, I don't need to worry about what I'll catch. Your sister, though, she thinks I ought to finally catch the big one, and I don't want to disillusion her."

"Ahh, Gilbert, you are a wise man. I don't suppose I could convince you to pull up stakes over there and get back to work? I've got a job for you. Extremely urgent. You'd need to leave tomorrow. Tonight, if you can. You could head to my place now, we'll put you up, and I can bring you up to speed."

"Tonight? How long you need me?"

"I'm not sure. Maybe as much as a few months. Might be longer. You'd need to move to Minnesota, and it could be dangerous. Possibly."

"Minnesota? The land of ten thousand lakes? Yeah, I might be interested in going that way."

Alex pursed his lips. "Ah, I don't know how much free time you'd have. It'd depend on what was happening."

"Where in Minnesota? Minneapolis?"

"No, farther north, the Brainerd Lakes area."

Alex could feel Gilbert's smile across the wire, and he knew he'd landed him.

"What is it I'll be doing there?" Gilbert finally asked.

"Let me ask you something. Can you cook?"

"Hell yeah, I can cook. Been cooking my entire life. Ask your sister if you don't believe me. Sometimes I push her to the side, take one of her *regular* meals, and make it what you might call delicious."

Alex smiled, envisioning that fight over the spice rack. "Well that's good, because I want you to work in a restaurant and bait shop. Be a cook, a waiter, a shopkeeper, whatever they need."

"I can do that."

"All right. Get your gear together. Pack casual, but plan on a long-term assignment. I'll arrange for a plane to fly you out of Teterboro tomorrow. I'll have a place rented for you, nothing too fancy, and a car waiting for you at the Brainerd airport."

"You're moving awful fast, Alex. Must be something pretty urgent going on in a small town in Minnesota. I can't wait to hear about it."

Alex rolled his eyes. "Just get here. I'll wait up, and Renzo and I will fill you in."

"Ah, the big guy. He in on this?"

"No. He stays with us. You're going in alone."

"Shouldn't be a problem. Hey, I don't suppose there'll be a boat waiting for me at my place? Like a signing bonus for all the scurry up and hurry."

Alex snorted. "I'll see you in a few hours. Drive to the office and leave your car in the garage there. Then taxi to my place."

––––––––––

It was hard to impress Gilbert Gorsky, but he had never been to his boss's Manhattan home, and he was impressed. From the front iron bars and hedged gates, the imposing, ridiculously large West Village home rose before him like something from the roaring twenties. But modern. And not in black and white.

Gilbert shook his head and pressed the button to unlock the gates. Hearing a buzzing sound, he pushed through. The gates clanged shut behind him with a finality befitting a prison cell. As he lugged his bags up the front steps, more metal bars greeted him, but these weren't locked. He calmly used the knocker on the door.

Gilbert's eyes opened with surprise when a strange man answered the door.

"Mr. Gorsky. Please come in," the man said formally. He extended his hand to help with the bags.

They've an actual butler?

"Hey there," Gilbert said, crossing the threshold, his eyes drawn to a large staircase nearby. Looking up what was probably five flights of stairs, he was unprepared for the hushed tones and wealthy elegance of the place. He knew the family was rich, but he couldn't imagine what it must be like to live in such a beautiful place.

"My name is Havish Khan. You may leave your things here by the door. Mr. Macchi and Renzo are expecting you. If you'll follow me."

Gilbert walked through the marbled gallery and past the grand staircase. As they walked, he turned his head and saw a vast dining room, which looked out onto a lighted terrace. He assumed a kitchen was nearby, but they turned down a hall and into a two-storied office where Renzo and Alex were seated by an actual wood-burning fireplace. Gilbert could smell the burning wood.

The butler disappeared, and Gilbert greeted each of them. "Alex," he said shaking his hand. "Renzo," he said, doing the same with the big guy.

"Thanks for coming, Gilbert. Have a seat," said Alex. "Can I get you something to drink?"

"Sure. You got a beer around here?"

"Yes," Alex said as he walked to an oak bar nestled between large bookcases. Going behind it and bending down, Alex rose and said, "We've got Heineken or Red Stripe. Sorry, no domestic here. I can get Havish to bring something else?"

"No. Heineken's fine. Nice place you have here, boss." Gilbert sat in a club chair near the fire and glanced at Renzo, who had his head cocked and was literally giving him an up-down with his eyes.

"Thank you," said Alex. "We haven't been in long, but it feels like home now. Took some getting used to. It's pretty big. Not like the place I grew up in Bay Ridge."

"Right. I knew your family was from Brooklyn." He crossed his leg, resting his ankle on his knee. His foot jiggled as Alex handed him the cold bottle then took a seat beside Renzo.

"Let's bring you up to speed," said Alex. "We have the real estate agent in Brainerd narrowing down the long-term rental options for you, but I've already got a couple listings that I think will work. The primary idea is to get you as close to your target as possible."

"Your target," said Renzo, "is the Backwoods Café & Bait outside Crosslake, Minnesota."

"That's where you'll get a job," said Alex. "Your residence will need to be close so it will seem natural you'd look for work there. As I said, I've got a couple listing options, there may be more, but why don't you look these over."

Alex handed him the MLS listings with pictures of the properties, and Gilbert looked awkwardly around for a place to set his beer. Spying a coaster nearby, he placed his beer on it, smiled sheepishly at Alex, and then looked at the papers.

"The first property," said Alex, "looks pretty rough. One bedroom, which is fine, but no lake access, just a place in the woods. Furnished—if you like orange corduroy and sponge. No Wi-Fi or cable, but it's got electricity there for ya." Alex smiled in a slightly amused manner.

"The second place," Alex pointed with his own beer toward the sheets, "is a bit nicer, on a lake, little private cove. One bedroom, a loft, has a big screen TV, a dish, looks like the furniture won't sag when you sit on it. Also, it appears they have a nice Striper Walkaround tied up in the cove. Comes with the place. Could be okay, but the first place is pretty sweet too. You decide. Like I said, we might have more options in the morning."

"If it were me," Renzo boomed in a deep voice, "I'd pick the quiet place. Deep, in-woods territory. No one knows I'm even there."

Gilbert looked at each of them and saw the smiles beginning to break out on their faces. He understood they were having fun with him. "Uh, huh. And you say I get to choose?"

Alex made a magnanimous gesture, indicating that was the case.

"I think I'll be okay on the cove, with the Walkaround."

"Your choice," Alex shrugged. "I'll set it up. I'll have the realtor leave the keys under the mat or something. You move in tomorrow, set up shop, have a look around, get the lay of the land. The next day, you head over to the Backwoods Café & Bait for their delicious breakfast and meet your assignment."

"Ginger Krueger," said Renzo, his eyes hooded. "She's a murderer."

Gilbert shook his head. "What?"

"She murdered a woman," said Renzo. "A real nice woman by the name of Penny Krueger. Penny Krueger was married to Ginger's second cousin, Clayton Krueger. Clayton Krueger has been arrested for the murder and he's awaiting trial. Clayton has a solid alibi though, so they've been looking for his accomplice. And we just found her. Ginger Krueger. Still loose. Living and working at the Backwoods taking care of her—what would you call her, Alex?"

"Her second cousin's kid?" Alex offered.

"Her second cousin's kid. An eleven-year-old girl named Violet Krueger. Violet Krueger is a close, personal friend of Petunia Carrows Macchi, and may be in danger."

Gilbert put up his hand. "Whoa. Maybe you should start at the beginning. I think I'm going to have a few questions."

They spent the next several hours talking, and over a dozen more beers, they worked out a plan. Best they could, not knowing what to expect.

The next morning, after an amazingly comfortable night on a mattress made of angel feathers, Gilbert found his way to one of the kitchens. Hearing little girl voices, he rounded the corner, and a very large dog launched himself at him.

Covering Gilbert with fur and saliva, the dog was being wrangled by the screaming girls, until Charlotte came to the rescue and pulled him away by the collar. "Oh, Gilbert, I'm so sorry. He's just a puppy and not that used to strangers, and we haven't got his manners in place yet. Down, Blue! Down!" She scolded the dog but lost control, and the dog bounded away, sliding wildly on the flooring while the girls scrambled after him, yelling.

"No problem. I'm good with dogs. How old is he? He a German Shepherd?"

"Yes. He's thirteen weeks old. We're in a heavy training period." Charlotte smiled.

"He's going to be a big dog." Gilbert raised his brows.

"I know. We may have bitten off more than we can chew." Charlotte looked down at the actual chew toys scattered everywhere around them.

"He's beautiful." Gilbert loved dogs.

"Both his parents come from long, healthy lines. Big and strong. Good natured too. Gilbert, let's get you some breakfast. Follow me. Havish has a nice buffet in the other room, and we can sit down for a chat before you leave."

"Where's Alex . . . and Renzo?" Gilbert followed her.

"They had to go out. They said to tell you to have a nice breakfast and to spend some time talking to Petunia."

He understood that Petunia and the family were intimately involved in the Krueger family drama. In essence, he would be protecting both Violet Krueger and the witness, Petunia, when the time came. He knew that

Violet and Petunia were friends and kept in touch, and it was important to understand the feelings of these young girls.

They spent a nice time getting to know each other, and it was fascinating to Gilbert how different he felt than on his arrival not many hours ago. Walking into the place, he'd been uncomfortable and nervous, unsure about who these people really were. After a breakfast with the girls and the large brute of a puppy, he almost felt like family. They were to the last, warm and real, and he was glad to know them.

He got hugs from all the women before he left with Alex to go to the airport.

Gilbert craned his neck and stared out the window at the Manhattan skyline. "You're a very lucky man, Alex. You know that, right?"

"Thank you, Gilbert. I appreciate the compliment, and yes, I'm extremely aware of how lucky I am. I'll share that compliment with the ladies if it's all right with you."

Pulling up to the private airfield and handing his luggage over to the pilots, Gilbert shook his boss's hand. He shook his head, too, as he looked over the small, private plane. "Alex. Thanks for the opportunity to help. I'll do what I can."

"Thank you, Gilbert. It means a lot to us, but especially to Petunia, knowing you're there, watching over her friend. Take good care of yourself."

With that, Gilbert boarded the luxury aircraft, as the only passenger, heading to the Backwoods Café & Bait, to ask a murderer for a job.

Chapter 26

Sheriff Tate Becker sat in his office waiting for the ballyhooed Macchi & Macchi guy to arrive. Given the travel arrangements, Gilbert Gorsky should be there any minute. Tate had told Alex Macchi that Mr. Gorsky's first stop was to report to him. Tate needed to test the obedience of the complete stranger who'd be infiltrating their delicate investigation. If the guy smelled wrong—or worse, disobeyed—Tate was ready to pull the effing plug. The Carrows Macchi's were a helpful bunch, but this was Tate's state and investigation, not theirs. He wondered what kind of character from New York the family had found who would blend into the country woodwork. Any sign of leather or cocky attitude would only give Tate more headaches.

His sergeant called within the expected window, announcing Gorsky's arrival. Tate told his officer to bring the guy back.

"Have a seat," Sheriff Becker said as he closed the door behind them and glanced at the blinds he'd drawn earlier to block the view into his office. The fewer people who saw this yahoo the better.

"Thank you," said Gilbert.

Coming around the desk, Tate eyeballed the man. Gilbert was a stocky guy with a rural kind of vibe, and he was certainly dressed the part. Wearing a faded T-shirt with some off-brand rod and tackle logo, the guy's baggy jeans even had a small stain on the knee.

"So you're the guy the Richie-riches sent to help us. The *Macchi & Macchi* man who's going to keep an eye on things at the Backwoods."

"I am." Gilbert nodded.

Tate liked that Gorsky kept his cool and didn't rile to Tate's supposed slight and sarcasm. He let the silence between them lengthen, but Gorsky sat there looking patient, cool, and obedient. "I suppose you got the full story from Alex?"

"Yes. You can speak freely around me, Sheriff. I'm in the know. You got a murderer out at the Backwoods Café & Bait. You got a young girl—the daughter, Violet—who needs some looking after. You got my boss's daughter, Petunia Macchi, as a critical witness for the prosecution against Penny Krueger's husband, Clayton Krueger. And you got his murdering second cousin, Ginger Krueger, who is looking after the Backwoods Café & Bait until this mess is sorted out and you get the shitheads locked up."

Tate nodded. "Yeah, that about sums it up. I understand you'll be asking for a job out there, from Ginger?"

"Yup. Shouldn't be a problem. I'll make myself useful." Gilbert scratched his two-day-old beard.

"And you're staying where?"

"A small place a few miles down the road from the Backwoods, on Bass Lake. I haven't been out there yet. I came straight from the airport. I'll text you the address and then you'll have my number so we can communicate."

Tate leaned his head back and cocked it. "All right. What are your intentions when you get to the Backwoods, other than what you said . . . making yourself useful?"

"My intentions are to keep my eyes and ears open and look for clues. If I see or hear anything that will help the case, I'll report it directly to you . . . and to Alex."

"You didn't bring any weapons with you or anything else I need to know about?" Tate asked harshly.

"I'm eyes and ears only, Sheriff. I'll call the cavalry if something goes down, but I'm not totally out of my depth if things become physical."

"So, we can count on you to do nothing to jeopardize the current case against Clayton Krueger?"

Gilbert looked down at his hands and considered. "Seems to me like you should have something more solid on him—but if a Minnesota jury wants to hang him on the circumstantial stuff, I got no problem with that."

"We don't have the death penalty in Minnesota."

Gilbert looked up. "Maybe you should look into that."

"Uh huh. Ginger Krueger is a dangerous woman. You need to be careful around her."

"Yup."

"I'd be open to any ideas you have once you get the lay of the land. Something we can do to trap her, get her to confess. We'd go for a search warrant, but I spoke with the county attorney, and we agreed that it might be better to wait and see what you could find. Clandestinely."

"Yup. I'm eyes and ears."

Tate lay his arms on his desk. "Okay, then. You stay in touch and let me know immediately if you discover anything you think might be interesting. Doesn't have to be big stuff either. We'll take anything you find."

Gilbert gave him a considered stare. "This woman, Ginger Krueger, she lured Penny Krueger out into the woods, bashed her skull in, and threw her into a hole in the ground. I'm about to meet this Ginger, get to know her, ask her for a job, and be her friend. I'm well aware that striking the grass alerts the snake, and I don't intend to spook this one. I got this, Sheriff. We're on the same team."

"All right then. Good luck."

———————

Gilbert left the sheriff's office and climbed back into the used Jeep Cherokee Alex had somehow purchased and delivered to the airport overnight, the keys in the console. He was getting used to the idea that big money could make anything happen.

He drove through the small town of Brainerd, checking out the scenery, and past a big statue of a baby blue ox. He wasn't sure what that was about, but something lingered from the storybooks. *Paul Bunyan?*

Crossing a bridge over the large, churning Mississippi River, the lushness of the heavy trees, still green, closed in on him. The scenery changed as he drove down the one-lane county roads, but tall, dense pines occasionally broke to reveal little jewels of lakes, each full of tasty fish.

Thinking about his interview with Sheriff Becker, Gilbert took in stride the things he neglected to tell him. Primarily, that Gilbert was, first and last, a company guy. He was a Macchi & Macchi man, and that organization had their own ways.

He'd do what Alex told him to do and report back to the sheriff only what Alex wanted him to know. Those were the rules and Gilbert understood them. After securing a job at the Backwoods, he knew his first big assignment would be to download illegal software onto any of Ginger Krueger's laptops or computers, which would allow Alex's hacker into Ginger's world. The second, a trickier one to accomplish, would be to clone her phone.

Alex told him to expect the tools he would need via FedEx. After that, he'd get a tutorial from one of the Macchi & Macchi tech guys about what he needed to do. Gilbert didn't give a crap about the illegal aspects or about getting caught by the sheriff. Macchi & Macchi would have his back on erasing his trail, but more than that, he had cause on his side.

He wondered too about Violet. If she was anything like Petunia, she'd be a young, emotional girl. He didn't have too much experience dealing with that breed, but figured he'd treat her like an injured colt. Soothing like and very patient. As for Ginger, he didn't know what to expect. A woman murderer? How would he manage her? She sounded like a lot of work.

Chapter 27

Hot, buxom, blond Skyler White Krueger flew down the road in her all-white convertible, a scarf wrapped around her head with the tail flying behind her. Smoking her cigarette and ignoring the cat calls coming from the other cars on the road—those simple passengers both lustful and jealous at the sight of her—she worked on her plot to eliminate the billionaire child who had unknowingly stepped onto the path of the hard-nosed and beautiful killer. She . . .

"Hey!" Ginger screamed as she woke from her daydream when cut off by a speeding driver towing some Ski-Doos. *Damn,* she thought as she looked down and realized she'd ashed and burned another hole in the carpet of her old Subaru Forester. Lost in her fantasy world, as usual, it was a real let down to come out of it. Tossing the last of her cigarette out the window, she popped a wad of bubble gum in her mouth and worked to get it going.

She wiggled her shoulders and then drove her hand under her shirt to readjust her bra. The damn underwires were gouging into her skin while attempting to force her massive breasts into a pleasing position. *It's so hard to look good!* Her hair was dried and thinning from the peroxide she'd been applying, but she couldn't afford to go to a salon to have the color professionally done.

Maybe she should. Her image was important. She could take some money out of the store's register and do it, but there was an audit coming up, and she didn't want any extra questions. The insurance company and the banks wanted to check things out. They were *nervous.* In the meantime, she was pulling the same salary as Penny had. Minimum-fucking wage. And room and board. It was bullshit. If she was patient, and after things settled down, and after Clayton came back, she was *sure* things would change for the better. But in the meantime, she'd just have to make do.

She pulled into the parking lot of the Long Prairie Library and parked. Her job today was research. For that, she needed the internet, and nothing traceable to her phone. She'd watched enough cop shows to know her searches could be traced.

The Kitchigami Regional Library System served five counties—Beltrami, Cass, Crow Wing, Hubbard, and Wadena. Since Ginger lived in Crow Wing County, she'd decided it was a wise idea to go outside the Kitchigami system, and this was on her third trip to a library—this one in Todd County, in Long Prairie. She thought she was covering her tracks. She didn't believe anyone would ever have the time or the technology to trace her research steps all the hell over Minnesota.

For a while, the difficult part had been getting time away from the Backwoods. She was beginning to hate the place. After the summer was over and Clayton was arrested, the volunteers had started to drift off, and Ginger had been looking for someone other than lazy-assed Violet to help with the load. That kid was turning into a real headache. Skipping school, crying, *not* helping around the place. She was either sleeping or reading, and Ginger didn't know what to do about it. The hours Ginger put in talking to social workers pretending like she gave a shit about the kid were exhausting! Work, work, work, all the time. Yes, the customers were still coming in, but it was just too much.

Full-time, reliable staff had been difficult to come by, and when Gilbert showed up out of nowhere, inquiring about a job, it was like an answer to her prayers. He came in for breakfast, told her he was new to the area and was looking for a job while he decided if he was going to stay. An outdoorsy type of guy, he liked to fish and hunt and was a bricklayer originally from Canada. He'd been to Minnesota several times and liked the lakes. Ginger thought his sense of humor was a bit dry, and his response time to her questions was agonizingly slow, but he was nice enough. Capable, she thought. Not bad looking either, if you liked 'em shortish and stocky. Her Clayton, he was a tall, thin drink of water, her model for all things hot.

Gilbert was working out nicely—even fixing crap around the place that needed maintenance. She didn't know how long he'd last, but she was glad he'd come around. A bit at a time, she'd increased his hours until he was finally doing the lion's share of the work. It *almost, but not quite* gave her time to watch TV again. She missed her old life. Cleaning cabins, hunkered down in her trailer after work, blinds closed, *not* dieting, a big bucket of Cheese Rings from the discount store between her legs. Oh, *God,* what she'd give to get that big bucket back!

Her research on the witness who could sink them began the day she moved into the house. She'd been watching Violet for clues and reading her text messages, but they were mostly boring. The Carrows girl and Violet swapped sad stories about how hard it was to have people *stare* at them, for people *to take pictures* of them, for people to talk behind their backs . . . What a bunch of whiners! She could almost understand Violet's problem, but Petunia Carrows? What a load of crap. No one should feel sorry for someone with a billion dollars in the bank. That was *not* a real problem.

Ginger sat at the Long Prairie Library and devoured all the intel and images she could find on the Carrows Macchi family. What a crew. As a pack, they were beautiful. Even the mother, the matriarch, Julia Carrows, was still beautiful, and she had to be old. They'd probably had lots of work done to keep them looking that good.

And the jewelry. *My God! Look at the jewelry!* It had to be real—which was mindboggling. Pictures of Whispering Cliffs in California, pictures of glamorous Carey Carrows, who just got married to that hottie Keanu Reeves-type from Hawaii. There they were strolling hand in hand on a beach somewhere with their perfect bodies. Why did God give so much to all of them? It was not fair.

Since Petunia Carrows' biological father had written two books about his daughter and his custody battle with Charlotte, it was easy to get lots of juicy insight into their family drama. The paparazzi had taken lots of pictures of the family during that time, and the candid ones, the ones of little Petunia, those were the best. Those were the ones that Ginger needed to study. She needed to memorize, *memorialize* her enemy's face. All their faces. She needed to know them on sight. The huge bodyguard in so many of the pictures with Petunia, his face too.

If there was a trial, and of course there had to be, the prosecution was sure to call Petunia to the stand. That meant that the Carrows Macchis would travel to Brainerd for the trial. Who would come with Petunia, Ginger couldn't say, but all their faces were now burned into her brain.

When they came to town for the trial, that would be her opportunity to do something. She couldn't fly to New York City and kill the kid on the street. That wasn't going to happen. It would have to be when Petunia stepped foot back in Minnesota. But how would she kill her? She'd have to think about that, and in the meantime, do research on methods of extermination, and keep tabs on Petunia through Violet.

It was interesting that Violet did not seem to realize Petunia might be involved in her father's murder trial. From the text messages she read between them, there was absolutely no mention of Petunia being involved as a witness. Maybe someone told her not to tell Violet. That meant that Petunia was lying to Violet, by omission. But that was okay, because it might work to Ginger's advantage.

If Petunia told Violet that she was coming into town and where she was staying, Ginger would have the advantage of *surprise*. She was a plotter/planner, and she'd be ready. She wasn't sure how, and she wasn't sure when, but her happily ever after depended on it. For now, she'd stay strong and play along.

Ginger finished her latest intel session and sighed—time to head back to the Backwoods Café & Bait to play supportive relative. She'd spend her drive time fantasizing, this time about Scenario B, the one where Clayton was convicted, and Ginger was stuck as surrogate mom at the Backwoods with Violet until Violet turned eighteen. She didn't like to dwell on Scenario B, but if Clayton went to actual prison, Violet would get her mom's insurance money, and it was only proper for the kid to have a beneficiary. Just in case something were to happen to Violet too. Maybe it was time for Ginger to ask her about it.

Always thinkin', always thinkin'. Ginger smiled as she packed up and left.

Chapter 28

Gilbert had no trouble at all insinuating himself into Ginger's life and the Backwoods Café & Bait. Once he low-balled a salary in exchange for a job and started showing up on the regular, he also went above and beyond helping on projects around the place. At that point, he was given the keys to the kingdom. And the thing was, Ginger and the Backwoods really did need the help.

It was a busy place, and between him, Violet, Ginger, and a couple of other somewhat apathetic employees, they worked to keep the place going. The enthusiasm of the volunteers he'd heard about had mostly dried up by the time he arrived, and now only a few came around once in a while to mow or take care of the landscaping around the place. It was nice of them, but Gilbert knew those days would come to an end soon. Community goodwill had an expiration date.

From what he could tell, the locals were ready to put the entire experience behind them and just burn the place down. If they didn't have to drive by it every day and be reminded there was a young girl there, left behind, that might have happened. Instead, they considered it helpful to eat and shop in the place to keep the doors open. Gilbert had raised hundreds of pans of cinnamon rolls, and while they were initially enticing and delicious to eat, his honeymoon with them was over.

Their big hope had been that the Macchi & Macchi hacker, whoever that was, would find some incriminating material on Ginger's cloned phone. But so far, Alex said they'd found nothing.

On arrival, Gilbert had discovered that Ginger didn't have a laptop, only a phone. Clayton and Penny had an old laptop they used for the restaurant, but that seemed to be used exclusively for the business. Regardless, both pieces of tech had been easy to hack.

Gilbert stood outside now on his short dock, looking longingly at his small, neglected boat. A blue-skied after-noon and all alone, he took the opportunity to call Alex and touch base.

"Well what's she doing on her phone? She's on it all the time. Whenever she has a spare moment, she's out back smoking and scrollin'." Gilbert paced in frustration at their lack of progress.

Alex responded, "According to our guy, Ginger has several sites that she visits regularly. She does a lot of calorie counting and checking on the calories of food, mostly junk food, fried food. She keeps a diary of what she eats each day. I'm assuming she's on a diet?"

Gilbert's entire face distorted as he glared with confusion at his phone. "On a diet? She eats constantly. If she's not eating, she's smoking or chewing gum, or sucking on ice. She's got something in her mouth all day long. A real oral fixation. I sent you a picture of her. She's pretty heavy, so if she's dieting, it ain't working."

"She's averaging around three thousand calories a day, but I don't know if she's telling the truth to her journal. She does a lot of research on diet drugs and has been looking at the side effects of a particular one a lot. Is she taking diet pills?"

Gilbert blew out some air and nodded. "That would explain a lot. She's a jumpy mess. Real fidgety. She's like going—you know, *going*—all the time. Her mouth, if it ain't got food in it, she's using it to gab. Sometimes I just walk away 'cause I don't have time to listen to her. I eventually learned that that's not a problem. When people walk away, she keeps herself amused by talking to herself. I've been listening hard, when I can, but I don't know what she's talking about sometimes. Weird shit. Like she's talking to fantasy people. She's a strange lady."

Alex's voice came through. "She follows a lot of celebrities and fan pages on Twitter. Her particular favorites are the actors from crime shows, which is interesting. A show called *Criminal Minds*, and she follows the actors from that show *Breaking Bad*. Ginger checks in every day with Anna Gunn's site. She played a character named Skyler White on the show."

Gilbert looked up at an eagle and watched it dive toward the lake. It skimmed the surface and came up with a fish gripped in its talons before it flew off. Deadly serious creature.

"Maybe she got her ideas about how to kill Penny Krueger from one of those shows," he said.

"Could be," said Alex. "If you want to be her friend, get her going in a conversation about them."

"There's nothing from her tech that we can use? Nothing suspicious?"

"Not that we can find, but it's troubling she's been searching sites about suicide in depressed teens and post-traumatic stress disorder. Do you think Violet is in trouble?"

Gilbert brushed a hand over his close-cut hair, then scratched it. "Oh man, it's hard to know. Violet's a twelve-year old girl whose mother was murdered by her father. I don't have a whole lot of experience with twelve-year old girls, let alone ones that are going through something like that."

"Well how does she seem to you?"

He shook his head. "Pretty distant. She's hard to engage in conversation. She keeps her head down and works hard while she's in the restaurant. I know she doesn't much like talking to the customers, and I know she doesn't like being stared at. And people *are* staring at her. Behind her back, in her face, from across the room. I can see it and she can too. We've talked about it, and I've told her that they'll lose interest eventually and that things will get better. I've given a couple of young punks the stink eye when I saw their antennas rise in her direction. That backed them down, but people are coming by, no doubt, out of curiosity."

"Does she have to work? Why can't she just be at home or at school?" Alex asked.

"I think she likes to work, at least in the kitchen. She says she feels close to her mom in there. I know she's been skipping school, that's obvious, and I tried talking to her about that too, but she said she feels like a freak there and the kids stare at her there too."

"So she doesn't have a safe harbor?"

Gilbert scratched a bug bite on his arm. "At home, in her room. She tells me she reads a lot. I guess she spent some of Petunia's money and got herself a Kindle, so she's reading a lot on that."

"What about her friends? Does she have friends she gets together with, or sports?" Alex questioned.

"I haven't seen much of that. Nothing regular. She told me she and her mom used to run, but I guess that's not something she wants to do anymore."

"Jeez. That poor kid. I'm glad she at least has something to read. I didn't think of the Kindle. I'll check on her account and make sure she has all the money she needs so she's covered. Is there anything else you can think of that we can do to help her?"

"She's lonely is what I see. I think she could use help, but I don't know what kind. With the trial coming up, it could get worse. I'm keeping my eye on her. It's just that I'm an old guy to her, and that might be weird for her. I know she likes to fish. We ain't got that much time left in the season, but maybe I can get her out on the boat with me."

"Do what you can and keep safe," said Alex.

"Yup. I'll keep you posted."

Chapter 29

It was October in Minnesota, the leaves fully turned, bringing beauty all around them. If Gilbert hadn't been on assignment, he might have been loving every minute of his time in the Crosslake area. It had been a warmish autumn, and he'd kept the boat on the lake as long as he could to be able to fish—but that was over now.

Deer hunting season opened in November, and he'd have looked forward to that too if he'd thought to bring his guns. It didn't matter though, as he wasn't going to leave the Backwoods for a long weekend of hunting. He was on the job. It was one thing to do a little fishing when things were quiet, another to drive off and leave for a few days. He had no intention of doing that.

He had been able to convince Violet to go fishing with him a couple times, and that pleased him. The two had spent some nice, peaceful hours on the lake. He'd packed sandwiches, and most often, when they caught something, they'd toss it back. Once in a while, they'd bring a few *eaters* back to her place and he'd cook them up for supper.

Neither were too comfortable with her hanging out at his place, but he was becoming a regular dinner guest with Violet at hers.

Ginger didn't usually eat with them. It was another weird thing about her; she was a snacker, but refused to sit down for a regular meal. At dinnertime, she'd often claim not to be hungry, but thirty minutes later he'd see her grab a bag of chips and her cigarettes and run outside with her phone like she had urgent business.

Once he knew she was checking her Twitter, following pointless tweets tracking celebrity movements, he opened up that conversation and landed a marlin. Ginger was all in.

After dinner, Violet typically excused herself, and he would linger longer, being helpful with the dishes, and really focus in on Ginger as she droned on and on about various actors and what they'd been doing, as if the information was vital to their well-being. In short order, Ginger learned he had never seen either of her favorite shows, *Criminal Minds* or *Breaking Bad.*

"Dammit!" she'd ranted. "You have *got* to see those shows! They're just the best damn television viewing out there. I can't believe we can't get the Wi-Fi here in the house. I used to stream them at my place, but we can't stream them here, and I can't afford to get premium cable. You've just got to watch them. I'm telling you, they'll change your life. Really, really superior acting. The scripts will blow your MIND! My God, have you ever seen Anna Gunn, the actress who plays Skyler White on *Breaking Bad?* If you did, let me tell you, you'd fall in love. Immeeediately."

On and on it went, until Gilbert got an idea and over-nighted the DVDs of *Criminal Minds* and *Breaking Bad* from Amazon. Presenting the boxed sets to Ginger, he thought she was going to have a stroke.

"GILBERT," she screamed. "Oh my God, you did it! You have got to come over and we'll all watch them together. Well, maybe not Violet—she doesn't need to see them—but you and me? Oh, I'm so glad you listened to me. You are not going to regret this."

From then on, each night and now into October, after Gilbert had dinner with Violet, and after they closed the Backwoods, he and Ginger would sit in the small front room of the house and watch her shows. He found he didn't mind the shows; they were actually pretty good, but twisted. What he did mind was watching Ginger view them. Like a woman in a trance, she knew a lot of the dialogue and would speak it before the scene played out. *Intensely*, like she was living in the episode, playing one of her favorite characters.

They started with *Criminal Minds*. There were 265 episodes to get through. How long would that take? Gilbert realized he had been dropped into hell, and he wasn't learning anything about Ginger relevant to the case, except he would take a blood oath and testify there was something really, really wrong with her. But that was obvious, of course. She was a murderer.

Chapter 30

Clayton Krueger had a trial date. Despite the pressure and threats, he had not agreed to a plea deal or turned over an accomplice. The trial was set to begin December 5th, and Gilbert was worried Violet would suffer even more while the spotlight was on her mother's murder trial. He felt tremendously sorry for the young girl, but he was proud that she had learned to trust him. They had become friends.

Gilbert knew everyone had been counting on him, hoping he would uncover something to help the prosecution's case against Clayton and find the key to arresting Ginger. Unfortunately, that hadn't happened.

After Clayton was arrested, the cops had done a thorough search of the Backwoods—both the business and home. They knew that whatever caused the blunt force trauma was disposed of long before Clayton's arrest, most likely in a lake, but they looked especially hard for a potential murder weapon.

Even though the taps on Ginger's technology were illegal and couldn't be admitted as evidence, it was still disconcerting to find nothing there either. Gilbert learned that Ginger had a trailer outside of McGregor. And while the sheriff may not have been able to secure a search warrant for that property, Gilbert wasn't so restrained. When the time was right and he knew Ginger was occupied at the Backwoods, he'd taken a road trip and broken into her home. Carefully searching, he looked everywhere for anything implicating her or Clayton, but came up empty handed.

It was all discouraging.

The trial was coming up, and Clayton had not cracked. In fact, the county attorney was wavering on the entire gamble. Conspiracy to commit was even looking like a stretch, but they were all hanging in, hoping the pressure of the trial and the actual faces of the jury would finally bring Clayton to the bargaining table. According to all the legal eagles, courtroom reality often made the difference.

In the meantime, Ginger, although erratic at times and hyper, didn't seem to be up to anything—at least nothing Gilbert could see. One night, while they were in between episodes of *Criminal Minds*, he prodded her with questions.

"Are you going to the trial?" he asked.

"I'm not sure. I haven't decided yet." Ginger shrugged.

"What about Violet? Is she planning to be there?"

"I talked to her about it, and we decided that it wasn't a good idea. It would be too upsetting."

"Not my business, but I got to agree about that one," Gilbert declared. Stocking footed, he rocked in the old, gray recliner.

"We'll have to see how it goes. I might need some time off around the trial, if it's okay with you. You can stay here and keep an eye on Violet, right? Make sure she's okay and not alone?"

"Sure, I can do that." Gilbert nodded.

"Good, good." Ginger pointed the remote at the DVD and paused the next episode of *Criminal Minds*. "Hey, I've got an idea, why don't we start watching *Breaking Bad*. We can come back to *Criminal Minds* later. It'd be a fun change. You'll see. You'll like it. I know you will."

"Sure. All right," he said, although he really couldn't care less. He was frustrated nothing was turning up, but then, nothing further bad had happened either—so that was something.

Chapter 31

December arrived, and the first-degree murder trial of Clayton Krueger was about to begin. The winds blew freezing cold weather into the area, and winter had taken a chokehold on the state. The snow was already deep, and the residents buckled up for what looked like a long winter season.

With the trial close, Ginger purposely stepped up her maternal efforts with Violet. Just now, she perched beside the young girl, who was lying on her bed. Ginger could tell Violet was mildly annoyed with her, but she didn't care. It was *go time*.

Channeling how Skyler White empathetically looked at her children when shit hit the fan in the White household, Ginger smoothed her hair and worked her motherly concern. Folding her hands primly in her lap, she said, "Violet, honey, I know we talked about the trial, but I just wanted to check again to make sure you still don't want to go."

"No. I don't." Violet had been in the fetal position with her back to Ginger but now rolled onto her back.

"Okay, okay, good, good," Ginger nodded and licked her lips. "How would you feel if I went? Would that bother you?"

"No. You can go." Violet looked toward her wall.

"Okay, good." Ginger shrugged. "I'll probably go a couple of days this week—you know, to show your dad our support."

"Whatever."

"So, hey," Ginger got up and went to Violet's dresser and grabbed a bottle of lotion. "I picked up this peppermint lotion today at Reeds. It's supposed to be real good for stress. You want to try it? Here, give me your hand and we'll try it." Ginger poured some onto her hand and extended the dollop of lotion toward Violet, coming back to the bed to sit beside her.

Violet held out her hand, reluctantly complying, and Ginger rubbed on the fragrant lotion. "Have you and Petunia been talking recently? I'm so glad you have a good friend to lean on right now. It's nice that you have a friend."

"Yeah, we talk."

"What do you talk about?"

"Stuff."

"Do you talk about the trial and your dad?" Ginger asked, using her shoulder to push back some hair which had fallen into her face.

"Yeah. She knows about it."

"What does she say about it?"

Violet pulled her hand away from Ginger and finished the job of rubbing the lotion in herself. She shrugged, "She wants to help me."

"How would she help you? I mean other than being your friend. I know she has lots of money. Is she going to send you something?"

"It's not about her money, Ginger," Violet said sharply, throwing her hands down beside her.

Ginger stood and rubbed in the rest of the lotion. "Oh, no, no, I get that. She's your friend. I'm glad she's your good friend. I was just wondering what was up with her. Since she can afford it and all, if she was going to visit you— maybe during the trial—to help, you know, really be there for you?"

Violet shrugged and pulled her phone, which had been lying beside her, to her face. "Yeah, she said she might be coming."

Ginger's pulse picked up. If she could, she'd have swooned in relief. "Oh! Isn't that wonderful. When is she coming? Where is she staying? Did she maybe want to stay here with you?" Ginger swept her arm across the room. "We could bring a cot in here, or we could set something up in the main room, or we could get another sleeping bag. You two could hang out."

"No, I don't think she's going to stay here." Violet looked at Ginger with dead eyes.

"Oh, well, she'd be welcome, you know. This is your home. I know it may not be much, but if you're embarrassed or something . . ." Ginger turned to a pile of clothes and plucked up a shirt to fold.

"It's not that. I think she's going to stay with her parents."

"Her parents are coming with her?" Ginger continued with the laundry and picked up a pair of clean matching socks from a pile and stuffed them together. *Oh boy, oh boy, oh boy.*

"Well, yeah, she's not coming alone!"

"Oh, I didn't know. I thought maybe a nanny or some-one . . ." she said off-handedly. She turned and picked up the bottle of lotion again and placed it next to an old jewelry box.

"No, her parents are coming with her."

Ginger turned to smile at Violet. "When are they coming? If they visit out here, I need to make sure the place looks presentable for you. Maybe we'll have some fresh cookies or something. We can bake something fragrant and make the place smell nice."

"I think they're staying in town. Petunia said she wanted to come by to see me, but I don't know what day yet."

"Are they staying at the Country Suites? You should let them know that it's really the nicest place in town. I'm sure they would appreciate that tip, you know." Ginger went back to sorting socks.

"I told her that. I think that's where they're staying."

"But you don't have a date for the visit? I really would like a little notice, Violet, so we can make sure the place is clean. I don't want to make a bad impression."

Violet put down her phone in frustration and looked at Ginger. "They're coming this weekend. She wanted to come after the trial started. I think they're just coming for the weekend, so I'll see her then. Maybe they won't even come out here."

"Really? But what about transportation? What if I'm busy and can't drive you into town? They should really come here for a visit, don't you think? Maybe they could just drop Petunia off for the weekend and you girls could hang out! We could get some movies, and I'll make popcorn . . ."

"I don't know what we're doing. Just don't worry about it. I'll bet they could pick me up."

"Violet, I don't want you to think I'm crazy or anything, but do you really trust them? What if they have some ulterior motive?"

"Like what?" Violet squished up her face, appearing angry and confused.

"I don't know, but people can surprise you. I mean I know they have lots of money, so they can afford to come all the way out here for a visit, no problem—but it's a lot of effort, you know. And what if they're followed! By paparazzi, and the cameras and stuff. You won't like that at all."

"Paparazzi in Brainerd? I don't think so." Violet frowned.

"Well, the trial . . . I'm just thinking. I worry about you, Violet. Sue me! I need to know where you are, especially during this month, which will be difficult for all of us. You need to tell me where you're going all the time. We need to be open with one another, Violet. I only want to help you. You know that, right?"

"I know." Violet looked back at her phone and began tapping away.

"Okay then. Let me know when they'll be arriving, so I can get the place real nice just in case they want to stop in. Be sure to let them know they're welcome here, okay? Your friends are important to me too."

"Sure. I'll let you know."

Ginger nodded and backed out of the room. She closed the door and smiled, wanting to dance a jig.

The Carrows are coming. They were coming this weekend, probably to put Petunia on the stand at the beginning of next week—the first full week of the trial. Violet was apparently too stupid to consider that they were coming for other reasons than to just give her a fucking hug. *Jeez.* I mean, my God, who did that?

The important part was that Ginger knew they were staying at the Country Suites—and she'd know exactly when they'd be arriving. Because Violet would tell her.

She had a plan.

Chapter 32

Three important things happened that first week of December. The trial began Thursday, the *Breaking Bad* marathon at the Backwoods continued, and the weather was terrible.

On Wednesday, the day before the trial was set to begin, Ginger walked into the kitchen at the restaurant and approached Gilbert.

"Hey, I was wondering if you could watch the place today while I go into town to do some shopping?"

Gilbert had been waiting for this week. His boss was coming with the family. If something was going to break, it had to be soon. Washing up the morning dishes, he nodded. "Sure, it's gonna be pretty slow today. Have you decided if you're going to the trial tomorrow?"

"I don't know. They'll just be picking the jury, won't they? I thought I'd go on Friday, though. Violet doesn't want to go, and it would be great if someone was around to keep an eye on her."

"Sure. What are you going into town for?"

Ginger looked up and to the right, then her eyes rolled down the stack of clean pans waiting for the rolls. "I thought I'd do some sprucing up around here just in case some of Violet's friends drop by—you know, just in case. She has that stain on her bed skirt. I thought it would be nice to get a new dust ruffle."

"Yeah? You think some of her friends will stop by? I haven't seen them around much lately." Gilbert glanced at her as he turned to stack some plates on a metal shelf.

"Well, I hope so. I mean, its crunch time for Violet, and friends should be there for each other. It's so important to take care of people. Just look at Walter White on *Breaking Bad* and what he's doing for his family. There he is, dying of cancer, and all he cares about is providing for his family. Taking care of them—leaving them enough money so when he dies, they'll be okay. He loves Skyler that much. So much that he risks his life cooking meth and selling it. That's real commitment."

Gilbert realized once again that all roads led to Ginger's favorite shows. Skyler White in particular seemed to fascinate her, and of course this obsession was supported by his knowledge that she followed the actress and several fan pages on Twitter. He didn't need confirmation from Alex's hacker to discover it; all he had to do was listen to Ginger talk.

Later that day, sitting at one of the cracking laminate restaurant tables and reading the paper, Gilbert got a call from Alex.

"Hey," he said.

"How's it going?" Alex asked.

"Okay. Really quiet. The weather's been bad, so no one's here at the moment. We can speak."

"How's Violet?"

Gilbert got up and looked out the window toward the house. "Quiet as usual. She's at her house, reading on her Kindle. Ginger went out shopping."

"How is *she?*"

"Ginger? The same. I don't see anything much going on. She went to get Violet a new bed quilt or something in case some of her friends come over. She's in town."

"Okay. Our tech guy is still monitoring her searches, and texts, and calls, and we don't see anything different either. You still hanging with her every night, watching her shows?"

"Yeah, onto *Breaking Bad* now. The woman is obsessed with the character Skyler White. Skyler's married to the main guy, Walter White, who's got a serious case of inoperable lung cancer. Walter goes into the drug business to support his family, and Ginger thinks it's the sweetest thing in the world. The show's good though. Probably better if you didn't have to watch it with Ginger, mouthing Skyler White's every line with her eyes bugging out. She's got the entire thing memorized."

"It's about cancer?" Alex asked.

"Well, it's about cooking and selling meth mostly, but that's the impetus—the big reason why this guy got into the drug business to begin with."

"Shit, Gilbert. I can't believe we didn't put this together before now. Petunia heard the murderer, the woman talking to Clayton, say something about the cancer not coming back. It never made much sense, and we've been worried that the defense attorney will twist the testimony around the cancer thing. But this might tie that up. Maybe Ginger was talking about the show?"

"Could be." Gilbert nodded, for the first time feeling he'd made a real contribution. "I'm not kidding about her knowing all the lines. She works Skyler White into *any* conversation she can. Probably dreams about her too."

"The cancer isn't coming back. That's what Ginger said that day in the bar."

Gilbert searched through what he knew about the show and real life. "Meaning what? The cancer or Penny?"

"Penny. This time she meant Penny, Gilbert. Goddamn. Nice job. I don't know if it will help, but it's a thread—it's something we didn't have before. We're coming into Brainerd on Friday, two days from now. We'll be staying at the Country Suites. Petunia wanted to have some time with Violet over the weekend so she can tell her in person she's going to be a witness at her dad's trial. We're not sure how Violet's going to take that. We're worried she might feel betrayed."

Gilbert paced the floor of the restaurant and glanced at the stain on the ceiling spreading from the corner. "Is Petunia coming to the Backwoods?"

"I don't want her anywhere near Ginger. I think we'll pick Violet up and bring her back to Brainerd with us."

"Who's coming in?"

"Charlotte, Petunia, Renzo, and myself. Lily's staying with my mom while we're gone."

"Okay. And Petunia is testifying on Monday?"

"That's the plan. Gavin Stewart is prosecuting this one personally, and he and Petunia have been on Zoom, preparing, but he wants to meet with her in person on Sunday."

"How long do you think you'll be in town?"

"Hopefully we're out again by end of Tuesday."

"How long do you think the trial will last?" Gilbert asked.

"Gavin Stewart thinks, after jury selection, a week—maybe two. They've got the medical examiner and the guy with the dog who found the body on Friday. Petunia is up on Monday. Then they have the bankruptcy attorney, a couple of Penny's friends, and a girlfriend of Clayton's, someone who willingly came forward to say she was having an affair with the guy. After that, it's the defense's turn, so we'll see."

Gilbert stared out the window into the blank whiteness of the snow. "You think they'll get a conviction, Alex?"

"It's problematic. Everyone's frustrated that Clayton hasn't cracked yet and given Ginger up in a plea deal. This nugget that the cancer bit may be related to a show Ginger's obsessed with might be useful if they put him on the stand. Or they might introduce it another way. They weren't planning on calling Ginger to testify. They were hoping to find a way to nail her. We'll just have to wait and see."

"I can't tell you how creeped out I am sitting next to this pig all day and night watching her get away with what she did to Penny and Violet."

"It's gotta be tough. Just keep up the pretense and keep me posted. I'll be in constant contact after we land."

"Sounds good. Give your family my best."

"Thanks for everything, Gilbert. We appreciate it."

Chapter 33

Ginger gripped the wheel as she slid on the ice; the backcountry roads were slippery and not as well maintained as the interstates.

"Goddammit!" she yelled as she dropped her cigarette onto the floorboard and used both hands to come out of a small spin. "Fucking roads!"

She glanced at yet another burn in her carpet and shook her head in disgust. It couldn't be helped. She needed to move fast. A fucking bed skirt shouldn't take eight hours to purchase, and her cover with Gilbert would be blown if she was gone until evening. She supposed she could bluff her way out of it, but only as a last resort.

She'd left that morning and driven straight to the Grand Casino in Mille Lacs County hoping they would have a computer café where she could do some clandestine research. It was such bullshit that internet cafés were no longer a thing.

The people at the casino looked at her like she was nuts. "We prefer our guests to be working with the *other* recreational machines on the property, ma'am. We don't have a bank of computers. We have free Wi-Fi, and most of our guests have smartphones."

Ginger stormed out of the casino after finding out where the local library was located. Going there, she was disgusted to learn she had to have a new library card to use the computers. Every county outside the Kitchigami regional system had asked to see her license before they'd given her access. All this security for some trashy secondhand books was fucking ridiculous. But they did have computers.

Ginger took a seat at the far end of the last aisle and struggled out of her jacket, hat, scarf, gloves, and heavy top sweater while she waited for the system to come up. She needed to do some critical research, and she didn't have much time. She wanted to know how to cut the brake lines on a car so it would leak slowly and not immediately alert the computer system. Thus, having the brakes fail when the car was traveling at high speeds.

It was all she had. She knew the Carrows were coming in on Friday and knew they would have a car. The weather report told her that another storm front was coming, and the roads could be dangerous. If Petunia wasn't coming to the Backwoods to stay overnight, then she'd have to get her another way.

She'd done all that research on poisons too! She'd plotted exactly where to go, what to get, and how to do it. Still a favorite daydream, her mind wandered again as she envisioned it all. *The poor kids, up late, snacking, chatting, and everything they ate, laced with poison. What a tragedy! What a terrible tragedy!* Plan B—the handy carbon monoxide accident with Ginger being the only survivor—she'd been ready for that one too.

But damn it all to hell, the billionaire's kid was not biting the invite. Now it was down to this—tampering with the Carrows' car and hoping for the best. A terrible accident. A big enough smash and boom that Petunia would be killed. And then, problem solved! Ginger couldn't believe her entire future hinged on the broken neck of an eleven-year-old girl.

Clayton had no idea how hard she'd been preparing to take out their witness, but she knew he would be supremely proud of her if he saw her in action. Her dedication was priceless!

Now that she knew she was capable of anything, her shackles were off, and the sky was the limit. So far, she'd played it smart, but felt angry that so much was out of her control. But then again, fate may very well be on her side. The Carrows would have to travel on roads during an icy winter storm. And on Saturday morning, they'd drive to the Backwoods to pick up Violet, who had no other means of transportation. *Poor needy Violet. Poor stupid Carrows.*

There was so much planning to do! But she'd be ready. And think of the sweet, sweet dreams!

Back in Brainerd later that afternoon, Ginger dropped by the local thrift store and purchased some fresh bedding for Violet. After that she drove to the Country Suites and slowly drove through the parking lot searching for cameras. There was a waffle place across the street with a direct line of sight onto the circular drive of the hotel main entrance and parking area. On Friday, she'd be back, and she'd wait for the Carrows to drive up to the entrance and see what kind of car they were driving. Later, while everyone nestled, snug in their beds, she'd come back to the hotel, slip under their car, and do what was necessary to ensure their destruction.

Ginger smiled at all the wonderful reconnaissance she'd accomplished that day and treated herself to a nacho platter at the Taco Bell drive-thru. Driving home, she ate the gooey chips and allowed herself the luxury of daydreaming about how it would all play out.

. . . *Saturday, when the elegant but simple-minded Carrows family came out to the Backwoods to pick up Violet, she'd make certain that Petunia was in the car for the drive. Somehow, Ginger-Skyler would make this happen. She'd work on Violet's end to double ensure it. All she had to do was get Petunia in the car and hope that bad brakes, a slippery road, and maybe . . .* Ginger licked some cheese off her fingers and shivered with delight as she colored in the details of the vision . . . *a large semi hauling gasoline would collide with the family on a backcountry road! Boom! Or better yet, maybe the brakes would give out at the exact moment their car drove over the arch bridge crossing the Mississippi River as they were leaving town.*

Oh my God! Ginger only wished she could be there in person to witness the explosion—or the car plunging off the bridge into the dark frozen waters below.

The vision was almost better than cheese.

Chapter 34

Flying through the darkness late Friday night, the Carrows Macchi's Gulfstream pilots nervously negotiated the bad winter storm and managed to land safely at the Brainerd airport. Alex and Charlotte thanked them for a job well done, and the two of them and Renzo and Petunia left the aircraft and made their way through the snow and into the waiting Ford Explorer. They hadn't been too fussy about the type of vehicle they rented, only that it had four-wheel drive.

"My God the roads are bad," Charlotte said from the backseat as Alex drove through town.

"They're a lot worse than I expected, but it's only seven miles. It's not like we don't have storms in New York. We'll just take it slow and easy, and everything will be fine."

Pulling into the circular turnaround of the Country Suites hotel, Renzo and Alex unloaded their luggage while Charlotte and Petunia made their way into the building. Once the bags were inside, Renzo stayed with the women while Alex drove through the parking lot, around the side of the building, and found a place to park. Jumping back into the cold, he left the car and ran, slipping his way back to the front of the building and went inside.

———————

While eating her second helping of waffles and fries at the restaurant across from the Country Suites, Ginger tried not to choke on her food when at roughly 8 p.m., she watched the Carrows arrive and enter the hotel.

Job well done, Skyler! she thought.

After observing her prey's arrival and where they parked the car, she slammed a tip down on the table and stuffed a few last fries in her mouth before walking back to her own car for the treacherous thirty-minute drive home to the Backwoods. On her way, she called Gilbert and lied through the details of an extended outing, explaining she'd been delayed because her friend showed up late for dinner and then she'd skidded off the road.

"No, I'm okay. This guy came by and took pity on me, used his truck to pull me out. I just wanted to let you know I'm on my way, so you wouldn't worry. It's real slow going out here. What's up there?"

She hardly listened to his response she was so pumped. The next step in her plan was to get back home and relieve Gilbert for the night. Once he was gone, she'd drive back to the hotel *in the middle of the night to do the deed.* She was certain the Carrows wouldn't be out driving around in their vehicle the rest of the evening or doing early morning sightseeing through little Brainerd. In this weather, they would only drive if they had to, and the only item on their agenda was to drive to the Backwoods the next day to pick up sweet, unsuspecting Violet.

It would be their last trip in the soon-to-be death trap of a car. The plan was perfect.

Chapter 35

Saturday dawned in Brainerd, and the family met Renzo and went downstairs to the hotel restaurant to get an early breakfast. None had really slept, and Petunia was especially anxious to finally see Violet.

She finished her pancakes in a hurry and listened while Renzo chatted with the waitress when she brought their check. "How are the roads? You been out on them this morning?" he asked.

The congenial girl poured him more coffee. "Yup, they made me come in. I don't live too far, so it wasn't that bad. More snow's coming though. I'm going to have to shovel my way out of the parking lot when I leave."

"Don't they plow the parking lot?" Alex asked.

"They do, but then it gets packed in around my car. I got a shovel in the trunk." She shrugged. "No biggie. You folks from around here?"

"No, just in town for a family thing," Charlotte interjected.

After breakfast, they went back to their rooms. While everyone watched television for a weather update, Petunia texted Violet.

"Mom, she said I should come out there and spend the night. What am I supposed to say to that?"

"Just tell her I said no. Make me the bad guy. Tell her I said you have to stay with us and *your bodyguard.*"

Petunia rolled her eyes and typed. "I can't wait to get her out of there. It's so scary to think she's living with that woman."

"Invite her to stay with us here. Tell her she can stay in your room, that we have a connecting room, and the two of you can go swimming. We'll order pizza or something."

"Can she stay with us until we leave?" Petunia asked.

Her mom let her eyes drop and uncharacteristically rubbed her arms as if chilled. For some reason, she was wearing all black today, and despite how pretty the turtleneck and trousers looked with her mom's dark hair, Petunia thought she looked really sad. Giving a small, rueful smile, her mom replied, "I don't know. I guess that depends on how she takes the news about why we're in town."

"The county attorney wants to keep socializing to a minimum. And they aren't going to be happy we told Violet in advance that Petunia is testifying," added her dad.

"One step at a time, Alex." Her mom shot him a hooded look.

The conflict between her parents wasn't lost on Petunia. She knew Violet was going to be hurt when the truth came out. She wasn't looking forward to the conversation, but she absolutely had to tell Violet before she testified against her dad on Monday. She'd betrayed her friend enough already.

There'd been so much lying by omission with Violet. Petunia felt sick about how secretive she'd been in their communications. She felt bad about testifying against Violet's father, but worst of all, she knew she was letting

Violet live with the woman she believed killed her mom! How could Violet recover from all that? This weekend, Petunia was finally allowed to tell Violet about her upcoming testimony, but still couldn't reveal anything about Ginger.

It was all so complicated. Her mom and dad had hired a local attorney to work with the judge and the other lawyers regarding her parents' demand she be kept anonymous. And mostly because of her age and stupid notoriety issues, they'd agreed the courtroom would be cleared of spectators—except Mr. Krueger, the lawyers and staff, and the judge and jury—while she gave her testimony. While everyone was hoping her identity wouldn't get out to the local or national media, they had agreed Violet was entitled to know.

Reading a text, Petunia said. "Violet said she asked *Ginger* if she could stay with us and *Ginger* said it would be okay, but she doesn't have a ride. They're up really early too, working in the restaurant."

"All right then, we can go out there and pick her up," said her mom.

"Mom," she rolled her eyes. "All four of us can't go, that would be intimidating. I mean, what? Violet packs into the backseat between me and you, with Renzo and dad up front? I mean, talk about overkill. What if just dad and I go get her?"

Her mom considered the situation, looking to the others for their thoughts.

"I think it would be all right if the two of us went," said her dad. "I don't think I'd need Renzo."

"Petunia and I could pick her up," Renzo offered.

Her dad grabbed his jacket off the back of a chair. "No, you stay here. We'll go get her. Text Gilbert and fill him in on the plan."

Nodding, Petunia texted and said, "Okay, I told her we'd be leaving in about five minutes, so we'll be there in about forty-five minutes—right? Like nine o'clock?"

"Sounds about right," her dad said as he put on the jacket and scarf and looked for his gloves.

"When you get there," said her mom, "don't get out of the car. Text Violet and have her come out. I don't care if it's rude; blame it on the weather."

"Got it," Petunia said, zipping up her parka.

Her mom gave her a hug and said, "We'll be waiting. I'll check into the pizza delivery options. We'll have a nice day with Violet. It'll be okay."

"Thanks, Mom," she said, letting go of her warm embrace.

"Alex, be careful." Her mom walked over and gave her dad a kiss and lingering hug.

"It'll be fine," he said. "We'll dig the car out of the parking lot and be back in an hour or two."

———————

Alex rode down the elevator with his daughter, making a few wisecracks to lighten the mood. He worried about what the next few days would bring but knew they were as prepared as they could be.

They walked out the front door of the hotel and were blinded by an icy blast of snow and sleet. Heads down, they marched through the parking lot and around the building to where he'd parked the car. He jumped in, started it up, and then opened the back looking for a shovel and a window scraper. The rental agency said the SUV was fully stocked with a roadside emergency preparedness kit in case they got stranded. Alex was concerned over the terrible weather but was determined to try.

Their breakfast waitress had been correct about the parking lot snow being plowed against their car, and while it was inconvenient, Alex supposed there was only so much that could be done, and everyone needed to be patient and pitch in.

He and Petunia got the job done, and once moving, the four-wheel-drive SUV had little trouble making its way out of the parking lot and onto the Brainerd roads. Few drivers were out, and those that were, were giving a wide berth to their neighboring drivers. Everyone was taking it slow, which was the only logical way to drive given the conditions.

Petunia looked at him and frowned. "I'm going to text her and tell her that it might take longer than I said."

"Good idea. Once we get there, we should text your mom and let her know how long it took, so she won't worry."

His own worries weren't easing, though, as the winter storm blew snow and ice on their car as they crept down the road. The Brainerd city boundary ended just as they reached the two-lane bridge that spanned the partially frozen and otherwise roiling Mississippi River. Alex felt the difference in road traction the second his wheels hit the bridge, but thankfully it had been recently plowed and salted. Breathing again after they made it to the other side, he was having misgivings about the safety of the trip and considered going back. However, he knew how important the visit was for the girls, and they continued down the road, picking up speed as they left the slow speed limits of the city and drove down the two-lane county highway.

Slowly accelerating, testing the conditions, now traveling around 50 mph, Alex spotted a road sign alerting him to a bend in the road and gently applied the brakes, but the car didn't slow. At the same time, a light on the instrument panel began to flash.

What the hell? His pulse rate ticked up as he continued to pump the brakes, slowly at first, hoping to not brake too hard and go into a skid, but still, no response. Realizing they were going too fast to make the curve, Alex's mind searched frantically for a solution but found none. He knew he was losing control as they began to slide around the bend.

"Dad!" Petunia shouted, her hands reaching out toward the dash.

His eyes grew wide as another car traveling in the opposite direction lay in their path, heading right for them.

Panic seized him as the SUV spun wildly out of control. Alex felt then heard the impact with the other car, his body punched and jolted as they flipped and rolled, air bags exploding all around them. The SUV landed on its side next to a tree in the ditch. His seatbelt still attached but straining from his weight, he felt his daughter's body under him.

"Petunia!" he yelled, fighting the seatbelt and flailing at the air bags, his heart beating out of his chest. Blood ran into his eyes as he maneuvered, pushing himself off Petunia and holding in place while he unbuckled his seatbelt. Nearly toppling on his daughter, he braced himself and pounded the passenger airbag, groping for her face.

"Baby, baby," he said inching her head gently toward him, only to see her eyes closed and not responding.

"God, *no*," he groaned, trembling, frantically searching his pockets. Finding his phone, supporting his torso, and searching for a position he could work in, he swiped blood from his eyes and barely managed with slippery and shaky hands to punch in his security code and then 911.

He gripped Petunia's arm, willing her to be okay as the operator answered, and Alex barked out the situation, begging for assistance. He put the phone down and shot his fingers down her jacket near her throat, feeling for a pulse. It was there. She was breathing, too, but still unconscious.

"Petunia," he whimpered, looking at her beloved face. "Dear God, please help her. Please, *Petunia*? Can you hear me, baby?" He didn't want to move her any farther in case of a neck or back injury. Glancing at his door, he knew there was no way he could get them both out without a lot of jostling.

"Help us. Hurry!" he yelled into the phone, which was still connected. The dispatcher was saying something but it barely registered. Alex wildly looked around, blood dripping everywhere, wondering what to do while waiting for the rescue vehicles.

He could think of nothing.

"Petunia," he moaned helplessly. "Please wake up. Can you hear me?"

He almost passed out when he heard her groan. "Petunia," he said quietly but with urgency. "Honey? Where does it hurt?"

She lifted a hand and he grabbed it. "Dad?" she whispered.

It was enough. For the moment. Alex couldn't help but drop his head. His shoulders jerked and he began to cry.

———

The firetruck and police arrived first. They handed a collar brace to Alex, which he positioned around Petunia's neck, then helped hoist Alex out of the car. Once he was out, they all worked to gently flip the SUV. It landed upright as the ambulance arrived and the paramedics carefully triaged Petunia before extracting her too. They put her on a stretcher, and Petunia and Alex were quickly taken away to the local hospital.

On the ride, she finally fully awoke, her sweet brown eyes immediately searching his. "Dad? You're bleeding."

"I'm fine, honey." He gave her a soft smile and squeezed her hand as the paramedic continued to triage her condition.

"How do you feel? Where does it hurt, Petunia?" the man asked.

"We were in an accident?" she whispered as her eyes looked around the vehicle. The lids rose in a bit of panic as she tried to lift her arms. The safety restraints on the stretcher had her locked down tight.

"Yes," he said, tears coming again in spite of himself. He sniffed, then hid his face as he rubbed at the back of his nose. Even with the cloth the paramedic had given him to hold on his head, blood dripped onto his face.

"You're *hurt*," she cried, brows furrowing and her teeth beginning to chatter.

"Baby, I'm fine, just a cut somewhere on my head. Try not to move. How are *you*? Tell us where it hurts."

"I'm okay. I don't know."

"You were unconscious. We're on our way to the hospital. They're going to check you out. It's going to be all right," he said, with hope for the first time that it might be miraculously true.

"Did we hit another car?"

"We did, but they're fine. Don't worry about them. They're being looked after."

"Daaddddd," she said as her chin quivered, and her body trembled. "I'm so cold."

The paramedic covered her with an additional warm blanket, and even though they'd been traveling at a fairly high speed, Alex saw him lean toward the driver and say, "Light 'em up."

Lights and siren came on, and Alex felt his stomach lurch as he looked to the EMT, begging for answers.

"She might be shocky; we need to keep her warm. Her vitals are a little low, but she's tough."

Alex reached down and gave her a kiss on the cheek but was horrified to see he left a trail of blood.

The paramedic fussed with equipment, but said, "Petunia, what grade are you in this year?"

"Seevvvvveeennnnthhh," she chattered, with her eyes closed.

"Good. What's the name of your teacher?"

"Mrs. Hunter."

"Is she nice? Do you like her?"

"Yeesss."

"Okay, dad," the paramedic got up and walked around to him. "Let me take a look at that head. We should be there in a few minutes."

"Petunia," the EMT said over his shoulder while attending him. "Do you have any pets at home? A cat or a dog?"

"A doggg."

"Wonderful! What's his name?"

"Bbbluue."

"Blue? What kind of dog is he?"

"He's a German Shepherd."

"Good. Okay, we're pulling in. Dad, Alex, will you wait while we get Petunia rolling?"

"Yes. Honey, I'll be right behind you, okay?"

"Okay. M-mom is going to be upset. And Renzo."

The siren stopped, but the lights were still flashing as the ambulance driver rounded the back and pulled open the door. The first EMT jumped down, and they rolled Petunia through the doors into the hospital's emergency bay. They then turned back and gave a hand to Alex as he walked down out of the rig, holding the bloody cloth to his head.

Following his daughter inside, he was still stoked with adrenaline and fear. They wheeled the gurney into an emergency room bay and the doctors and nurses began to examine Petunia.

Someone sat him down and looked at his scalp wound and shined a light into his eyes.

"Sir, can we get you to lie down on the table next to your daughter? We need to check your vitals and look more closely at your head."

"In a minute. How is she?"

The doctor near his daughter answered. "She looks good. Her blood pressure is a bit low, but she's responsive. I think they'll want to scan her, but so far, it looks good."

"Thank you," he said humbly, feeling his throat close as another wave of tears threatened. He fought them back and went to her side to hold her hand. Never in his life had he felt so absolutely helpless and at the same time, so filled with love. "Honey . . ." he began, looking at the trail of blood streaked across her freckles and down her precious face.

"I'm okay, Dad," she smiled weakly. "Did you call Mom?"

"No. I'll do that in a minute. Don't worry."

"Petunia," said a doctor, "do you mind if we take a look at your dad on the next table? He's not going far. He'll be right over there. You have a neck brace on, and we'd like to leave that for a little while until we can get some X-rays, so don't turn your head. Your dad will be right there," he said again, pointing at the next bay.

"Okay."

"I'm right here," Alex said as they guided him, laying him down. He wanted her to hear his voice so she could gauge he was still close by.

The two of them were well looked after in the emergency room, and as his daughter was taken down the hall for a CAT scan of her head and neck, Alex stayed in his bay while the doctor discussed options for stitching together his scalp and forehead.

"We could wait for the plastic surgeon on call to do this, but it might take some time. Your decision."

"Just stich it. I'm sure it'll be fine."

The last stitch was in place as Petunia's gurney was brought next to his, and they were able to check in with each other.

"Mr. Macchi," the doctor said, taking off his gloves. "It's your turn into the machine. I'd feel better if we get some pictures of your head too."

"Really?" he frowned.

"Dad, it doesn't hurt," Petunia said with a little spunk back in her voice.

Smiling at her tone, he said, "I'm not afraid of the machine, honey, I'm afraid of your mother. I'll get my head scanned and then give her a call. I'll be right back."

"Tell her I love her and that we're just fine."

"Got it," he said as they rolled him away. Once out of earshot he said, "Can you wait up? How were her films?"

"We don't know. The doctor is looking at them," said the nurse.

"Let me just give her mom a call. We've been gone a long time."

"Five minutes, and then into the machine."

"Right," he said as he tapped her number.

"Alex, where are you? I've been calling!"

He swallowed hard and spoke with a strong voice. "Charlotte, I'm afraid we were in a little accident, but we're both just fine."

"What!"

"We're *okay.* We're at the Brainerd Hospital, and we're being looked after. Petunia told me to tell you that she loves you and that all is well."

"Alex! My God! You're hurt?"

"Yes. Some stiches, some bumps on the head. I'm heading into a CAT scan right now, just as a precaution, but I wanted to give you a call because I knew you'd be worried."

"We're on our way."

"Honey, you don't have a car," he said.

"We're on our way," she repeated firmly.

He could hear Renzo in the background say, "Shit."

Alex continued. "All right, we'll be waiting. I guess I don't have a car now either, come to think of it."

"Oh my God. Are you really certain you're both okay?"

"We are. Try not to worry, and don't steal a car or anything."

"We're coming."

"Be careful."

"I love you, Alex."

"I love you, too."

Chapter 36

Never in Charlotte's life had thirty minutes of madness and negotiations gone so agonizingly slow. Controlling her emotions, her mouth utterly dry, her fingers fumbled with her jacket zipper as her legs somehow walked her through the corridors of the hospital, to the emergency room, where she was finally led to the bays where her loved ones were. Glancing between the bloody faces of both, she hurried to Petunia and leaned down to hug her. The smell of her, the gift that she was alive and safe overcame her.

"Angel. My baby, I'm so sorry," she whispered, feeling her daughter breathe.

"Mommy," Petunia said, returning the embrace. "We're okay. The doctors said so."

Pulling back and looking at her innocent face, a neck brace in place, Charlotte's felt her hands tremble as she pushed back her daughter's hair, examining her scalp, looking for more blood. She kissed Petunia's forehead. "Are you bleeding somewhere?"

"What?" Petunia said.

"I think that's mine," Alex said. Charlotte released the grip of her focus and looked over to the next gurney to see the smiling but blood-stained, stitched up face of her beautiful husband.

Leaving Petunia, she went to him. "Oh, Alex," she whispered, holding him. "I love you so much."

"I love you too," was all he managed.

She stood up as Renzo moved in and neared Petunia. He leaned down and gave her a kiss on the cheek, and Charlotte heard him mumble, "It's good to see you, kid." Raising to his full height, he wiped the back of his hand across his face, unsuccessfully hiding his tears.

Renzo cleared his throat. "So what happened out there? You hit a deer or what?"

Charlotte went back to Petunia and held her hand as Alex told the story.

When he was finished, a dark rage built as her mind raced through the possible reasons why the brakes failed. She grabbed her bag off a nearby chair. "I'm calling Sheriff Becker."

As she pushed past Renzo and out of the bay, she heard him say, "I think Charlotte just stepped up to bat. There's a new sheriff in town. Becker better watch out."

She called Tate Becker, and he answered on the first ring. She kept the conversation matter-of-fact but got her message across. Spying the doctor pushing back the curtains to Petunia's bay, she hung up on Tate and followed the doctor inside. Relief flooded through her as he shared the news that the films on both of them looked pretty good, but they'd like to admit Petunia for observation.

"Does that mean I can take the collar off now?" Petunia squirmed.

"It does," he said, walking over to remove it.

"How long will she need to stay, Doctor?" Charlotte asked.

"Just overnight. She lost consciousness and she has a mild concussion, so we'll watch her. She can leave tomorrow, late morning. We'd just feel better if we had her here for the next twenty-four hours."

Her stomach tightened as her jaw clenched. *She lost consciousness?*

"What about Alex," she said, glaring at the floor, not daring to meet anyone's eyes as her fury built.

"No concussion. Just the head wound, unless I'm missing something?" The doctor queried Alex as they all turned to observe him rubbing his neck.

"No. I've got a headache. A neckache."

The doctor nodded. "We'll give you some Tylenol."

Charlotte contained herself from further questioning the details of the accident and their conditions until arrangements were made for Petunia's stay. Once they got her daughter to her room, Renzo planted himself in a chair next to her and Charlotte and Alex went out in the hall to talk.

She leaned against a wall and sank down a bit, her eyes communicating her glaring determination to find out what happened. Alex, she saw, was on the same page. It was time for answers. She gritted her teeth. "Sheriff Becker said he'll look at the car. He said he'd go to the lot personally and check it out. How in the world, Alex, could your brakes go out?"

"That's a good question. I texted Gilbert to let him know we weren't coming, but I told him to play dumb, and not to say anything to Violet or Ginger. I didn't give him any details about what happened either."

Charlotte ran a hand down his arm, nodding at the good reasoning of his plan. "Okay then. Let's wait for Sheriff Becker."

Chapter 37

A bit after twelve o'clock noon, Sheriff Tate Becker walked alone into Petunia's hospital room. Apprehensive about what he'd find, he removed his hat and greeted the battered and angry-looking family. Inquiring after their health, he felt encouraged to see Petunia sitting up, eating ice cream, but felt a heated glare coming from the huge bodyguard, Renzo. Gesturing out the door, he asked Charlotte and Alex into the hallway.

He held his hat in his hands and glanced around, sure they couldn't be overheard. "We have a situation. I'm afraid to say that it looks like your brakes were definitely tampered with."

"Are you kidding me?" Alex barred his teeth, practically hissing.

Tate inhaled. "It appears the brake line was cut, not so much that you lost everything while the vehicle sat in the parking lot, but when you got it up to speed. Then it just broke open. Clean cuts."

"Is there any *natural* way this could have happened?" Charlotte asked. She too, looked uncharacteristically feral and ready to pounce on him.

Tate pursed his lips and slowly shook his head. "I don't think so."

The Macchis glanced at one another until Charlotte spoke in a steely voice. "Do you plan to arrest Ginger Krueger, now that she tried to kill my husband and daughter?"

He dropped his head and made a small gesture, his hat coming up with his eyes. "It's not that easy, Mrs. Macchi. We need to conduct an investigation, and that will take some time."

Charlotte, always well-mannered in the past, took him off guard as she leaned into his face. "That's a load of crap. We all know who did this."

Tate shuffled an inch or two back. "Most likely, yes, I agree—it was *probably* Ginger Krueger. So let me ask you some questions. What do we know about her movements yesterday? Have you spoken with Gilbert? What time did you arrive in town?"

Alex reached out to touch his wife's arm. She stepped back, nearer to him, as Alex held his voice low and ran him through the details of their arrival and Gilbert's observations. "Ginger got home around eight-thirty last night. She claimed her friend was late for dinner and that her car went off the road into a ditch, but a good Samaritan helped her out. After that, Gilbert left them and went back to his place. He texted me again this morning at five a.m. reporting in for the day. He found Ginger in the restaurant's kitchen, putting the rolls in the oven."

Sheriff Becker devoured the valuable information as the two formidable Macchis continued to glare at him. Somehow, he needed to manage this before one of them exploded and ruined everything. Tate focused on Alex, who was a least sticking to the details. He didn't know what to think about Ginger being involved. He had to follow the evidence. "So Ginger was in Brainerd last night. The timing's awfully tight here. How would she know where you were staying?"

"Petunia may have told Violet," Charlotte said quietly. She lifted her chin, challenging him to scold her or her injured daughter for this potential lapse. He did not want to go there. Instead, he waved his hat back toward the door.

"I think we should ask her." Sheriff Becker looked between them.

They went back into the room and Charlotte's voice turned soothing as she approached Petunia. "Honey, did you text Violet yesterday or the day before and tell her where we would be staying?"

Petunia's eyes got large. "Yes, because I wanted her to come stay with us and I knew she knew the hotel because they had the volunteer center there."

Charlotte nodded. "Of course, no problem. Did you tell her when we'd be arriving?"

Petunia paused, her face looking pained as she began realizing where this was heading. Her face paled as she answered. "Yes."

Charlotte picked up her daughter's hand. "Okay, listen to me, you didn't do anything wrong. One more question. Do you know if Ginger reads Violet's text messages, or if Violet talks to her about you?"

Petunia's eyes grew truly wide, this time in fear. She jerked up. "Do you think Ginger did something to our car?"

Charlotte put her hands on Petunia to settle her back.

Tate tried to calm them. "We don't know anything for sure right now, Petunia. We just need some answers."

Petunia said, "Violet told me that Ginger borrows her phone a lot because she has an unlimited data plan and Ginger doesn't and she runs out in the middle of each month."

"So she knows her password and she can look at her texts if she wants to?" The sheriff asked.

Petunia nodded. "I guess so."

"Did you text her, or did you tell Violet about our schedule, honey?" Charlotte asked.

Petunia's face contorted in pain; tears formed in her eyes. "I told her. We talked."

Alex moved to the foot of the bed. "So there was nothing on Violet's phone that Ginger may have *read*?"

"I don't remember. Where is my phone? We could check."

"It might still be in your jacket pocket," Charlotte said as she crossed the room and searched the jacket hung in the closet.

As Charlotte pulled out the phone, Petunia held out her hand. "Mom, I need to let Violet know what happened. We never showed up!"

Charlotte crossed the room to her daughter but didn't relinquish the phone. Instead, she leaned over and kissed Petunia's forehead. "Maybe we'll do that in a minute, honey. Let me talk to your dad, okay? And Sheriff Becker. And we'll come back in. Violet's okay. Don't worry."

Charlotte gave Renzo a stern look as she, Alex, and Tate in the rear went back into the quiet hallway.

"Has Gilbert texted or called since you didn't arrive, Alex?" Tate asked.

"I texted him. Told him we weren't coming but to keep it quiet."

Tate thought that logical as he watched Charlotte open her daughter's phone, plug in the security code, and begin scrolling through text messages.

Alex got his phone out of his pocket. Tate didn't miss the fact that there were smears of blood on it. He watched while Alex wiped the phone on his pants before he tapped it open and began his own scrolling.

"Did she text Violet the itinerary?" Tate asked.

Charlotte looked up. "She did not. But she recalled telling her, so Violet must have told Ginger."

"You're pretty confident this was Ginger Krueger." Tate raised an eyebrow, trying to slow this down and stick to the facts. There was no hard proof Ginger knew the itinerary.

"Of course it was. Who else would do this?" she snapped.

Tate took a step back. "No, I agree, it makes sense, but you being who you are—I was just wondering . . ."

She glared hotly at him as she clenched a fist and dropped her arms to her sides. "You need to tell me right this minute just what in the hell you've been doing in your investigation of Ginger Krueger. You haven't come up with squat yourself. *We've given you* everything. Ginger is dangerous. She's a *murderer.* She almost killed my family. What the hell have you done about her?" Charlotte shook off Alex, who had reached out again, trying to interrupt, but then grabbed his hand and jerked their locked fists in front of Tate's face.

"Does Ginger have a background in automotive espionage?" Charlotte tilted her head in a mocking manner as Alex brought their hands down. "Where did she go to school? Any other dead bodies in her past? Does she have many friends? Where does she hang out? Has she been visiting any internet cafés? Do you have her under surveillance when she leaves the Backwoods? Why the hell *didn't you* have her under surveillance once we got to town?"

Tate colored but held his ground. "We didn't know if Ginger knew about you—or specifically your daughter and her travel schedule. Unless Violet told her, which means Petunia was communicating and speaking with Violet against our wishes."

Charlotte's green eyes flashed daggers at him. "You will not blame this on her! *You're* responsible for our safety! You! What the fuck have you done about her!"

Somehow shocked at the graceful woman using that obscenity, he said, "We did look into her background, and no, there was not a trail of bodies. You—and by *you*, I guess I mean Gilbert—has somehow uncovered what Ginger's interests are and what she searches for on her phone. We have no access to that information. I'm just going by what you tell me and how Ginger conducts her business. At one point, we did check the Kitchigami Regional Library System, which supports the counties around here—Beltrami, Crow Wing, Cass, Hubbard, and Wadena—and Ginger Krueger has not been using the internet in any of those libraries. She could have borrowed someone's tech device, or gone somewhere else, but we have no knowledge she knew anything about you or your family being involved."

Charlotte forced him to take another step back down the hall as her aggression heightened. Alex just stood there. "She obviously knows about us and she's looking somewhere. It's also obvious she had some knowledge of our movements yesterday, which means she could have followed us from the airport and to the hotel. After that, she could just take off and come back in the middle of the night to tamper with our brakes. Why was no one watching her?"

"I assumed Gilbert would have that end covered. Where did you think we might hide an officer to keep an eye on her? In the woods?"

"Okay!" Alex said, stepping in as Charlotte's face reddened further and her fists came up. "So, we believe Ginger did this—which means she knew our schedule, which we can assume she got from Violet. She somehow knew how to tamper with the brakes, and she had to learn that from somewhere, unless it's something she picked up in her youth. Which I doubt. She must know we are a threat to her, otherwise why try to kill us? She must know that we, or possibly that Petunia is the witness. Which is either good guessing on her part, or you, Sheriff Becker, have a leak. Either way, she's been planning this. She's been doing some groundwork, and she's not doing it on her tech devices at the Backwoods or in the local libraries. If you will excuse me, I need to give someone a call."

Alex gave Charlotte a hard look and squeezed her arm. The two of them communicated an understanding before he walked down the hall, thumbing his phone. Charlotte turned her attention back to Tate and crossed her arms, challenging him.

Holding up his hands he said, "I understand you're upset, Mrs. Macchi. I'm sorry. We're going to put protection on you for the rest of your visit. I'll speak with Gavin Stewart and let him know what happened. We'll get some patrol officers on rotation until we get this done."

She shook her head. "No. You're not, Sheriff. We're going to wait for Alex to come back, and we're going to make a plan—together. The only thing going for us right now is control of the information. No one knows what happened to us, and we're going to keep it that way until we decide what to do."

"Is that right?" He cocked his head.

"Don't test me, Sheriff. We can be on a plane out of here in the morning. Don't think I won't do it. Right now, we wait."

He looked away from her, down the hall to Alex, and wondered just who in the hell he was calling now.

Chapter 38

I want everything, Bacon. Everything," Alex whispered urgently into his phone. "The Sheriff here said they checked the Kitchigami Regional Library System, so start somewhere else. Think. Pretend you live here. Where else could she find a computer? I want you to think hard about that and find her. Break through any system you need, but find her and her search history. Pull up a map. We need this now. Right now—within minutes. You got it?"

Alex listened impatiently as his nasally challenged hacker gave him a little grief about having other projects to work on and that it could take a really long time, but eventually he came around. The Carrows and Macchis had made the guy rich. They both knew he would drop whatever he'd been doing and get to work.

Alex pulled Charlotte away from the sheriff after he got off the phone with Bacon. Sheriff Becker seemed both irritated and concerned, but Alex didn't care. They had to prove it was Ginger and do something about it.

"We need to step up surveillance and somehow nail her for this. What kind of car did you get for us? How did you get here?"

Charlotte gave him a half smile. "I got a plow."

"What?"

"There was this guy, in the parking lot of the hotel. He was plowing snow. I ran out and asked him if he wanted to make some extra money and we negotiated. I hopped in the cab with him and explained about the accident and that he could name his price for the truck. He said he had obligations, a business to run, and so forth, but I told him I would pay him $3,000 cash if he would let me use the truck for the day. I told him I'd return it as soon as I could. He took the deal, I gave him the cash, took him back inside the hotel, and told the front desk clerk to arrange for a couple of new rental SUVs to be delivered. I told her to give the plow guy one of the cars. I told her to charge it to my card and gave her $100 to get it done. We all swapped numbers, and Renzo and I took off."

"I'm awfully glad you carry so much cash around with you, darling," he said, giving her a kiss. "I'm going to ask Renzo to take the truck and plant a GPS tracking device on Ginger's car. I think it's time we took charge of her destiny."

Charlotte glanced back at Sheriff Becker, but then squared her back on him. "I'm assuming you have an idea?" she said.

"Not yet, but we will." Alex smiled.

"Let's do it." Charlotte walked back into Petunia's room, and they watched her tell Renzo to go out to the hall.

"Sheriff," Alex said, gesturing him aside. "We were wondering if you might happen to know where we could get our hands on a GPS tracking device. Quickly. Like right now."

Tate looked at Alex and opened his mouth to make a quick response, but then closed it. He hesitated, but Alex could almost see the sheriff's mind whirling through the possible uses. "Sure, I might know a guy."

"Good. Give him a call and see if he can swing by with it or if Renzo can stop at his place and pick it up."

Tate looked over at Renzo, standing near Charlotte. "You're going to send Renzo out to put a plant on Ginger's car? Don't you think she'll notice? It's not like it's a big place, and he's the size of grizzly. She'll see him coming."

"Gilbert will distract her. We'll work it out."

Alex waited while Tate mulled it over. Finally, he nodded. "Okay. Let me make a couple calls."

It was afternoon before Alex finally texted Gilbert again. He knew the man was probably going crazy, but he'd probably go even more wild once he learned the news. Poor Gilbert Gorsky was going to have to summon all his acting skills to deal with this one.

Do NOT let on you're getting information on our status. We are okay but had an accident. We believe Ginger sabotaged our car. Brake lines tampered with. Ginger and Violet are probably worried we didn't show up. Let them worry. I'll get back to you with more details. First part. Renzo is coming that way to plant GPS on Ginger's car. You'll need to distract her. Think of something and make it good. I'll keep you posted.

Chapter 39

Whether or not Tate was going to go through with the surveillance plan, he wasn't sure, but he could get the ball rolling and get the equipment. He arranged for his friend—the manager at the local Best Buy—to drop what he was doing and bring a GPS monitoring system to the hospital. He knew the guy would have the gear, but Tate didn't tell him why he needed it, and the guy didn't ask.

Staying clear of the Macchis, Tate called Gavin to fill him in. The Macchis may not have wanted him to do it for fear of leaks, but screw that. The leak wasn't coming from his friend, the county attorney. Also, there was no way Tate would legally jeopardize whatever information might be coming their way. Gavin had to get a warrant for the GPS. It was as simple as that. The two tossed around the problem, but in the end, Gavin thought he could sell it to a judge.

He knew the Macchis were anxious, but logistics took time. The device delivery came before the warrant, but he waited until he had both before he walked back to Petunia's hospital room. He glanced down the hall before going inside. Alex was deep in conversation with someone, and he didn't look happy. He waited for Alex to finish the call.

Alex shoved his phone in his pocket, seemingly upset, as he waved a finger at Tate and walked past him. "Excuse me, Sheriff. I'll be right back." He went into his daughter's room.

Moments later, he came back out with Charlotte and Renzo, who was holding his winter jacket. "Walk with me," Alex said leading the group to the dead end of the hall near a stairwell.

Alex said, "I just got a report back from our guy, and Sheriff, I don't really give a shit what your ethics are on this, but he told me he found Ginger Krueger's browsing trail in at least two places. Two libraries in neighboring counties. Apparently, she's done a shitload of research on our family. More importantly, she's done heavy research on poisons, carbon monoxide poisoning, and how to tamper with the brake lines in an SUV."

Shit. Tate put his fist to his mouth. *Fucking Ginger.* Conflicted about the illegal nature of the intel, his eyes scanned the intense group while he considered the implications and whether he even needed to tell Gavin about it. They already had the warrant for the GPS, but the Macchis didn't know that yet.

Tate thought he heard a growl somewhere from Renzo's direction as Alex continued. "There's no doubt at all she tried to kill us today. Her problem is she couldn't know if she'd be successful, so she has to have a backup plan. Didn't Violet invite Petunia to stay out there with them? To spend the night?"

Charlotte swayed, putting her hand on Alex for support. "My God."

Alex nodded. "She definitely knows Petunia's the witness—or she's got a pretty good idea. She knows all about us. Or everything she could find about us on the internet. She was ready, and her big opportunity just failed. But she doesn't know that. She's out there, at the Backwoods, right now, with Violet, who is probably extremely worried we didn't show up. And Ginger's probably delirious thinking she might have succeeded in eliminating a damaging witness for the prosecution. We have got to use this to our advantage. Right now. Renzo, I believe Sheriff Becker has a package for you. A GPS tracking system. You're going to drive out there, very carefully, mind you, and plant it on Ginger's car. In the meantime, we'll figure out how to use it to set her up. If she falls into our trap, Sheriff, I hope you'll agree it's time to arrest her."

Tate nodded several times at the three tense faces daring him to challenge them. Tate's anger was on high too, but he didn't want to tell them he'd already spoken with Gavin about getting a warrant. "I agree, but I'm worried about the legalities. It's time to call Gavin Stewart. He may even want to bring in the judge for a warrant."

Alex seemed to seriously consider the merits of the suggestion. "All right, let's think about that. In the meantime, let's get Renzo on the road and at least get it planted. Renzo, I'll text you the make and model of Ginger's car. You'll most likely need to go in on foot. Park down the road where she can't see you coming. When you get in position, text Gilbert, and he'll distract Ginger and Violet long enough for you to plant the GPS. Give me a call when you're on your way back and I'll tell you what we've decided to do."

Tate didn't look into Renzo's face but handed him the bag of equipment. He doubted Renzo would need a tutorial on how to use it. If it wasn't clear to Tate before, he now understood clearly that the Macchi organization wasn't used to playing by the rules, never mind the law. He'd stay close on this one, making sure that whatever plan they concocted would stand up in court and, hopefully, nobody would get killed.

Alex and Renzo walked side by side down the corridor toward the exit. Tate watched people move out of the way as they marched.

Chapter 40

Alex glared across the table in a small conference room. On the same floor as Petunia, the hospital had given them the space for a private conference, and as he sat there, Gavin Stewart and Sheriff Becker frowned back. Alex had been reluctant to bring in the county attorney. He didn't want to beg for permission to go forward with his plan, but legal reasoning won out. It was face off time between his plan, the cops, and the law. He mustered a calm, cool demeanor as he began laying it out.

"Charlotte is sitting with Petunia, but we put our heads together, and we've come up with a plan."

Gavin Stewart held up his hand. "Mr. Macchi, I understand you have a legal background, so you must be aware these discussions are legal in nature. I'm here to listen to the allegations against Ginger Krueger and to ascertain whether there is enough evidence for an arrest. After Sheriff Becker and I spoke, I can guess there may have been some illegal search activity conducted by you. You may lay out your plan, and then the sheriff and I will decide what steps can *legally* be taken going forward."

Disgusted at being asked to tread carefully while Ginger Krueger was still at large and wildly dangerous, Alex shook his head and crossed his arms in defiance. "My daughter is a prosecution witness in a murder case, there was an attempt made on her life—that fact has been verified by your sheriff. The sheriff's office provided no protection for my daughter or my family against a woman who we all believe to be a murderer. We came into town in good faith believing you had Ginger Krueger under control. That was not the case. My family has been generous with its time and has gone to great expense to help your investigation, and today we nearly paid for it with our lives."

Sheriff Becker opened his mouth, "Alex . . ."

Alex pointed a finger in his face. "Don't. Petunia heard Ginger's voice over the phone and identified her to you as the woman she heard Clayton speaking with. The woman who killed Penny Krueger. You wanted to wait, to use this against Clayton, or Ginger, and gather more evidence against her. In addition, *we supplied you* with more information about her guilt, provided to you by our private investigation corroborating everything Petunia heard at the diner, even explaining the 'cancer' references. You believe Ginger Krueger was the murderer and got a search warrant to look for evidence against her, but you didn't look deep enough or hard enough.

"Ginger set a plan in motion to harm us so Petunia would be unable to testify at the trial. We are in danger. She needs to be stopped. In New York, the police have no problem using undercover officers to capture and secure evidence against suspected criminals. I'm really hoping you won't have a problem with that today.

"We've created a plan to trap her, but I agree we need your involvement and cooperation. If we're successful, I need your word you will arrest Ginger and see that she's charged with the attempted murder of my daughter . . . at the very least."

Gavin stared down at the table, drumming his fingers on his legs while he processed. His head came up; his lips were pursed. "You're a private citizen, Mr. Macchi, but you're still required to work within the law. Did you illegally hack information on Ginger Krueger's activities on the internet? Before you answer, I warn you, your answer could incriminate you."

Alex wanted to explode. "I don't give a shit about that. We did."

Gavin nodded like he was satisfied. "I see. And would you please describe what you found out about Ginger Krueger?"

Alex rolled his eyes, his head beginning to pound. It was so much easier to get things done without needing the law or permission. Being a Carrows by marriage had changed him. "I found out that she's been looking for information about digestible poisons, about carbon monoxide poisoning, about tampering with and cutting brake lines, and searching for anything she could find on my family."

"This evidence was obtained by you how?" Gavin raised his brow.

Alex threw up his hands. "I hacked into some internet sights and found her trail."

"Hacking is a crime, Mr. Macchi."

Alex pounded the table. "I don't give a shit! Come after me! Give it your best shot! I don't think the state of Minnesota, or the judge in the case, or the governor's office, or the people at large if they find out, will give a shit either—but it's entirely up to you if you want to press some kind of charges. I'm telling you I have credible evidence, and I will tell you where to find it. In my opinion you already had enough credible evidence, but now I've just given you more! Get a search warrant, which shouldn't be a problem since you did this once before, and I'll point you in the direction of the information. In the meantime, Ginger is out there at the Backwoods with an *innocent child* who is in danger. We can catch her, but we need to move on it."

Gavin rubbed his hands together. "All right, I agree we'll set aside the hacking for now. Tell us your plan."

Alex sat back, feeling exhausted, and rubbed his head. Sheriff Becker cleared his throat and looked at Gavin. "We need to make sure we have the search and surveillance authorized for the GPS so it won't get thrown out. Will warrants be a problem, Gavin?"

Gavin gave Sheriff Becker a quizzical look. "Ah, no, Tate. I don't think that will be a problem."

Sheriff Becker plowed on, nodding vigorously. "Because we need warrants for the GPS, and we should check the 'tip-line' intel on Ginger sightings." Tate put tip-line in quotes.

"What?" Gavin said.

Alex thought he was seeing a sheriff who was trying to come up with a workaround. He'd already confessed to hacking, and apparently the sheriff didn't give a shit about that either.

Timing was important. Alex continued describing his plan. "Okay, so as we speak, my guy, Renzo, is out there, putting the GPS tracking device on Ginger's car. When he's done, we'll be able to track her movements on the computer. What we need to do is hot tip her, forcing her to do something to cover her tracks. If she takes the bait, we'll follow her and arrest her. The bait will be something that will implicate her for tampering with the brakes on our car."

Alex knew he had their full attention. "My idea is this. We tell Gilbert to encourage Violet to call Petunia."

"Hasn't Violet called her already?" Tate interrupted. "Christ. It's nearly three o'clock. You told me she was expecting Petunia to pick her up this morning."

Alex shook his head, then grimaced a bit, in pain. "The last time I checked, Violet hasn't called. She's texted, but Charlotte has Petunia's phone, and my wife hasn't responded. As I said, Violet calls Petunia, but this time— *Renzo answers*, all flustered. He can do flustered. He gives Violet the bad news. Petunia can't come to the phone because she's in surgery, at death's door. She's been in a very bad accident. The police think someone cut the brake lines, but they found a glove in the parking lot so they might have DNA and they'll find whoever did this. He'll cut off the call, and Violet, sitting there all upset, will report the news to Ginger, who will do her best to look surprised, and to Gilbert, who will also look surprised, but he'll know differently."

Alex paused to make sure Tate and Gavin were tracking before he continued. "But before this big, upsetting chat with the flustered Renzo, Gilbert will go to Ginger's car and leave one of Ginger's gloves on the seat. Only one. He'll keep the other.

"After Ginger hears that the cops are looking for a matching glove to the one they have in evidence, Ginger will be uncertain, *worried* even. She'll try to remember which gloves she wore last night when she tampered with the brakes."

Alex went into Ginger mode. "*Could it be possible?* She'll look in her jacket pocket where most people keep their gloves, and they won't be there. She'll panic. She'll go out to her car, and she'll look for them. And she'll find *one*—only one, and it will drive her crazy. We hope. Now, she knows she needs to get rid of the glove because the cops are looking for it. It's not too much of a stretch that the cops will be looking at her because you fellas have already talked to her—and the Macchi family, whose brake line she cut, were on the way to her home!

"She'll need to dispose of the glove, but we have Gilbert watching her. Staying in her way, keeping her busy, making sure she doesn't chop up the glove in the house, until finally she makes a break for it and leaves the house. Gilbert will let us know when she does, but we'll already know that too because we can watch her movements on the computer. You'll have an undercover car ready to follow her when she makes her move. She's got to hide it or dispose of it. We just need to be there when it happens."

Alex pointed at the county attorney. "If Ginger takes this bait, based on the false information that the cops are looking for the owner of a glove used in an attempted murder, then you should have enough to bring her in."

Alex stopped speaking and waited. He could see Sheriff Becker liked the plan, a smile forming, but he needed Gavin's approval.

Gavin too, for the first time, seemed to brighten. "I think that would be enough to arrest her. If she attempts to dump a spare glove thinking it is *evidence in the crime of attempted murder,* then I'm okay with charging her."

Alex breathed a sigh of relief. "Then get the judge on the phone now. Get the warrant for the GPS. Get the warrants to find her searches. Get someone you can trust ready to head out to the Backwoods area to wait for Ginger to move. We'll have a heads up when she leaves, so they can park nearby. Once Renzo's done with his part, we'll make sure the technology is working. We can do that together from here if you have a laptop."

Gavin Stewart pushed back from the table. He shot Tate a quizzical look, then pulled out his phone and left the room. Sheriff Becker pulled out his phone and turned to Alex and said, "I'll call one of my officers and get him up to speed. We can trust him. He'll use his own car, not a patrol car. I'll send him to O'Toole's now."

Alex nodded and exhaled, glad they were finally going to do something about that woman. Hopefully Ginger Krueger would take the bait and do something stupid. "I'll tell Charlotte we're working the plan." Alex got up to leave, his neck and body aching with every move.

"Alex," said the sheriff. "Thank you. I'm sorry this happened, but once again, we appreciate your help."

Alex reluctantly nodded and left the room to see his wife and daughter.

Chapter 41

Gilbert Gorsky was worried. Alex and Petunia hadn't arrived at the Backwoods.

That morning, Gilbert arrived at the restaurant early and found Ginger working in the kitchen. They'd opened the restaurant like any other day at six o'clock, ready to serve breakfast. He'd expected the arrival of his secret boss sometime that morning and was looking forward to at least putting eyes on him since he'd been alone for months on his assignment. But by 10 a.m., when they closed the restaurant after breakfast, Alex had yet to arrive.

Ginger seemed anxious too, but she was typically high strung—at least as long as he'd known her. Since she didn't own a gun and there were no other guns on the property, Gilbert didn't really think there was anything Ginger could pull off once his boss and daughter hit the parking lot of the Backwoods. Violet, initially waiting at the house, had come over to join them at the restaurant when her friend had not shown up. She was worried too.

They were all curious about what happened. Violet texted Petunia a couple of times and tried calling, but she got no answer. Gilbert's nerves had also been flying as he'd watched Ginger counsel Violet, trying to soothe the poor girl, telling her she was certain they would hear from them later.

"Maybe they got tied up," Ginger said hopefully to Violet.

Violet shrugged and took off her jacket and sat down to wait. They all watched the newscast from the television suspended from the ceiling in the restaurant. The weather reports were dreadful.

"I'm sure she'll call soon," said Ginger, going back to the kitchen.

———

And mercifully, Alex did text Gilbert around 11 a.m. But the message was cryptic, saying they weren't coming but for him to play dumb about it. *Don't say shit or let on. I'll text again soon*, Alex had said. Some time had passed when the second text from Alex came. This time, when Gilbert felt his phone vibrate, he stepped into the men's room to take a look.

Do NOT let on you're getting information on our status. We are okay but had an accident. We believe Ginger sabotaged our car. Brake lines tampered with. Ginger and Violet are probably worried we didn't show up. Let them worry. I'll get back to you with more details. First part. Renzo is coming that way to plant GPS on Ginger's car. You'll need to distract her. Think of something and make it good. I'll keep you posted.

His blood pressure shot through the roof as he paced in the small space, trying to calm himself before he went back out, forced to look at the murdering bitch. "Fuck me," he whispered to his reflection in the glass. He wanted to strangle Ginger. She'd done all this on his watch.

Once back in the store and restaurant, he kept himself busy, doing a whole lot of not-murdering-Ginger while Violet read a book and worked her phone. The poor, stood-up girl sat dejected in one of the restaurant booths while Ginger worked on the dough for the next batch of rolls in the kitchen.

Now that he knew Renzo was coming to plant a bug on Ginger's car, Gilbert thought through the how-tos. He knew that her car was parked near the house. Not directly in sight line from the restaurant, but both she and Violet would definitely be able to see it from the bar or from the front window of their home. They couldn't see the car from either the restaurant or convenience store, so he had to keep them in there. When was Renzo coming? He had to be ready.

"Hey, Gil," Ginger said, coming out of the kitchen and untying her apron. "Maybe you want to take off for the day. It's going to be slow, and I might even close down the store early if it keeps up."

Gilbert knew she was right. Hardly anyone had come to the convenience store after breakfast, and only a couple of customers stopped in the off-sale bar to buy beer.

But he needed to stay with them. He searched for a reason. "Nah. Hey, I was just in the restroom, and there's a leak back there. I was thinking about giving it a look, see if I could get that fixed for ya."

He watched Ginger consider this, but he saw that she was looking for a reason to get him gone. She wanted to be alone. Why? If she knew the Macchis weren't coming, then she'd be alone with Violet for the rest of the day. Would she hurt her too? What else was she planning? She seemed anxious, but upbeat. *Sneaky bitch.*

Finally she shrugged. "Okay. You got what you need?"

"No, I'm going to head out to the shed and get some tools. I'll be back."

Leaving them, he scoped the area and tried to figure out what he was going to do to keep them wrangled and distracted when a guy the size of Renzo came creeping into the area. He'd have to wing it when he got the call.

The weather was keeping the worry of further customers away, and thankfully, Ginger and Violet continued to hang out in the restaurant while Gilbert, who was not a plumber, came back inside with his tools and did some purposeful damage to the restroom plumbing. He made a mess, and since it was such a small space, he was able to keep track of them while he pretended to work. Ginger kept encouraging Violet to be patient for her friend's arrival and talked about how she was looking forward to meeting them.

Oh God, Gilbert groaned. *That can't happen.* His mind wandered to knives, or whatever Ginger's backup plan could be if the poor Macchi family had somehow escaped her attempt on them and actually showed up. While trying to figure out how long he'd need to goof around on the bathroom floor, his phone buzzed, making him jump. He stood up pulled it out of his pocket. *Shit.* It was Renzo.

I'm here coming in on foot on your go

How long do you need?

Ten minutes of cover

Do what you can about tracks. On my clock, go now.

Gilbert put his phone away, took a deep breath, and threw a wrench at a pipe. He hit the floor and screamed. Ginger and Violet came running into the restroom.

"Gil!" yelled Ginger as she entered and saw him lying on the floor. "Are you okay?"

Gilbert groaned and held his leg, "Dammit! Dammit! I was hitting the pipe and missed, and the damn wrench came down on my leg!"

Ginger looked around at the mess on the floor; Gilbert groaning in the middle of it.

Violet knelt beside him and put a hand on his arm in concern. "Is there something I can do to help?" she asked.

"Just give me a minute," Gilbert said, breathing hard. "Damn! I thought if I could get that pipe loose, I might be able to look inside and see if there was something blocking it! Ginger, would you grab that flashlight over there and take a look in the pipe?"

Ginger stepped around some tools and knelt on the floor to retrieve the flashlight. She tried turning it on but nothing happened. She banged her fist against it and said, "It's dead. It's going to need some new batteries. I'll go over to the store and grab some."

"NO," Gil shouted, horrified that he might have made a huge mistake. He didn't want her leaving his sight. "Here, just give it to me, let me look at it."

Ginger did as he instructed, but with a smirk—clearly not seeing the point. Gilbert took his time pulling himself into a sitting position and then became conversational. "This is my best flashlight. You wouldn't believe the distance this thing can shine," he said as he accidentally dropped it further under the pipes and watched it roll to the back.

"Oh man," he threw his hands up in frustration.

"I'll get it," Violet offered. She bent down to get the light.

"Here you go," she said, handing it back to Gilbert.

"Ah, darn, it's a little wet. Ginger, would you hand me a couple of paper towels?"

Ginger did as instructed and watched while Gilbert wiped down the light and inspected it. Continuing his dialogue, he said, "You ever see this light advertised on one of those late-night info commercials, Ginger?"

She shrugged. "I don't know. Maybe."

"This light, I ordered it kind of spontaneous-like one night. I was watching this show on TV, and through the entire show, they had these advertisements for stuff like cooking pans, and huge cupcake pans, and this light. I just couldn't resist. I love this light!" He mustered up enthusiasm while he slowly began to open it up. He threw in a few complaining noises too as he moved his leg. "Sometimes, you see, I purposefully turn the battery heads around inside the gizmo, to save the battery. My dad showed me that trick."

"How would that save the battery," asked Ginger.

Gilbert stared at her, thinking. "You know what, Ginger, you're pretty smart. That's a pretty smart question. When my dad, he first told me that story, I wasn't smart enough to ask him that question. You know what I said?"

Pausing, he looked at the two of them and waited for a response. Ginger finally prompted him with a terse, "What?"

"I said . . . well, hell. What did I say? Damn," he said, rubbing his head. "Maybe I bumped my head too when I fell. Just give me a minute. Hey, Ginger! You know what though, that infomercial, the one for this light and the big cupcake pan, you know what I was watching? I remember I was watching an episode of *Columbo*. Hey, do you know what show I'm talking about?"

Ginger perked up, almost smiling. "I love that show. I've seen all the episodes."

"Yeah? Violet, you ever see *Columbo*?"

"I don't think so." Violet shook her head.

"Ginger? Hey, you know what we should do? We should buy us some *Columbo* DVDs and show them to Violet."

"I already have a season!" said Ginger.

"What? Really? Which season?"

"Season three. I think it's the best one. You know, I think it takes time for a show to hit its sweet spot. Like season one might not be the best. They don't know how to use the characters. But by season two, and especially by season three—if the show lives that long—they have the budget for some really good writers."

"Huh. Which shows are on season three of *Columbo*?"

"My favorite is the one with Jack Cassidy. He's like a publisher, and he's mad at one of his authors who wants to leave him, so he hires this guy to kill him. You know he's real smooth. And then the killer, he shoots the guy, and then the Jack Cassidy character, he kills the killer to cover his tracks. Columbo has to come in and figure it all out." She seemed satisfied with her recollect and fond memory.

"Wow. You're not going to believe this, but I think that was the *exact* episode I was watchin' when I ordered this flashlight!"

Ginger smiled back at him, and Gilbert said to Violet, "You think you'd be up to watching some old classic shows with us sometime?"

"I don't know," Violet said, clearly losing interest in all of it.

"I think you'd enjoy it, Violet. Don't you, Ginger? It's like a mystery, right? And you watch this smart guy come in and look around for clues. How would you describe him, Ginger?"

"He's old, well not that old—thirties, forties. I think the show ran for like ten seasons. Anyway, he's kinda rumpled, and forgetful—at least, he makes people *think* he's forget-ful, but really, he's not."

"And," Gilbert said, jumping in with enthusiasm, "he's got a glass eye! For real. Something happened to this guy, and so he's got one glass eye, and it's hard to tell which is the fake and which is the real one. Ginger, I'll bet you know."

"I don't know," she said, squinting and looking up, trying to visualize the actor's face. "Maybe his right. He lost his real one when he was little."

"What happened to it?" Violet asked.

"I'm not sure. Cancer maybe?"

"That's gross," said Violet.

"Hey," said Gilbert, wagging a finger in her direction. "It happens. As a matter of fact, a friend of mine from Canada, did I ever tell you about him? We were laying drywall one day . . ."

The tall tale about the drywaller from Canada soaked up another ten minutes since Gil stopped frequently to fact check with Ginger on the geography of a northern town on the border, and the name of a taco place in Manitoba north of Minnesota. His story about the taco memory alone probably distracted them long enough for him to be safe on time, but he didn't want to make another mistake that day. He got his part done, and he assumed that Renzo had too.

Now all he needed to know was what the hell his boss was up to. He figured he'd find out when they told him.

Chapter 42

Alex took the call from Renzo.

"I'm on my way back, boss. I don't think I was spotted. Is it working?"

"We'll find out. Good job, Renzo." Alex said.

"I'm hurrying, but the roads are still bad."

"Why don't you plow the roads on your way back?"

"S'pose I could, but it'd slow me down."

"I'm joking. Take it easy out there and get back in one piece. It's going to be a long night."

After Renzo got back, he reclaimed his spot in a chair next to Petunia, who was watching TV. Alex and Charlotte went to the small conference room to regroup with Sheriff Tate and Gavin Stewart.

Assured the warrant was in place, Alex pulled up the feed of the GPS plant, something he'd done many times in his life. They all watched the screen. "It looks good," Alex said, relieved. "Up and running."

"Gavin." Sheriff Becker turned to the county attorney. "How did it go with the judge on the rest of the plan?"

"He's sending a signed arrest order back to me. We've got a green light to plant an allurement, watch her movements, follow her, and make an arrest for attempted murder—if we can pull it off and she takes the bait."

"Sheriff," said Alex. "You got your guy set up at O'Toole's, down the road?"

"He should be there any time. He's taking his personal vehicle. A truck. He knows what to do."

"All right then," said Alex, "it's time to make Ginger nervous. I'll text Gilbert instructions and let him in on the plan."

Done with the previous subterfuge in the bathroom, Gilbert was still in there, pretending to work. Frustrated he'd have to call a real plumber to clean up his self-made mess, he shut the door when his phone vibrated. He read the text.

Plant in place. Working fine. Got an unmarked truck and cop at O'Toole's ready to trail Ginger when she leaves. Warrants in place. We need her to implicate herself. Eyes on you now. Find the gloves she wore last night. We want to make her believe she left one in the hotel parking lot when she was cutting our brake lines. She must have a pair of gloves, ones she was wearing last night, maybe in her coat pocket or still in car? Find them, steal one and hide it. We'll need it as evidence. Take the other glove and throw it in her car . . . maybe on seat like it fell out of her pocket last night. Text me when it's done. Then encourage Violet to call Petunia's phone again. This time it will be answered. By a distraught Renzo, who will tell Violet about the terrible accident. He'll slip in that the police have a glove found in the parking lot with brake fluid on it. They're looking for the person, a MANHUNT has begun. Ginger will leave, we hope, and hide remaining glove or dispose of it. Keep an eye on her and make sure she doesn't cut it up and try to flush it or go outside and burn it somewhere on the property. You gotta make her leave with it in the car. Cops will follow her, watch her movements, and nail her for attempted murder. Let me know thoughts. Does she have gloves or mittens? Does she have usual ones?

Gilbert nodded, liking it. He texted back:

Good plan. She has favorite gloves. Usually keeps them in pocket of coat. I know where they are. Can do it. I understand. Will text when done.

Gilbert looked around at the mess in the bathroom and recognized the plan was a good one, but now he needed to figure out how to distract them again to get it done. He opened the bathroom door and took a gander at the coatrack. *Shit.* Her jacket was across the room, and she'd just been talking about closing down the place and walking back to the house with Violet. He needed to get to that coat before she did.

Chapter 43

Okay," Alex announced to the group, "he thinks it's doable. He'll let us know when he's done."

Alex looked at Charlotte. Her head down, looking at her watch. With her dark, shoulder-length hair worn loose and black clothing, the only color was her small gold earrings. No matter what occasion, though, his wife had a natural elegance.

"Honey," he said.

She looked at him, reminding him her eyes, too, held color in their emerald beauty, but he saw the stress and worry as well. It had been a long, terrible day for all of them.

He held her hand. "I'm afraid we're going to need Renzo in here. He's up to bat. Would you give him Petunia's phone and ask him to come down here?"

Charlotte pushed back her chair. She stood looking down at him and gently touched his still slightly bloodied, stitched, and now horribly bruising face. She frowned, leaned over, and kissed him gently on his lips. "I'll swap places with Renzo and arrange for some food. How do hamburgers and fries sound?"

"Are you planning to drive the plow truck through a drive-thru?" He smiled up at her.

She barely returned the smile, then looked at Tate and Gavin. "I'll order something for you as well. I'm assuming you'll stick around and be here for a while?"

"As long as it takes, Mrs. Macchi," the sheriff said.

Nodding, she left them.

Sheriff Becker gave Alex a short look, but averted his eyes when Alex tightened his own and gave him an angry glare. Alex was calling them out for fucking up. He'd almost lost his family today. It was time for someone to pay.

———————

The big man, Renzo Castrogiovanni, walked into the conference room and sat down, adding an uptick to the hostile energy in the room. Folding his arms across his massive chest, holding Petunia's pink phone, he glared at the sheriff and county attorney in a challenging manner.

Alex let the unspoken tension permeate the room until he broke in and said, "Renzo. Hell of a job out there. We appreciate it. Now we need you for Act II. This is going to require some theatrics on your part. Very soon, Petunia's phone is going to ring. When it does, it's going to be Violet Krueger on the other end. She'll be surprised to hear your voice instead of Petunia's. She's been worried about Petunia all day. Your conversation will be many layered. In short, you'll need to be flustered, confused even, maybe harried, panicked, and with an emotional tone."

Renzo looked down at the table, his tongue in his cheek. Alex plowed forward. "Here's the message you need to deliver. You will tell Violet that poor Petunia was in a terrible accident. She's in surgery. You don't know if she's going to make it . . . at which point . . . maybe you even sob?"

Alex grimaced as Renzo's head popped up, but the man's face was made of stone.

Continuing, Alex said, "Okay, well, then you need to tell her the sheriff is here, and he just told the family that they've been investigating the accident and discovered the brake lines were cut on the car. The good news is that they found the perpetrator's glove with brake fluid on it in the parking lot of the hotel. Maybe you could get angry here?" Alex balled his fists and shook them in a theatrical gesture.

Renzo, still not responsive, nodded for Alex to continue.

"So yeah, then just say the cops are going on a *manhunt* the likes of which this town has never seen. If something happens to Petunia . . . well, maybe some more sobbing at this point or something, and then just hang up. Any thoughts?"

The big man looked around the room and placed his hands on the table. He turned to the sheriff and the county attorney and said, "You fellas wanna give me a moment to practice with Mr. Macchi—in private?"

The two men nodded and left. Renzo sagged when the door was closed. He grimaced with real concern and shook his head. "Damn, boss, you want me to cry? I ain't no actor."

Alex smiled at him and patted his arm gently, "You'll be fine. We'll playact it. I'll be Violet, you be you. We'll work out the kinks as we go along."

Renzo pulled Petunia's phone to his ear and began some voice clearing sounds and said gravely, "Okay, I'm ready."

Outside the door, Tate and Gavin stood with their backs to the conference room door and watched as a hospital staff worker sprinted past them toward the parking lot, zipping up his winter parka as he ran.

"What was that about?" said Tate.

"You get the feeling we're not actually in control here, Tate?" Gavin said. He crossed his arms across his chest, then dropped them as they both turned their heads back to the door, surprised to hear Renzo inside, sobbing.

Tate raised an eyebrow. "I get the feeling that this isn't their first rodeo."

Gavin nodded. "Good, because we can use all the luck we can get."

Chapter 44

Gilbert didn't overthink the situation. He just called to Ginger from the bathroom and apologetically asked her to get him some new batteries from the store. She shrugged, and as soon as she was gone, he walked over to the coat rack, took the gloves from her jacket pockets, and hid them in his own winter coat. He pushed them down in an inside pocket. Violet, thankfully, had her head in a book and noticed nothing.

Relieved he'd done it, he walked back to the bathroom. As soon as she returned, he put the new batteries in his flashlight. Pronouncing himself done-in, he encouraged the two of them to go back to the house and relax. He told them he'd close down the Backwoods and then pitifully asked if it was okay if he hung around for dinner and some serial TV.

Thankfully, Ginger agreed and told a completely dejected Violet it was time to call it a day. They grabbed their jackets off the coatrack and pulled them on for the short walk back to the house.

Gilbert stood near the window watching them walk through the snow with their heads down. It was dark out now, but the outside lights were on. He held his breath, hoping Ginger wouldn't reach into her pocket and search for her gloves. She didn't. He breathed a sigh of relief. Now he had to get one of the gloves into her car without being seen. It was parked right outside the house, in clear view through the front window of the house.

He knew everyone was counting on him, waiting for him, but he had to do it right. The first thing he did was put everything back together in the restroom and then turn on the closed signs over the restaurant and store. He put on his own outer gear with Ginger's gloves inside, grabbed the toolbox, locked up the joint, and headed to the house.

Along the way, he muttered under his breath, "Jesus help me with this one. Get me through this and get this devil locked up before she hurts anyone else." He wasn't really a praying man, but it felt good.

More confident, he walked up to the house and peeked in the front window. Not seeing anyone around, he dropped the toolbox, put his hand in his pocket and pulled out one of her gloves. He walked over to Ginger's car, quietly opened the driver's side door a few inches, and threw it in. He closed the door just as quietly, walked over to the tools and looked again in the window. Nothing. Backtracking through the snow, retracing his steps as he neared the vehicle for the second time, he pretended to lose his balance and scrambled the snow around his feet before making his way to the nearby shed.

Leaving the tools in the shed, he walked back to the house wondering if Ginger would make her move tonight or wait for the morning. He'd text Alex after he made sure the coast was clear when he got in the house. He'd use the privacy of the bathroom to conduct that business.

He knocked on the front door as a courtesy and opened it at the same time, announcing himself. "Hey, guys, I locked it up. What do you want to do about dinner?" he yelled as he pulled off his boots and hung up his jacket. He recognized the sound of the stove vent and the smell of tobacco mixed with something frying in a pan. He made sure the zipper of his coat pocket was closed on the remaining glove and walked into the small den in his stocking feet. Ginger was a few steps further on, past the den, in the kitchen.

"Hey," he said coming around the corner, his hands casually placed in his back pockets. "What do you want to do for dinner? You hungry?" He looked at some sausage meat cooking on the stove and the makings for queso dip on the counter. Velveeta and Ro-tel.

She turned to him and said, "Yeah, I thought we'd celebrate. I mean, I thought I'd take a night off from dieting, you know? Make something to cheer up Violet since her friend stood her up."

Gilbert watched as Ginger took a long drag on the cigarette and blew it toward the vent fan, as if that was all it took to keep the smoke out of the house. Relieved that he seemed to have gotten away with the glove drop, he looked around and said, "Is Violet in her room? Maybe we should watch something together tonight. You know, something she might like?"

Ginger shrugged as she opened the cans of Ro-Tel on the counter and added them to the cheese slowly melting in another pan. "I guess. We can ask her."

"Sure. Anything I can do to help here, or you got this under control?"

"I got it. Why don't you see what's on TV?"

"Sure," he said, leaving the room and pulling out his phone. He didn't need to use the restroom for this one. He just stepped out of her line of vision by the large television, used the remote to turn it on, then shot a quick text to Alex.

One glove in car, other hidden in my coat. In house waiting to see Violet at supper. She'll call within next 30 minutes?

Gilbert put his phone back in his pocket and picked up the remote and began to scan through their selections. The first contender he came across was *The Parent Trap*, the one with Lindsey Lohan. He watched for a moment, the mother and daughter were hugging. He realized that Violet might be pained by that movie.

Gritting his teeth as the remembrance washed through him: Ginger had killed Violet's mom and dumped Penny Krueger into a hole. *God damn you, Ginger. And you too, fucking Clayton. Look what you did.*

The adrenaline of the day's events as well as the fresh wave of anger coursed through his veins, and he realized he needed to relax. He sat on the couch and tried to give the television line-up his undivided attention. There had to be something on that would be emotionally safe and interesting to compel Violet to come into the room. Eventually he found it—*Harry Potter*. What a stroke of luck. He knew Violet loved those books.

"Hey, Violet," he shouted down the hall. "*Harry Potter*'s on TV and Ginger's got a special treat for supper. You wanna come out and watch it with us?"

Nothing happened for a bit, and then thankfully, Violet, looking sadder than he had seen her all day, came slowly down the hall and into the room to see the TV.

"Hey," he said gently. "Hey, Violet, it's going to be okay. You'll see. Hang in there for me, all right?"

She didn't respond but took a seat on the sofa.

"Ginger is making some queso. You like queso?" he asked.

She shrugged.

"I love it. With some sausage and chips, it's going to be good," he sat in his regular reclining chair nearby. "So which one is this? Tell me about it," he encouraged, gesturing at the TV.

"*The Half-Blood Prince.*" She rolled into the fetal position and grabbed a pillow to hug.

"Yeah? I haven't seen them all, but maybe sometime we could watch them together?"

"I don't have them. I just watch when they come on TV."

"Oh. Got it." He thought he should stop talking for a moment and wait until Ginger was in the room for the next part.

Ten minutes later, Ginger yelled at them over the loud noise of the vent fan that dinner was ready.

"Come in here and get it. Grab a bowl."

Violet and Gilbert got up and went into the kitchen just as Ginger shoved a chip with dripping cheese into her mouth and some dribbled onto her chin. Wiping it with the back of her hand, she finished crunching and then returned to her cigarette while she watched Violet and Gilbert load their bowls.

Gilbert began, "So when was the last time you called Petunia, Vi?"

"This morning. About an hour after she said they'd be here."

"When was the last time you texted?"

"About the same time. She hasn't responded."

"Yeah, I see that. Maybe before we sit down to eat you should try her again?" He could see that he had her full attention, and he could also feel Ginger's piercing eyes on his back, watching him.

"Wouldn't that be rude? I mean, she knows she stood me up. *She* should call *me.*" Violet blinked hard and fast, her emotions building while Gilbert helpfully spooned some more cheese into her bowl.

He nodded at her. "No. You're right. You're absolutely right. I just think you deserve an explanation. I don't think it would be rude to reach out and try again. Not at all. It's been several hours, so maybe she's available now? Who knows what happened! She came here to help support you, right? That's awfully nice."

"She's rich," barked Ginger. "She could fly back and forth all week and it wouldn't matter to her. She shouldn't treat Violet like this. Going back and forth on her promises, standing Violet up. I think it's rude."

He felt like a heel for doing it, knowing what was waiting for poor Violet, but he pressed his case. "Yeah, well, I just think you should go ahead and call her again. Hear her voice, you guys can talk. I think you would feel better if you talked with her. Worst case, she doesn't answer again."

Violet put down her bowl and picked up her phone, which was never far from her reach. The adults watched her retreat from the room as she used her thumbs to dial.

Gilbert did not follow but proceeded to load his bowl with chips as Ginger walked past him into the other room to listen.

"Hey! Is Petunia there?" Violet said, confusion as well as excitement in her voice.

Gilbert heard an intake of breath and a loud exclamation. He dropped his bowl and went to see what was happening. Violet had her phone to her ear and looked like she'd seen a ghost. Her eyes were wide, and her free hand was clenched and pulled tight against her chest. Looking to be on the brink of tears, she listened and then disconnected the phone and started screaming.

"She's dying! She's in the hospital! She's *dying*!"

Ginger looked sincerely alarmed herself at the exclamation. Her body jerked.

Gilbert grabbed onto the doorframe, watching in horror as the pain on the young girl's face intensified. When she dropped to the floor and threw her hands up to cover herself, he swallowed with difficulty, knowing the pain was partly his fault.

Eventually, Ginger got on the ground too and began coaxing Violet for details.

Violet gulped out, "She was in a car accident! She's in surgery! She might be dying!"

"A car accident?" Ginger sat up straight. "Oh my God, that's terrible! Oh, Violet, I'm so sorry. We had no idea, all this time! She's in the hospital? Who answered the phone?"

"A guy. He said she's in surgery and they don't know if she's going to make it! Oh my God, oh my God, not her too! She's my best friend! I love her, I love her so much!"

"Violet, you need to stay calm," Ginger said, rubbing her back. "Gilbert, would you get some tissues, please?"

Gilbert fled the room and ran to the bathroom to grab a box while listening to Ginger, the murderer, try to calm one of her victims. This was all too much.

"Thank you, Gil," Ginger said, reaching up and taking the box and handing it to Violet. "Now you've got to stay calm, Violet. Did the man say anything else?" Ginger laid a hand on Violet's back like a python stroking her next meal in a deadly embrace.

Violet sat up, tears streaming down her face as she slammed the tissue box onto the carpet. "Yes! That someone did this on purpose! Someone cut the brake lines to the car. Oh my God, who would do that to her?"

"What else did he say?" Ginger removed her hand from Violet's back.

The child was riding a wave, another spasm of grief, and didn't seem to hear them. Sobbing wildly and then pounding her fist on the floor she screamed, "WHO WOULD DO THAT TO THEM! WHY IS THIS HAPPENING TO ME! WHO WOULD DO THIS!"

Ginger shook her head and yanked several tissues out of the box in quick succession, thrusting them in Violet's direction. Gilbert saw a tension in Ginger's jawline before her face disappeared under a shroud of white-blond hair, as the woman moved closer to Violet's face.

"Are they sure that someone did this on *purpose*? Who did you talk to?"

"A guy. It was Renzo. Her bodyguard." Violet's chest heaved, each sentence an effort.

"So *he's* okay? Who was with her in the car? Was anyone else hurt?" Ginger prodded.

"I DON'T KNOW! I DON'T KNOW! He said that the police found a glove with brake fluid on it where they parked their car at the hotel and they're searching for the person. A MANHUNT!"

Gilbert watched as Ginger pulled back from Violet, no longer faking her concern. Her eyes were wide, stunned by the news, and she looked off toward the front window.

"What else did this guy say?" Gilbert asked helpfully, speaking for the first time. So far, Violet had delivered the news like a champ, she just didn't know it. Her pain was all too real.

"Nothing! Oh my God! I've got to get to the hospital! Ginger, Gilbert! Take me to the hospital!"

Gilbert watched the two of them on the floor. Violet, her face red and splotchy, looking close to a nervous breakdown, and Ginger, silent, contemplative, not yet recovered herself. He hadn't seen this request coming. He knew he couldn't take her to the hospital. Petunia was there, not at death's door or in surgery. If he brought her over there, what would happen?

Ginger, got off the floor. She began pacing and finally said, "Violet, you can't go to the hospital. Not tonight. Look outside at the weather. The roads are dangerous! Clearly! And there's nothing you can do there. Her bodyguard is with her. Were both Petunia's parents in the car with her? Both Charlotte and Alex?"

"She said they were coming, but she didn't say with who. Take me to the hospital, please, Ginger!" Violet pleaded, jumping up.

"NO!" Ginger suddenly screamed back, startling them all. Staring into the face of her frightened charge, Ginger approached Violet, grabbing her shoulders and giving them a shake. "Violet! It wouldn't be appropriate. They don't need you there. They have enough to deal with and don't have time for you! My God, I wonder if the press has gotten wind of this?" Ginger looked off into space, lost for a moment in some kind of sick fantasy.

Violet saw none of that and ran from the room and slammed her bedroom door. Gilbert and Ginger heard her wailing through the door, and both of them, each with wildly different agendas, took a seat on the sofas.

Gilbert knew there was no way he was going to leave Violet alone. She was hysterical, and it scared the crap out him.

Ginger began to chew on her thumbnail, her eyes roaming back and forth, thinking hard. "Gilbert, would you check on the dinner, make sure I turned off the stove?"

"Sure," he said slowly, like the earth had just stopped shaking and they needed to go back to business. Getting up, he knew what she was going to do, and he was going to give her the time to do it. "This is terrible. Would you mind if I made myself a drink? You've got some vodka out there, right? And some Diet Sprite? You mind?"

"No! Not at all. Make me one too! Maybe cut up some limes, huh?" Ginger brightened.

Gilbert looked hard at Ginger, and the two momentarily checked one another out until she put her head in her hands and mumbled, "Oh, sweet Jesus."

Gilbert sucked down his rage as left the room. He heard her get off the sofa and walk, he knew, toward the front entry to check the pockets of her coat. He opened the freezer and made a big racket with the ice and grabbed some glasses, making their post-apocalyptic cocktail.

They were in Hell.

Chapter 45

A glove? *What the fuck?* Ginger thought hard. She didn't leave a glove under the Macchis car last night! But she presumed she was the only one who had cut the brake lines, so who else could it be? Coming out of her ruminations, she caught Gilbert standing there staring with his eyes all wide. Regardless of her surety, she knew she had to check for the glove to be sure.

"Oh, sweet Jesus," she said, before putting her head in her hands, hoping to look worried and not scared shitless.

She couldn't check for the glove in front of him; it would be too obvious. She needed to get rid of him.

Mercifully, Gilbert went to the kitchen to mix drinks, and she grabbed her jacket. Discovering her gloves missing, her mind flew over the last twenty-four hours, trying to remember when she'd last worn them. She was convinced she had them on last night on the drive home.

No way she left them behind! One? No way! She could see her hands on the wheel, driving through the storm. Two gloves—at least part of the time. The rest of the time her hands were uncovered as she chain-smoked and rocked out, celebrating her clandestine achievements.

But where are they now? She began to sweat, her mind reeling. Thinking hard, she dug further into the closet.

People in cold climates often have many pairs of gloves. And mittens, and hats, and scarves, even boots, that accumulate over the years. They get dirty, they get scratchy, get holes, and often get lost: dropped in a random snowbank, fallen from a pocket, carelessly and quickly stuffed away, forgotten on a warmish winter day. No one likes to wear gloves or mittens. They get in the way, and they make using your hands and fingers difficult. Some gloves fit too tightly, some too loose, sometimes mittens are the better option, but then you have almost no use of your fingers. But what usually happens is the unconscious, repeated use of your favorites, the ones you like best.

Ginger was no different and had worn the same gloves, nicely broken in, since the beginning of winter, and she almost always kept them in the pocket of her coat. But, like everyone else, *sometimes* she didn't. Sometimes they were left in the car, taken off in haste for some reason, or thrown in a bag, or on the seat. Sometimes they were in the house, forgotten on a chair, or on a floor vent to dry when they got wet. Gloves could be difficult creatures.

Her eyes were like saucers, lost in the storage files of her memory, trying to think smart and recall her hands, what they were wearing, when she last had gloves on, and where she put them. It was crazy making. Even if she was absolutely sure she got home and put them in her coat pocket, the point was *they were not there now.* Her coat pockets were empty. She looked on the floor, she pushed through the boots, scattering melting puddles around the small, tiled entryway. She looked in Violet's coat pocket, in the hall closet, and came up with nothing.

Oh, God! She couldn't be found searching the coat closet. How would she explain that to Gilbert? Hey, Ginger, what are you looking for? Oh, my gloves, can't find them. Huh, what a coincidence, maybe I should call the cops and tell them you lost your gloves!

Fuck.

She backed away from the closet, returned to the sofa, and looked out the front window. She needed to get outside to her car and check there. *Stay calm, Ginger. They're in the car.* She looked outside and saw snow falling. The sky darkened early in December. She had to get out there.

Fuck what Gilbert thinks. She grabbed her jacket and was putting on her boots as she yelled to him in the kitchen, "Hey, Gilbert. I think I left a new pack of bubblegum in the car. I'm going outside to get it."

She left, slamming the door, and tramped through the snow to her car. She opened the door, and the first thing she saw was one of her gloves thankfully sitting on the seat. But where was the other? Her heart lurched as she searched the floorboards and between the driver's and passenger's seat of her Subaru, coming up with some candy wrappers, a few Cheetos, coins, ashes, but no glove. She jumped in the driver's seat and slammed the door, her breath fogging the window as she laid over the seat and searched thoroughly under her seat and the passenger bay. She twisted her neck to look in the back and saw nothing. Pounding frantically on the steering wheel—*It has to be here!*

Her heart racing, she got out and shot a look at the front window of the house. Seeing no one, she dropped to her knees in the snow and searched again through the open door, under her seat, into the back seat, everywhere, and then began digging in the snow. *Ginger! Stop!* She looked like a wild, guilty woman. But where was it?

She needed to get inside so Gilbert wouldn't start to ask questions. Looking toward the Backwoods, she realized it was possible, maybe, that it had dropped out of her pocket while she walked to and from the restaurant that morning. Maybe. But the new snow had covered it up. She probably wouldn't find it until spring, unless she got a shovel and started to excavate. But she couldn't do that with Gilbert or Violet watching her. But just in case, she ran quickly down the path she'd taken to and from the Backwoods, her eyes scanning the ground, searching. Not seeing the glove, she made her way back through the snow to the house.

Once inside, hands trembling, she took off her boots and jacket as Gilbert came around the corner from the kitchen with two cocktails.

Sipping from one, he said, "Do you think we can get Violet back out to watch *Harry Potter* with us?"

God! Violet? She didn't have time to think about that hole; she had problems of her own. Counseling herself to shake it off and think straight, she said, "Ah, maybe, but I think she needs to be alone right now. Here, give me that drink." She walked toward him with her hand outstretched.

Clearly, Gilbert had not noticed anything unusual in her behavior or even the wet knees of her jeans. She plowed past him into the kitchen and cranked on the vent fan and lit a cigarette. Her temples throbbed and she put the beverage on the counter and inhaled the nicotine deeply, trying to alleviate the pressure and organize her thoughts.

Okay, Ginger. Go there.

Worst case scenario. *I HATE worst case scenarios!* Okay, let's say the glove somehow, by a *goddamned act of magic*, fell out of my hand and I just fucking left it behind under the fucking car. How stupid was that? It was like every stinking crime show she'd ever watched. They always say you can plan one hundred things right, but even the smartest person forgets something in the heat of the moment. On every damn episode of *Columbo*, he nailed them for forgetting about one simple, trivial thing. Something they neglected to consider, didn't notice, or slipped up. She couldn't believe she would be so stupid as to leave her glove behind—under the car?

Okay, but *if* she did . . . *Focus, Ginger.* She put out her cigarette, already fully inhaled, and dipped a chip into the queso and crunched. *Okay. So what would that mean?*

The cops had a glove, abandoned in a hotel parking lot, in winter! It could be anyone's glove! But obviously some-one in the car accident was still alive and working with the cops. Someone who knew where the car had been parked the night before. That could only be Alex. Renzo hadn't parked the car, so he couldn't point out the spot, and Charlotte had gone inside with Petunia—she didn't know where the car was parked either. That could only mean that Alex was alive and showed them. Since Renzo answered the phone tonight, he was apparently okay. And Alex was well enough to work with the cops, and that meant he was okay. So only Petunia was hurt? Or was Charlotte in the car with them? Did she hurt *Charlotte Carrows* too? Maybe! That was exciting to think about . . .

Wait. Don't get distracted. Back to the glove. So the cops had it and it had brake fluid on it. What the fuck? Was this turning into *CSI Brainerd?* Go with it. That's what Renzo said.

So the cops knew the car was tampered with—well, that was obvious—and they had a glove that may have been involved. It could have been there before. Before Alex Macchi even parked in that spot, there could have been a glove, just lying in the snow. But the cops are looking for someone. The person who owns the glove. They would want to find that person and interrogate them to see if that person might be involved. How would they do that?

Ginger came out of her trance and looked around the kitchen, trying to gauge how long she'd been standing there, but all was well. She could hear the movie going in the other room. She gulped down her drink and decided it was helping steady her nerves. She needed another one. The diet pills made her so nervous, and she had to work so hard to appear calm all the time. Just like Skyler White. She must have been a bundle of nerves all the time too. It was almost like the two of them were twins. Except the real Skyler was thin.

Screw it. She made herself another drink, this time a huge one, and began to think again about the cops. They would begin by asking the surviving Macchis if anyone wanted to harm them. Probably, would be the answer. You didn't get to be as rich and famous as they were and not make enemies along the way.

"So who knew your schedule?" the cops would ask. "Who knew you would be in Brainerd, staying at the Country Suites ? Who knew your car?"

Ginger's stomach tightened as she composed their list. The pilot, the family, whoever the fuck else they told, and Violet Krueger. If Petunia was the witness, in town to testify, then the cops obviously knew this. Or were told this. Who would benefit from the Macchis being hurt? They would ask this. Where were you headed when the accident happened? They would ask this.

The answer to both questions sickened her.

They would be coming.

She needed to get rid of the other glove, fast. She slammed back her drink and put the glass on the counter. Time to improvise.

Walking into the den, she looked at Gilbert, sitting in his recliner, and said lightly, "Hey, I think I should go into Crosslake and pick up something to help poor Violet sleep tonight—you know. Poor kid."

"Like what?" he said cocking his head in curiosity.

Fuck, always improvising. "Oh, I read somewhere that chamomile tea and melatonin, they're really helpful, especially mixed together, and I'm sure they sell that at the drugstore."

Crossing the room and grabbing her jacket again, she continued speaking while she geared up. "I'll drive over and pick some up. Poor Violet."

"The weather's looking pretty bad. Want me to go instead?" Gilbert sat up and asked, looking at her.

"Naw, I got this."

"Really, I'm happy to help."

Shut the fuck up, Gilbert. "Naw, thanks, but I'm just going to head in, and I'll be back in a jiff. We'll get poor Violet calmed down, and then I'll feel better."

"Okay, but drive carefully," he said, sitting back and sipping his cocktail.

"Oh, I will. See you soon," she said as she stumbled out the door. The cold wind hit her as she lurched for the car.

———————

Gilbert licked his lips and forced himself to stay in his chair sipping his drink until he saw the lights of her car and heard her engine start up.

She's shook up. Now they would need to catch her. *God, this night's never going to end.* He texted Alex.

She took the bait. Go now. She just left house

Hoping to slow her down and give the sheriff stationed down the road at O'Toole's a chance to catch up, he ran to the front door and yanked it open.

"Ginger!" he yelled, waving at her as she backed up.

"What!" she yelled, her window down. Her face looked pissy as the snow fell all around her.

"Hey, so my knee, it's hurting a little, and since you're going to the drug store, you think you could pick me up some of that special Icy Hot stuff? I'll pay you back."

"Sure," she yelled, the window going back up.

"Hey," he waved again and watched her jaw drop as she rolled the window down again.

"Would you mind picking up something else for me too?"

He didn't say anything, knowing it would rile her as he waited for her reaction.

She slammed her hand on the wheel in frustration. "What! What!"

"Oh, just some Twizzlers. You know, we can cut off the ends and suck the vodka through them like you like."

She rolled her eyes and this time, truly left.

He watched her turn onto the road in front of the house and drive past the Backwoods, where she came to the T intersection at the highway. No traffic coming, she took a right turn heading toward Crosslake. Gilbert continued to watch, and within moments saw another vehicle, a truck, pass, which he prayed was the sheriff.

He went inside and reported what happened to Alex.

She just left, panicked, heading north toward Crosslake

In the next text he said:

Saw a truck not too far behind, hope its the cops

Gilbert was nervous and grabbed his empty cocktail glass and went into the kitchen. He finally turned off the noisy vent fan and looked at the counter, strewn with ashes where Ginger had missed the ashtray.

The vodka bottle stood on the counter, the level much lower than he remembered. Ginger had put back several ounces in the last thirty to forty-five minutes. That could be helpful too. He looked at the greasy, congealed mass of queso in the pan, ashes floating in it, and thought he might be sick. He got a spoon and cleaned out the ashes on the off chance Violet may want some later. Poor kid.

He left the mess behind and went down the hall and knocked on Violet's door. He got no answer.

Chapter 46

Ginger flew through the snowy night, her concentration intense as she focused on the problem. She lit a cigarette, turned down the music, and squinted through the smoke and wiper blades beating back the falling snow.

How should she dispose of the glove? There was a roll-off dumpster site a few miles down the road. She could pull in there and open a dumpster lid and toss it in. Maybe even reach in and bury it under someone else's trash. *Hmmm.* Then there was town. Crosslake was dead ahead, and there were a lots of trash cans at the gas station, out front of the grocery store, the ice cream store . . . lots of dumpster options too.

She could just toss it out the window and let the plows and salt take care of it. If she rolled down the passenger window, how far out could she toss it? Not far. Would the wind take it to the shoulder? It might just drop, but still, it would look like a random sock in the road. Who would give it a second glance? She looked in the rearview mirror; a vehicle was not far behind her, lights beaming into the back of her car. If she tossed it out the driver's side window, would they see her toss it and get pissed she was littering? People hated littering. They honked sometimes. The glove wasn't like a cigarette butt out the window. For some reason, people didn't get as pissed about that, but a glove? But still, even though the headlights were on her, whoever was in the vehicle behind her couldn't possibly know it was a glove she was tossing, or for what reason.

Dammit. *Should she?*

There were lakes all around her, but they were frozen. But the woods—hell, the road she was on had woods on both sides, broken only occasionally by some retail places. She glanced over to the glove sitting on the seat next to her and it seemed pulsing, like it had a heartbeat. Gray with a black leather palm, it shimmered like a phantasm glowing eerily, shrieking at her to make a decision.

"Fuck!" she screamed and pounded the steering wheel. "Shit!" The damn glove was radioactive, and she needed it gone.

Not overthinking it, she decided a random place in the woods was better than a dumpster where it could sit for days. She couldn't imagine Brainerd cops would search every trash can and roll-off place in the area—she was already miles away from the city, but just knowing it was out there in a can, waiting for pickup, glowing, throbbing, waiting to be found . . . No. She couldn't do it.

The woods. The woods were a better option because there were hundreds of miles and millions of trees, and it was snowing. No way they could find it in the middle of nowhere. But where exactly? Not directly off the highway; that was too easy. Up ahead was the turnoff to access Scott

Creek. In the summer months, people would rent inner tubes and float down the creek, but right now it would be frozen. There were steep embankments on either side of the creek, which could not be seen from any road. She'd be able to dispose of it over the side, but near the top, in a place no human would ever need to look.

It felt good to make the decision. A few miles later, she turned right and drove down the Scott Creek road toward the tube rental parking lot. She wasn't surprised to see the area deserted, but the parking lot hadn't been plowed and she didn't think she'd make it in or out. It would be another disaster if she got stuck in the snow. Who would she call for assistance on that one? Gilbert? He'd wonder what in the hell she was doing stuck in the Scott Creek parking lot. How would she answer that?

At the last minute, she just pulled over to the side of the plowed road nearest the creek, as the truck following her passed by the turnoff and continued down the road. *Shit!* Had he seen her pull in? *Who gives a shit!* Why the hell would some random stranger care if she pulled off the road. *Get a grip!* Grabbing the glove, she got out of the car, knowing she needed to move fast.

As she started the trek into the woods toward the embankment, she worked hard, plodding through the snow-covered terrain, her breath coming out in a fog, until she finally stopped at the base of a large tree hanging over the creek. She got on her knees at the base, toward the creek-side, pushed back a mound of snow, threw the glove in, and covered it back up.

Done.

She tried running back to the car, the adrenaline and the alcohol pounding through her, but got winded from the exertion. Eventually she made it, got inside, started up the Subaru, and considered the tracks she'd left in the snow toward the embankment.

Who was going to look there? And why would they care? Making a U-turn in the road, she got back to the highway, and once again headed toward Crosslake.

Now that the glove was no longer in the car, she breathed a tremendous sigh of relief and started to relax. *It's over, Skyler, you beautiful girl. It's over.*

No one would ever be able to find that glove. Not in a million years.

Chapter 47

Alex, Charlotte, Sheriff Becker, and Gavin Stewart were in the conference room surrounded by boxes of takeout, eyes glued to the computer screen as they watched the movements of Ginger's car.

"She stopped," said Alex. "What is that spot?"

Sheriff Becker answered. "It's right by Scott Creek. A short road, it cuts between a couple of highways. Nothing much down that road except a parking lot and a stand where they rent inner tubes in the summer to float down the creek."

"Any reason you can think of that she stopped there?" Alex asked.

"Only one reason I can think of. I'll call Deputy Sorenson."

They listened to the call on speaker. "She stopped. You see her?"

"Yeah. I followed her north on the highway toward Crosslake. If I'd been in my patrol car, I would have pulled her over. She swerved a few times. I saw her exit east toward Scott Creek and looked down the road as I drove past. She'd parked her car on the side of the road. I didn't see her outside the vehicle but kept on driving. I did a U-turn out of her sight down the road and killed the lights. I went past the Scott Creek road, did another u-ey, drove up, and watched. I saw her come out of the woods on foot. She got back into her car, drove back to the highway, and headed north again. Looks like she's headed to Crosslake. I'm just making my move to follow her."

Sheriff Becker pumped his fist. "Okay, stay with her. She may have seen you on the drive-by at the creek, so be careful. I'll check back."

Tate disconnected the call and turned to the group. "You think she dumped it?"

Alex glanced at Charlotte, who nodded. "I do," he said. "There was no reason to turn down that road. There was no reason for her to be out in the woods. It's there. By the creek. We need to get someone down there fast, before the snow covers up her tracks and we can't find the glove."

Sheriff Becker grabbed his coat and said, "I'm heading out. You call me if anything else interesting happens out there."

"Are you taking your sheriff's car?" said Alex.

"Thought about it. Why?"

"You sure we want your car driving around Scott Creek? What if she drives by again and sees it? She might not have a chance to move the glove again, but Violet and Gilbert are still at the house. They could be in danger if Ginger loses her shit."

A side of Sheriff Becker's mouth turned up. "Yeah, I was thinking about our options earlier. I called Buster Finlayson, the guy who found Penny's body, and asked if he'd be available over the next twenty-four hours to do a little tracking. He's waiting for my call. I'm going to light it up on my way out there to his place. He's not far from the Backwoods. Maybe he and his coonhound can give me a lift out to Scott Creek in their vehicle. Call Gilbert, let him know what's happening, and see if he can slip out and leave an article of Ginger's clothing where we can pick it up on our way to Scott Creek."

Gavin Stewart stood and grabbed his coat too. "You're going to need another witness. I'm coming with you."

Alex nodded. "We'll keep in touch. Good luck."

After they left, Charlotte and Alex looked at the GPS and saw Ginger Krueger had stopped again—this time in Crosslake.

"Do you think they'll find it, Alex?" Charlotte asked with concern.

"I do," he said, grabbing his phone and calling Gilbert. "They have the general vicinity and a good tracker. They'll find it."

Chapter 48

Hearing no response from Violet, Gilbert uncomfortably opened her bedroom door and saw her small body heaving as she sobbed into her pillows, muffling the sound. Not wanting to intrude, and not having a clue what to say, he closed the door and went back to his chair. And waited.

The call came from Alex. Gilbert answered in a quiet voice. "Hey."

"Hey, so good news we hope, she stopped, up by Scott Creek. The sheriff's picking up a tracking dog and heading over. As we speak, Ginger's in Crosslake, so you have a few minutes of cover. We need you to get an article of clothing, something of Ginger's they can use to track her scent. Maybe put it in a plastic trash bag on the side of the road."

"You got it. I'll text you the location."

"Thanks, Gilbert. We'll be in touch."

Alex hung up, and Gilbert looked around the room, trying to spy something of Ginger's. Digging in a pile of random stuff near her chair, he was startled when he heard Violet behind him saying, "What location? Who was that?"

He spun around and saw her standing there, puffy from crying, holding her phone and a blanket. "Violet! I was worried about you. I hope you don't mind that I popped my head in earlier to check on you."

She shrugged and walked past him to the sofa. "Where did Ginger go? Gilbert, do you think it's a bad idea for me to go to the hospital too?"

Gilbert desperately wanted to have this conversation with Violet, but he knew he needed to get the bag ready and out to the road before Ginger returned.

"Ah, I'm not sure. Maybe. I think we should wait and call back in a bit, ask this Renzo guy for an update?" The expression on the poor kid's face was breaking his heart. He went to the sofa, dropped to his knees, and gently took her hand.

"Violet, I want you to listen to me. Everything is going to be all right. Believe me. I'm here to take care of you, and we'll get through this together. I'm not leaving here tonight, and when the time comes, I *promise* you I'll help you see your friend. Okay?"

He watched as the tears slid down her face. She nodded, her mouth in a tight line.

He nodded back at her, his brows lifted in encouragement, then stood and fast-scanned the room, patting his pockets like he forgot something.

"So Ginger, she went into Crosslake, and she'll be back soon. Hey, I need to use the bathroom. I'll be right back." He stepped backward and turned down the hall.

Once in the bathroom, he shut the door and looked around. He got lucky. Sure enough, there was a small pile of clothes on the floor, and he recognized a shirt and jeans which belonged to Ginger. As he grabbed them both, he realized he needed to get them past Violet and into the kitchen where they kept the trash bags. He gently folded the clothes into a clean towel, flushed the toilet, and walked briskly out with the wad under his arm. Violet thankfully had her head bowed, looking at her phone.

Walking into the kitchen, opening the cabinet door and finding the trash bags, he grabbed one, tossing the items inside. Putting the Ginger bag on the floor, he pulled the bag out of the trash bin and tied it off. Grabbing both bags, he walked back through the living room, past Violet, who looked up as he headed toward the door.

Shoving his feet into his boots, he said, "I'm going to take the trash out. I'll be right back."

He didn't wait for a response as he left. He went behind the house to the large trash container and threw the real trash inside. Then, unseen from the back side of the house, he ran toward the Backwoods and around the front toward the road. He dropped the bag with Ginger's clothes near the front of the building, nestling it by a front hedge. He bent to open it and grabbed the clean towel out of the bag, then tied it closed.

As he headed back to the house, he stopped at his car, quietly opened it, and threw the towel inside. Trying to stay calm, he texted Alex:

Shirt and jeans in white plastic garbage bag in front of Backwoods, next to the building, roadside, near large hedge

He hoped it was enough. Now, he wanted to talk to Violet. She deserved better than this shit, and tonight, he knew he was her only friend.

Chapter 49

Later that evening at the Krueger house, Gilbert glanced out the front window as headlights hit the window and Ginger returned home. He watched her throw a cigarette into the snow then get out and unload some bags from the back seat of her car. He went to the door, opening it, letting cold air and bits of snow inside.

"Hey, I'm back. Gilbert, take these," she said, extending the bags.

He grabbed the bags and closed the door as she maneuvered inside and pulled off her wet things.

"How are the roads?" he asked as he held the bags, waiting for her to finish.

"Wet," she barked, retrieving the bags then walking past him.

"Hey, Violet," she greeted the kid as she walked into the kitchen. "Did you get any of the queso?"

Violet didn't bother answering as Ginger went right on talking from the kitchen. "Hey, come see what I brought for you," she said, poking her head around the corner, looking at Violet, who had her head in her phone.

Ginger stomped her foot. "Violet! I went all the way to Crosslake in a snowstorm to get you some things. Come here!"

Violet dragged herself off the couch and Gilbert followed.

"Look." Ginger held up a box. "I got you some chamomile tea! It's supposed to help you relax. And I got these pills? They're Melatonin. They're supposed to help you sleep!"

Gilbert couldn't help notice that the crazy in Ginger's eyes seemed exacerbated. Since Violet stayed mute, he jumped in, offering a response. "Hey, Ginger, swell, that was nice. Did you get the other stuff?"

Ginger shot Violet a disappointed look when the girl couldn't work up any grateful enthusiasm. They watched Violet retreat back to the living room.

"Yeah, right here," Ginger said, slamming items out of the bags onto the counter.

Gilbert was mildly surprised to see a massive canister of puffed cheese balls, but only said, "Hey, thanks," as she unloaded the Icy Hot and Red Vines. He thought Ginger needed some calming and gestured with his chin toward the bottle of vodka. "You gonna make any more of those?"

"I am. Why? Did you want me to make one for you too? Anything else I can do for the two of you tonight? When is it going to be *my* turn for someone to think about *my* needs!"

"Hey, sorry. I appreciate all the trouble you've gone through. Why don't you go sit with Violet, and I'll make us a couple more drinks."

"Fine," she said, and stomped out of the room. "And bring me a bowl of that queso too."

Gilbert did the appointed tasks, and then they sat, Ginger in her own recliner, still giving off angry vibes, still feeling unappreciated. She pounded back her drink, cheese ball canister between her legs, while Gilbert and Violet sat nearby watching the *Harry Potter* marathon.

At one point, Violet brought up reaching out again to Renzo, but Gilbert said maybe they should wait a bit longer. Violet reluctantly agreed.

Gilbert's phone vibrated in his pocket, and he got up and went to the restroom. It was a text from Alex.

Glove Found! Sherriff Becker and Sheriff Sorenson and DA Gavin Stewart ready to arrest her. More backup coming. They are now on the road waiting your go. Any ideas? You need to protect Violet. Can we get Ginger outside? They can take her down out there

Gilbert threw his head back, his eyes closed in relief. It was almost over. But he needed to think of a way to get Ginger outside alone and then help Violet through the next stage of her living hell. How was he going to do that? How could he compel Ginger to unwedge the canister of cheese balls from between her legs, put on her boots, and go outside? Something at the restaurant she needed to check on? The store? He recognized that Ginger was on a bender and would probably be drinking for some time. He knew what to do.

Give me a few minutes. I'm going to send Ginger to the liquor store at the Backwoods. I'll text when she walks out the door

Passing the girls in the living room, he went into the kitchen, where the bottle of vodka sat on the counter. Looking in the cabinet below the sink, he took out another and quickly shoved it into a high cabinet behind some pans.

He heard the recliner creak and Ginger call out, "What you doing in there?"

"Hey," said Gilbert, making a racket. "I thought I'd make some pasta, in case we get sick of queso. That okay?"

He heard her mumble, but she didn't come into the kitchen. He pulled out a big pot, making sure the backup vodka was concealed, put the pot on the stove, and threw the open vodka bottle onto the floor, shattering it.

Ginger and Violet came running. "What the hell!" screamed Ginger. "What the hell did you do?"

"Oh man, I'm so sorry!" Gilbert said, standing in a puddle of broken glass and vodka. "It fell!"

"I can shee that it fell," she yelled, now slurring her words.

"Violet," Gilbert held up a cautioning hand. "Don't come in here. You'll cut your feet. Ginger, hey, I got this. I'll clean it up."

"Yeah," Ginger said, resigned to the mess now that she knew she wasn't going to have to deal with it. But it did register that there may be an alcohol situation. "Hey, we got another bottle of vodka under the sink, right?"

Gilbert threw a couple hand towels on the floor and swiveled in his socks, opening the cabinet where they kept the booze. He moved a few bottles around and said, "Nope, sorry, don't see any."

Ginger, brow furrowed in confusion and anger, stomped her foot. "What the hell! Will this night never end? I could have sworn there were two under there."

"Look for yourself," he pointed at the cabinet, but they both looked down doubtfully. The path to the cabinet was wet and filled with broken glass and liquid.

"Shit!" she said.

"Hey, that's the beauty of having a liquor store. You don't even have to drive. Just walk over and grab another one off the shelf."

"Whatever," she mumbled, but he popped his head around the door and watched her put her feet into her boots, ready for the task.

"It's locked up. Take the keys," Gilbert said.

"Have that cleaned up by the time I get back," she yelled as she opened the front door.

He yanked out his phone.

COME NOW. She just went outside

Gilbert took a long jump over the vodka and glass and into the living room to check on Violet. His socks were soaked; he pulled them off, killing time. "I think I'll put on my shoes while I clean up. It'll be safer that way."

He strode past Violet and looked out the front window. He could see movement by the front side of the store close to the road. Ginger was halfway there, walking with her head down, arms bundled around her since she hadn't stopped to put on her coat. When she was almost to the side gate of the liquor store, someone popped out of the shadows with a gun pointed directly at Ginger and yelled, "Hands Up! NOW! NOW!"

Ginger threw her hands up, but then made a break for it, running toward the gate entrance to the liquor store. Even muffled through the glass, Gilbert heard the sheriff scream, "STOP! SHERIFF! STOP NOW!"

Ginger did not stop, and as she pulled open the gate, a cop shot a warning into the air. She disappeared behind the gate, and Gilbert saw two more men run up as another shot rang out.

Holy Hell.

Violet had jumped off the sofa and was at the window beside him.

"What's going on?" she screamed.

"Let's get back from the window." He extended his arm, trying to corral her away from the scene.

Not listening, she placed her face near the window. "Oh my God! What's going on out there? Was that a gun?"

Gilbert took her by the shoulders, turned her, and planted her in a chair. "Yes. Stay calm. The police are here. It's going to be okay. They're here to arrest Ginger."

"What?" she screamed, flailing back. "What's going on?" she wailed. Jumping back up, she ran to the window.

Sirens began wailing in the distance, but Gilbert couldn't see what was happening to Ginger because of the fence.

Violet, beside him, began jumping up and down, her hands moving over her mouth, and eyes and ears. She seemed in a panic. He tried to put a calming hand on her arm, but she pushed it away.

"Violet," he tried, in a soothing voice. "It's okay. It's okay."

"It's NOT OKAY! WHY ARE THEY ARRESTING HER? What did she do?"

Just then, a sheriff's car, sirens and lights blazing, pulled into the Backwoods lot and two officers, weapons drawn, jumped out, each running in a different direction. Gilbert could make out yelling, but through the window of the house, couldn't hear the words.

He couldn't pull himself back from the window either but patted the air and tried to keep his cool. "I'm going to explain everything to you in just a minute. Stay calm. The police have it under control."

Three men came back into view from behind the wooden gate of the liquor store. They were shoving Ginger, hands cuffed behind her back, into the back of the squad car. One of them slammed the door behind her, leaned inside the front, and shut off the siren. The other two officers joined them, and the five of them spoke near the vehicle.

Violet held her face in her hands. "GILBERT! What's happening? What did she do?"

He nodded aggressively. "Give me a minute here, Violet, and we're going to sit down and talk about it. I promise I'll explain everything." He pulled out his phone and texted Alex.

Ginger in custody, Violet safe but scared.

He looked up and saw one of the men break off from the group and approach the house. He went to the door and opened it. Sheriff Becker walked into the entry and said, "Everyone okay in here?" He shut the door behind him.

Gilbert nodded. "We're fine."

"What's going on?" screamed Violet. "Why won't anyone answer me?"

"The sheriff and I are going to answer all your questions right now. Let's sit down," he said. He took her shoulders again and gently led her to the sofa. Sheriff Becker stood in the entryway watching while Gilbert took a seat across from Violet and began.

"Violet. You've been so strong, and I know this is going to come as another shock, so please try to stay calm. The first thing I need to tell you is that Petunia Macchi is fine. She's alive. She's in the Brainerd Hospital, but she was never ever in any surgery. She and her dad really were in a car accident this morning on their way out here to get you, but both of them survived."

Violet's chin quivered as her tears began to flow.

Gilbert continued, "Alex got some stiches, and Petunia had a mild concussion, but they're both going to be okay. Renzo lied to you on purpose. He told you that Petunia was in surgery, hurt bad, and all the rest because he wanted you to share that information with Ginger."

Gilbert glanced at the sheriff for some kind of solution to this hellish scene as he watched Violet's body begin to shake. He got up and grabbed a blanket and wrapped it around her.

Seated again, this time beside her, he reached out and held one of her hands. "You see, Violet, Ginger was the one who cut the brakes on the Macchi's car. I'm so sorry, honey. It's a long story, but we know she did it, so Renzo told you about a glove they found and that they were looking for the mate. That, too, was a lie. But the lie worked. It made Ginger believe the cops would find the other glove. When she went into Crosslake for groceries, they followed her and watched her hide the second glove. This implicated her. Do you understand? She wouldn't have a need to hide her glove in the woods if she wasn't worried the cops had the mate, with brake fluid on it. Ginger cut the brake lines. We have proof. She's just been arrested for attempted murder."

Violet had tears running down her face as Sheriff Becker, still dripping in the entry, said, "Violet, I'm afraid Ginger Krueger is a very bad person, and you'll no longer be living with her."

Her head fell back, and her eyes closed as she moaned. "But where will I live?"

Gilbert put his arm around her and gave her a hug, then reached down and took her hand. "It's going to be okay, Violet. I'm sure of it. You need to trust us, okay?"

She began to truly sob, and Gilbert held her for a while. Sheriff Becker finally removed his boots and walked into the living room. "Violet needs to come with us, and I'll have to call Social Services."

Gilbert shot him a discouraging look, warning him to back off.

"I'm so sorry this happened to you." Gilbert turned to Violet, feeling helpless. "I'm really, truly sorry. More than you know."

She looked at him, her face a mask of confusion. "How did you know about it? You knew about the arrest coming? And the Macchis?"

Gilbert nodded. "It's all a part of the longer version of the story, honey, but I promise I was only here to protect you. Like I told you earlier tonight, there are a lot of people out there who care deeply about you. I'm just one of them."

She shook her head. "I don't understand."

Sheriff Becker said, "Gilbert, why don't you help Violet pack an overnight bag and follow us back into town. Violet, there are some people waiting to see you. I've been told to give you a lift once you were safe."

She looked at him, then wiped at her face, her bottom lip trembling. "Who wants me?"

"The Macchis, honey. The family is waiting for you at the hospital."

Violet fell into racking sobs as Gilbert held her.

God damn you, Ginger. He gathered up a bunch of nearby napkins they'd left from the dinner and handed them to the poor little girl.

"Smells like booze in here," Sheriff Becker cleared his throat and said once Violet quieted a bit.

Gilbert did a chin jut. "The kitchen. The distraction. Watch your feet. There's glass all over the floor."

Sheriff Tate walked to the kitchen doorway, inspecting the debris. "Guess we should do something about that before we go?"

"Violet," Gilbert said, gently hoisting her to her feet. "Come on, let's you and me go pack a bag. Sheriff Becker will clean up the kitchen while we're getting ready." Gilbert smiled over his shoulder in the sheriff's direction as he guided Violet to her room.

Sheriff Tate Becker smiled back.

Chapter 50

T hey're on their way." Stroking Petunia's brow, Charlotte felt relief for the first time that day, knowing no one else was going to get hurt. Renzo, seated in a chair near Alex, hung his head, most likely feeling the same way.

Charlotte worried, too, about Alex's condition, but knew there was no way to convince him to go back to the hotel until Gilbert and Violet arrived. Nevertheless, she wanted him to at least close his eyes. Assigned a double room, Alex had been sitting on the empty bed.

She walked to him now, gently coaxing him to recline. "Come on, Alex. Lay down for a few minutes. Close your eyes. It's over."

He did as instructed. For the moment, Charlotte thought, it would do, but knew there was an emotional scene to play. Young Violet, betrayed by another relative with whom she had been living, had yet to hear the worst of the news. They all worried for her future.

The door opened. Sheriff Becker entered, followed by Violet and Gilbert.

Violet scanned the room until her eyes landed on Petunia.

Charlotte smiled, and her heart leapt a bit as Petunia threw back the covers, jumped out of bed, and ran into Violet's arms.

The two girls hugged tightly, Petunia saying, "Violet, we've been so worried about you."

When they finally let go, Charlotte stepped forward for her hug. The young girl was much thinner than she remembered. She looked into Violet's vulnerable eyes. "We're so glad that you're safe. I'm so sorry for everything you've been through."

Gilbert and the sheriff stood against the wall as Petunia grabbed Violet's hand and led her to her bed. She scooted to the top of the bed by the pillows and pulled Violet next to her. "We need to talk. How are you feeling? Although I suppose that's a stupid question after everything you've been through."

A look of concern washed over Violet's face as she frowned. "I should ask you how you're feeling. You were in a car accident today, with your dad?"

"Yes," Petunia put her head down and shook it sadly. "It was terrible, but we survived. Thank goodness for airbags, right, Dad?"

Violet looked over at Alex. His head was stitched, his face bruised, but he was smiling. "That's right."

Violet's face contorted in confusion and pain. "Did Ginger do this to you?"

Charlotte licked her lips, sensing the girl's desperation and guilt. She stood in her line of sight near the foot of the bed. "I'm sorry to say that she did, Violet. But it had nothing to do with you . . . it wasn't your fault. So don't go there.

Ginger did this because Ginger was scared. She wanted to hurt Petunia, and she tried to kill her."

"But why?" Violet asked, not understanding. "Why would she do that?"

Charlotte gripped the guardrails of the bed. "She had a reason, and we were going to tell you about it today after we picked you up, but we didn't get the chance. We couldn't tell you before today because, well, for lots of reasons . . ." She trailed off, thinking how they'd wanted to find evidence against Ginger, and in doing so, they'd put young Violet in harm's way by allowing her to live with her mother's murderer. It felt shameful.

"Violet," Alex's voice came through soft yet strong as he came to stand beside Charlotte. "Petunia is a witness for the prosecution in the trial—against your dad. This summer, she overheard something, and when your mom was missing, we came back to Minnesota to meet with the sheriff and the county attorney. We were told—and we agreed—to keep the information a secret, because the police needed to investigate. After they found your mom, we came back again, secretly, and Petunia testified before a grand jury. We believe her testimony was a big part of the reason they got an indictment against your dad."

Violet jumped off the bed and spun back to face Petunia. "You've been lying to me too?"

Charlotte saw tears of desperation spring into her daughter's eyes. Looking destroyed, pleading, Petunia said, "No! Yes. I couldn't tell you the truth. It was part of the trial. They wouldn't let me, but it didn't have anything to do with our friendship, our conversations. I just couldn't tell you!"

"You lied to me! All of you!" Violet's eyes darted around the room.

Sheriff Becker walked closer and said, "They did what they had to, Violet. For your mom. For Penny. They helped us, the Macchi family, all of them. They helped us figure out who killed your mom, but they were—are—very, very worried about you. We all were. They may have had to lie to you sometimes, but they only did it for your *mom*, for everyone's protection, and to solve the case. They've done nothing wrong, and I think you should give them a chance to explain."

Petunia folded her hands and shook them in a pleading manner. "They told me I could tell you this weekend. I'm supposed to testify on Monday. The courtroom will be closed, only the jury and the lawyers and stuff while I'm testifying, but I wanted to tell you before I did it. I've been *bursting* to tell you the truth, all of it, but I couldn't."

Charlotte went to Petunia, worried about the effect the stress of this conversation was having on her. She rubbed her back and told her to stay calm.

Violet threw her hands up. "Why did Ginger want to kill you? How did she know you were a witness?"

"She figured it out," said Alex. "She was a close friend of your dad's, she knew there was a witness, and she knew if the witness was dead, Clayton might not be convicted."

Violet shook her head in confusion, her eyes squeezed tightly, as Alex continued. "But I'm afraid there's more, Violet." He waited until she opened her eyes to look at him.

Alex continued. "Ginger was able to put the pieces together because she knew what happened the day your mom disappeared. She knew . . . because Ginger was there that day. We believe she was the one who actually killed Penny."

With the sterile walls gleaming too bright, the fluorescent lights, the strangers, the hot stuffy air, the chaos and pain, Charlotte shouldn't have been so surprised when she saw the young girl swoon. Renzo got to her first, right before she hit the floor. He picked her up like a feather and carried her gently to the now vacant second bed.

Gilbert ran out the door, calling for a nurse, as the adults fumbled with what to do. Thankfully, Violet was out only momentarily, and a nurse was there within moments to check on her.

Charlotte scolded herself for not being prepared as the nurse gave Violet some water. Not long after taking her vitals, the nurse left, saying she was confident she would be all right, but they would keep tabs on her condition.

Violet wasn't speaking, her face pale as Renzo brought her a blanket from the closet. He wrapped her into it like a small papoose and then patted her on the head. "Supposed to be a sensory thing. Calm you down."

Charlotte knew there was more to come and nodded at Gilbert to come forward. He pulled up a chair near Violet's bed and sat in front of her.

"Violet, my name is Gilbert Gorsky. That part's true. What you don't know is, I didn't randomly show up at the Backwoods looking for a job. I was sent there, on purpose, to look after you and to see what I could find out about Ginger. I live in New York, most of the time, and I work for Alex Macchi. He hired me to come to Minnesota to protect you. I've really enjoyed getting to know you, Violet, and I think you're a very special young girl. I hope you believe we're friends. *Really* friends, and that you can depend on me. I'm very sorry for everything that's happened to you, and I suppose in a way, I've been lying to you too. But just like Petunia, and the rest of the people in this room, we did it, we hope, for the right reasons. I'm sorry I couldn't be honest with you, but I am honest about thinking you're special, and I enjoyed our time together. Especially the fishing."

He gave her a hopeful smile but didn't get much in return.

"Violet," Gilbert said, softly. "It's time now for your questions. We're all here, ready to tell you the truth. Ask them."

"Did Ginger really kill my mom?" she asked weakly.

"Yes," Gilbert nodded. "We believe she and your dad planned it, but that Ginger was the one who killed her. Since then, we've been trying to find evidence, so we could bring them to justice."

"My dad really did it?" she whispered, holding the blanket close.

"Yes," Gilbert continued. "I'm afraid he did. I'm truly sorry."

Violet's eyes squeezed closed and cried quietly, her abdomen heaving under the blankets. Petunia handed Gilbert some tissues, and he used them to dry her tears as they fell. Violet made no move, and didn't ask to be released from the tight blanket so she could do it herself, but she allowed Gilbert to help her.

Charlotte wasn't sure what more they could do and turned when the sheriff spoke.

"I've got to get over to the station. We got Ginger cooling her heels in an interrogation room waiting for me." He walked over to Alex and held out his hand, "Thank you, Mr. Macchi, for everything. You all get some rest tonight, and we'll speak in the morning. Would you and Mrs. Macchi walk me out?"

In the hallway, Sheriff Becker said, "Social Services has to be involved with Violet, but it's fine if she stays with you tonight. I'm officially releasing her into your custody. Are you certain you want that?"

"Yes," said Charlotte. "We'll take care of her."

Sheriff Becker nodded his head a few times, so much unspoken but not really necessary. He put on his hat and left.

Back inside the room, Charlotte walked to Violet and ran a soft hand down the girl's swaddled arm. "I hope it's okay with you, but Sheriff Becker has given permission for you to stay with us until this is settled. Are you comfortable with that?"

Violet nodded, still crying, her lip quivering, trying to pull it together.

Petunia said, "I need to stay in the hospital tonight, Violet. I'm like, under observation or something. You can stay here with me if you want."

"Okay," Violet whispered.

It was time. Charlotte turned to her husband. "Alex, you're leaving. I'm going to have Gilbert take you back to the hotel, and you're going to get some sleep. You look awful, and I know your head is killing you. Renzo, I'd appreciate it if you would stay here with me and the girls this evening. We'll make sure you catch up on your sleep tomorrow. The sheriff said they would be sending someone to look after us as well, so there should be no concerns about our security."

Alex put up his hand, ready to open his mouth and protest.

Charlotte pushed him toward the door. "I'm not having a conversation with you, Alex. I'm telling you. We need you, but more importantly, we need you well. Go back, get some sleep, shower. We'll all be here in the morning." She kissed him gently on his cheek. Releasing him, she gave him a look that communicated that the discussion was over.

Alex rolled his eyes and looked at Renzo. "You okay with this?"

"I'm good, boss. I'll take care of them."

"All right. Gilbert. Let's head back to the hotel."

They watched as Gilbert leaned over Violet and kissed her on the forehead. "Hey, kid. Your mom would be very proud of you. You've been a brick. I'll see you tomorrow."

Once the adrenaline left the girls' bodies, they both fell into a deep sleep. Renzo and Charlotte sat on either side of them and watched over them through the night.

Chapter 51

Alex had set the alarm for eight a.m., hoping he wouldn't need the wake-up call. That the alarm woke him was a surprise, but worse, his head still pounded, and there was yellow, purplish bruising all over his face.

Anxious for an update, he called Charlotte and learned the girls had slept well through the night, but breakfast had come early for all four of them. The doctor had just left, pronouncing both Petunia and Violet fit for discharge. They were waiting now for the paperwork, and once done, Renzo would drive them back to the hotel.

Encouraged by the news, he set the small coffeemaker going and got into a hot shower. He was dressed and drinking his first cup when there was a knock on the door. He opened the door of the two-room suite and let his family inside.

While jackets and boots were being shed, Alex turned to Renzo and told him to hit the sack. Gilbert had his own room at the hotel, and he'd stay with them today. After Renzo bid them goodbye, Alex turned to the girls.

"Violet," said Alex. "Is there anything you need? Anything I can arrange for you? If you've forgotten something, please tell me and we'll get it. I don't know if you girls will do any swimming today, but if you want to, I'm up for it."

Petunia looked at Violet, who shook her head no.

His beautiful Charlotte had dark circles under her eyes, and he pointed toward the bedroom. "You. To bed." Turning back to the girls, he said, "You two can hang out in your room or out here in the living room. We can order pizza, or we can go out later for dinner. Your choice. I'm going to hang out, right here, all day, and get some work done on my laptop."

"Am I still going to testify tomorrow, Dad?" Petunia asked.

"I think we should assume yes unless we hear otherwise. I'm sure the county attorney, Gavin Stewart, will be in touch today. Violet, you should know the original plan was that Petunia and the county attorney would spend time together today, but we'll wait to hear from him. If he needs to meet with Petunia, we can arrange that it be done elsewhere in the hotel. You won't need to be a part of it."

Charlotte walked toward her bedroom but stopped and turned. "I know yesterday was a nightmare for you, Violet, but I hope you understand what influenced our decisions."

They all looked expectantly at Violet, wondering how she felt now that she'd had a bit of time to absorb all the shocks.

"What happens when you leave? Are you leaving tomorrow after court?" Violet asked.

Charlotte answered, "I don't know. There's quite a lot that needs to happen, a lot of people we need to speak with. Today, I think, we should take things one at a time. You had too much coming at you yesterday. Today is for information gathering. After that, we'll make some decisions . . . together. Does that make sense?"

"Yes," said Violet, nodding, but her face was clearly worried.

"Go now," Alex pointed again at Charlotte, then to their bedroom, but they got a knock on the door. Alex looked through the peephole and opened the door for Gilbert.

"Hey, good morning!" Gilbert said brightly as he entered the suite. He rubbed his arms and bowed quickly in the direction of the girls. "Violet, ladies, good to see you! I wasn't sure what the transportation story was, but I see everyone made it over here in one piece. You got an early release from the hospital?"

"Yes," said Charlotte. "The doctor was in at six. Breakfast and discharge papers, and then we just walked out. We had a rental at the hospital."

"Charlotte was just leaving us for bed," said Alex as he shooed her out of the room. "Renzo has his own room next door and I'm sure he's snoring as we speak."

"Well, you want me to hang around for a while? Ladies, do you need anything? Violet?" Gilbert queried with a smile.

"No," said Violet.

Gilbert clapped his hands. "Okay, Alex? You need anything? You want me to hang around?"

"Yeah. I'm expecting a call from Gavin Stewart, so I could use your help keeping an eye on the girls with Renzo and Charlotte clocked out."

"Sure, sure," Gilbert said. He sat down and rested his ankle on his leg, his foot jumping.

"Good night, everyone." Charlotte left the room.

Gilbert threw up his hands. "So anyone hungry? I haven't had breakfast. There's a buffet downstairs." He jerked his thumb, indicating out the door.

"I'm hungry," said Alex. "But the girls have eaten. Would you go down and bring some food back up here?"

"Sure." He hopped up. "Ladies, anything? Violet, did you want to come with me?"

She shrugged her shoulders and said, "No, I'm okay."

"All right then." Gilbert bit his bottom lip. "I'll see you in a bit. Alex, text me if you need me."

"Come on, Violet," said Petunia. "Let's go see what's on TV and check out the pizza delivery places. Dad? What time do you figure they deliver pizza around here?"

"I should think around eleven?"

"Plan on it," Petunia said as they left the room.

Chapter 52

Tate Becker picked up his coffee cup and brought it to his lips. Empty.

Damn. He needed to get some food before he put any more of the thick, awful-tasting brew into his empty gut.

Gavin Stewart wandered into the office, his weary eyes half lidded, his clothes rumpled. Tate realized his friend had not been home either.

"Tate," Gavin said, collapsing into a chair in front of him. "Fill me in."

Tate rubbed his temples. "The paperwork is killing me, but I gotta get it done while it's fresh."

"When I left here last night, Ginger was screaming for a lawyer, so I'm assuming you guys called the interrogation quits. Where is she?"

"In a cell. Last I heard, she was being a pain in the ass puking her guts up. Her attorney said he'd interview her at eight and meet with us after. I slept on the couch, but it wasn't great." He gave the stink eye to his deeply swayed, uncomfortable leatherette sofa, living way past its expiration date.

Gavin yawned. "We need to talk about strategy. I'm prepared to file two counts of first-degree attempted murder against Ginger for the Macchi hit. That's a life sentence, but with the possibility of parole—she's in for maybe twenty, thirty years. We'll hold that up in front of her, see how she takes the news. The second issue is Penny Krueger's murder. Ideally, both Ginger and Clayton go down for it forever, and we throw away the key."

"Or switch the fucking flip," Tate growled as he pulled a bottle of Tums out of his drawer.

"Yeah, well, reality is, there is no death penalty in Minnesota. We have an active trial already in process against Clayton Krueger for conspiracy to commit murder. He's looking at ten to twenty if we get a conviction. We knew going in that the case was circumstantial, but we hoped he would turn in his accomplice and we'd get them both. So far, he's called our bluff."

Tate rocked back in his chair, his hands behind his head, focusing. "But now we have Ginger in custody. She's looking at even more time than Clayton if we get a conviction for the attempts. Lay it out for me, prosecutor."

"All right, let's talk about Ginger. She killed Penny Krueger. Violently, brutally killed a young, vibrant mother, and with no apparent remorse. Ginger shoved her in a pre-dug hole and walked away. She then moved into the home of the victim's daughter and played the role of surrogate mother. Sick. Twisted. Oddly enough, she had no priors, but who knows what other crimes she's good for. So we want her. Right now, if convicted for the attempts on the Macchis, she might serve twenty years. Are we happy with that? Is that enough?"

"No," said Tate. "But let's focus on Penny's murder."

"Let's say Clayton and Ginger both keep their mouths shut until the bitter end. Neither giving up the other on their roles in Penny's murder. We don't have enough on Ginger for the murder. Petunia is our best hope, but I don't think we can nail Ginger just because she has a hang-up with *Breaking Bad* and uses the word 'cancer' and the words 'I'm cool, I'm cool' in her everyday conversations. I don't see it. So, if Clayton doesn't flip, and nothing else shakes out, we don't have Ginger for it yet. Attempted on the Macchis is our best bet."

Tate was following along. He picked up his coffee cup, belatedly remembering its awful and mercifully empty status. He put it down as Gavin carried on.

"Then there's Clayton. The conspirator. The husband. He set this thing in motion. No doubt. He wanted the insurance money, and he coerced Ginger into doing the dirty work. Are we going to get a conviction?"

Hearing Gavin pause, Tate prompted, "Well . . ."

"There's a *maybe* out there. If we get Clayton on the solicitation of his wife's murder, he's doing thirty years. I'll fight for the maximum. So Clayton, he's sitting in county lockup right now, his trial is underway, and maybe he's scared and maybe he's not, but so far he hasn't been willing to take a deal. We offered him ten years if he gave up his accomplice—hell of a deal, but the prick said no. So far, he's rolling the dice and taking his chances. He's hoping he walks, but he can't be sure. We want him too."

Tate got up and moved his tired muscles, getting the circulation going. Stretching, he took up the thread. "Now we've got both these jackasses sitting in the same building, but neither knows what's going on in the other one's head. How desperate are they? How scared? Which one is more frightened? Clayton or Ginger?"

"Right," said Gavin. "What happens if we put a deal in front of each of them. We tell Ginger today we have her dead to rights for the premeditated attempts. That's big. And we can use the Carrows angle. We tell her I'm going to be working with the best investigators in the country. Budget problems? Over. Expert witnesses will be flown in from China to talk about that particular brand of brake fluid. Surveillance, her movements on GPS, the tracking dog, the witness, *Gilbert*—all of that will shock the shit out of her. She had no idea that Gilbert was working for us, living with her this entire time. We'll tell her Gilbert heard her implicate herself a number of times. Doesn't even have to be true. She'll pee in her pants trying to remember every conversation she's had with him over the last few months. We tell her we've got search warrants, and we're going over to the Backwoods and out to her trailer in McGregor today. We're going to find something.

"But the problem is this. Why would she cop to another crime? Admit to a first-degree murder. She wouldn't. She'd get life without parole. There is no reason in the world she would take a deal, at least not on the surface. Maybe a profiler could give us something, but we can't get someone here fast enough. Not before we interrogate her, and our leverage with Clayton is happening now. Before the trial is over, while it's ongoing and he can't predict the outcome. Clayton is still our best hope to get Ginger."

Walking back to his sofa, Tate sunk down in it. His friend and colleague may be tired, but he was laying it out like sugar road. It was Gavin's turn to stand and do the pacing as Tate took the baton. "We have to get Clayton to give Ginger to us. He doesn't know what's happening with her right now. He doesn't know she's been arrested for attempting to murder a witness. If we tell him Ginger is in the next cell and willing to sing, confess to Penny's murder and testify to Clayton's masterminding it all if we drop the charges on the attempts, then what will Clayton do?"

Gavin nodded his head. "He might believe it. Next, we tell him that the first one to confess gets the deal. We're offering it to both of them. The first one who spills gets five to ten years shaved off their sentence. That's a big deal. We make sure they understand that the deal's on the table today, and today only. Before the trial resumes tomorrow. Before Petunia Macchi gets on the stand and tells the jury she overheard Clayton conspiring with a woman to kill his wife.

"If they take the deals, Clayton and Ginger, they each get twenty years for the murder and nothing on the attempts. Is it good enough?"

Tate put his head back and took a deep breath. He let it out, exhausted and frustrated. "No. It's not good enough, but I think it's the best we're going to get."

"You don't think we should discuss this with the Macchis before we go for a deal? They might be really pissed we're offering Ginger a pass." Gavin raised a questioning brow.

"No. We're doing what needs to be done. Sometimes the victims don't get the justice they deserve, but we do all we can. The Macchis would have helped to build a case for a kick-ass prosecution, though. I liked your thought about a profiler."

Tate felt that nugget percolate. Something was there.

"Who do we approach first?" Gavin was saying. "I might be able to get a delay in trial, but we gotta make something happen today."

Tate looked at his friend, a smile creasing his face. "You know what? I've got an idea on how to play this. And I know exactly who to call." He stood up. "We're going to need some better coffee."

Chapter 53

Late that afternoon, Charlotte and Alex went down the elevator and walked toward the hotel conference room to meet with Social Services. Renzo would stay with the girls.

As they got off the elevator, Alex said, "I wonder what's happening at the jail."

The thought of the plan going down upset and worried her too, but right now, she had to focus on Violet. Social Services had asked that Violet be present for the meeting, but until she and Alex understood the situation, they'd begin without her. The poor girl didn't need any more stress.

Entering the small conference room, Charlotte saw two women seated at the table, their heads together. They looked up all big-eyed and stood to greet them.

Monica Gilstad and Gloria Marshall were seasoned professionals, having worked with family victims and children for many years. They claimed there was no longer much that surprised them, but in this case, the circumstances were extraordinary.

After introductions and pleasantries were out of the way, Monica said, "Violet Krueger must have adult supervision, either through the foster care system, or from a family member or friend. After Penny Krueger's death, when Clayton was arrested for the murder, we reached out to the few relatives on both sides. Sadly, there was no one either appropriate or willing to take in Violet. When no other friends or family stepped forward, we were relieved when Ginger Krueger volunteered to manage her support. Now, Ginger is out of the picture, but if Clayton Krueger is found innocent, custody would automatically be returned to him."

They sat digesting that unacceptable outcome. She and Alex had already put that piece together. The only reason they would agree to have the attempted murder charges dropped, was to ensure that Clayton would lose custody.

Monica continued. "In the meantime, until the trial ends, we can award you an emergency temporary arrangement of custody, assuming you're interested in taking responsibility for Violet."

Charlotte gave Alex a short look, but quickly answered, "Of course. We'll take care of her."

"Mr. Macchi? How do you feel about taking responsibility for Violet Krueger?" Monica pressed.

"She's been through too much already. My family and I will take care of her, and we'll get her any help she needs. But we don't live in Minnesota, and we'll be leaving for New York as soon as the county attorney allows. Hopefully, tomorrow. So how do we make that work? Can we take Violet with us?"

"Yes. We can make that happen. We'll be in touch with the state of New York as the receiving state. They'll conduct a home study on you, assuring themselves that Violet will be emotionally and adequately provided for. They'll make a recommendation back to us, and if approved, you can legally become Violet's foster parents and she can reside with you in New York."

"If you really want her," Gloria inserted.

"But if Clayton walks," Charlotte said, ignoring Gloria, "we'll need to bring her back?"

Monica shook her head. "Despite my own personal beliefs about his guilt, I'm afraid so. If he's found not guilty, then he's innocent and Violet is his daughter."

Gloria piped in. "We'll check on her from time to time."

Charlotte opened her mouth, ready with words of rage, but stopped herself in the nick of time. The thought of the young girl living with her murdering father was too much. "Would it really be in Violet's best interest to live with a man—granted, her father—whom she believes killed her mother? Living a short distance from the site of her mother's murder? In a small town filled with people who will suspect that Clayton is the murderer and possibly shun the family for life? What about Ginger Krueger? When she goes on trial for attempting to murder a witness, won't that add to the negative notoriety? Wouldn't it be better for everyone concerned if Violet were given an opportunity to get away from all her murdering relatives and a town where no one has the decency to take her in? Won't she feel the ridicule and become hardened and bitter? She's struggling right now—with confusion and almost no hope."

She glanced at Alex before continuing. "What that child has gone through is obscene. All you need to do is look in her eyes—she's in there, scared to death. She's grieving for her mother. She's going to hate her father. And she's going to withdraw ever further inward. But she wants to be loved and feel safe, and she deserves that. I think Penny Krueger would want her daughter to be given a chance at a normal life. We all know Clayton and Ginger Krueger planned and murdered Penny. You can't tell me that Violet, if the world stops spinning and Clayton walks, would be better off living with him at the Backwoods."

"No, Mrs. Macchi," said Gloria, "perhaps not. But it's not up to us. We'll just have to hope that the truth comes out in a Minnesota court of law."

Monica glanced at her colleague and took over. "If Clayton *is* convicted, I don't see any reason why you couldn't become Violet's full-time foster parents. Assuming you were interested in that position—not in a temporary capacity, but long term?"

"If Clayton is convicted," said Charlotte, "we'll adopt her."

There was silence around the table as the social workers glanced at each other. "Mrs. Macchi," said Monica, "we all agree, she's been through enough, but I think it's time we speak with Violet. We need to explain the options to her, and I sincerely hope your commitment to her helps."

Charlotte stood up from the table, ready for them to go upstairs to see Violet. Once outside the room, she stopped and pulled Alex aside. She kept her voice low. "I'm so sorry, Alex. I know we didn't talk it over, not really, but I hope it's okay with you, what I said in there?"

He gave her a small smile, her heart melting with the compassion in his eyes.

"It's more than okay. It reminds me why I love you. You have a generous heart and a commitment to do the right thing. I think you're wonderful."

She held him, beyond relieved, and heard Monica, not too far out of earshot, say, "Violet Krueger may have a bright future ahead of her after all."

Chapter 54

Gilbert stood before the interrogation room window in the sheriff's office, looking for the first time at the wretched face of Clayton Krueger. Clayton didn't know he was being observed. Well, he might know—the man glanced at his side of the one-way mirror often enough—but he'd never guess that a security guy from New York who'd moved into his life was staring back.

Gavin Stewart said, "You know what to do. It's time."

Gilbert turned from the window and looked at Sheriff Becker and Gavin Stewart. It wasn't going to be easy, but he'd give it his best shot.

Sheriff Becker led the way out of the room, and they stopped in front of the door to the room next door. The sheriff waved Gilbert forward, encouraging him to enter alone. "It's hot in there. We turned up the heat."

Gilbert opened the door and looked straight into Clayton's eyes. The murderer, shackled to the floor with a cuff around his ankle, sat behind an empty, unmovable table, which was secured into a utility-colored green wall under the one-way mirror. He was long, lean, and looking pale, almost washed out in his orange county jailhouse uniform.

"Who the fuck are you?" Clayton grunted.

The room didn't exactly smell like what they say fear smells like—whatever that is—but it did reek of unwashed body odor, and it wasn't coming from Gilbert. He lifted his arm, his T-shirt tight on his bicep, and smelled his own pit.

"Nope. Not me."

Clayton had a two-day beard. Gilbert rubbed his own clean-shaven face, realizing how good it felt.

"How you doing, Clayton?"

"What do you want?"

Gilbert crossed his husky arms and paced near the table. He knew Ginger was down the hall, her lawyer on standby after the initial visit. Gilbert didn't know who he'd rather face down, Clayton or Ginger. If asked, he knew he could kill them both.

"Ahh," he sighed loudly pulling up a chair. "It's decision time, dumb ass."

"Decision time for what?"

Sheriff Becker's bright idea to bring in a profiler had been floated past Alex earlier that morning. On the off chance that the ever-resourceful Macchis may have access to one on short notice, Alex, once sold on the idea, upped the ante proposing that after a consultation with his person, they send Gilbert in to cut a deal with Clayton.

And so, here Gilbert sat, the smell of a killer's stink in his nostrils, his own head full of shit from the profiler telling him what a person like Ginger Krueger was made of. He had to transfer that shit to Clayton and make it stick. Clayton was not aware of last night's events, or the fact that Ginger had been arrested.

"My name is Gilbert Gorsky. I'm here to give you some news."

"Are you a cop?"

Gilbert pursed his lips and shook his head. "Nope. Not a cop. I may be too stupid to be a cop." He winked at Clayton and watched the man's head jerk back in surprise as Gilbert let out a loud whoop of laughter while slapping the table.

"Ah, sorry, Clayton. Didn't mean to scare ya," Gilbert said. "No, the fact is that I've been living your life. Ever since you've been here, ever since Ginger moved into the Backwoods, into your old bedroom, doing God knows what between those sheets, I've been living there too."

Clayton relaxed and settled back a bit. "Oh, you're *that* guy. I heard about you from Ginger. What the fuck are you doing in here?"

"Like I said, I got news."

"Then fucking spit it out! Did something happen to Ginger or Violet?"

Nodding, Gilbert said, "You could say that. But let me ask you a question. Are you and Ginger doing something cousins shouldn't be doing? And a follow-up, how the hell do you manage to finish the job with Ginger's sick, ugly face staring back at you? When you kiss, do you taste lingering bits of Cheetos through the thick layer of tobacco on her tongue?" He licked his lips. "Yum."

Clayton leaned back. "I didn't sleep with Ginger."

Gilbert's eyes popped wide. "Really? That's not what she says. She once told me you two were going at it every night for like a week straight at her trailer in McGregor. That you two have been lovers going way back to when you were little kids."

"That's a lie," Clayton said, his color rising.

He raised his hands. "Just repeating what the sick fuck told me, Clayton. I can't control her twisty, beady imagination any more than you can."

"What is going on here?" Clayton gnashed his teeth at the two-way glass.

"Okay, okay." Gilbert patted the air. "I'll tell ya. Last night, Ginger was arrested for attempted murder."

Clayton's eyes flashed surprise as Gilbert jerked his thumb toward the door. "Yup. She's down the hall. Puking up a bunch of nasty shit, last I heard. Vodka, Cheetos, queso, Twizzlers, God knows what else. I'm sure it don't smell too good down there either."

"I don't believe you," Clayton said, licking his teeth, his mouth smacking dry.

"You better believe it. She's got that mop of burnt-out white hair sticking up every which way, trying like hell to look like her favorite character, Skyler White. My God, what a mess. It's always about *her*, isn't it?" he said, cocking his head as he asked the question. "She's a real package of twist. Narcissistic as all get-out, conniving, self-indulgent, sprung tight on a rotating diet of pills, alcohol, and lard. She's *unstable*, man. Completely manic. I even looked stuff up. She has something called *egodystonic* behavior. It means that her behavior isn't in line with her goals. No kidding, right? You should have seen her last night when they arrested her. They had to put her in a straitjacket. She was un-fucking-hinged."

"Who the hell did she try to kill?"

"My boss." Gilbert said, deadpan.

"And just who the fuck is your boss?"

"Alex Macchi. Owns Macchi & Macchi Security out of Manhattan, London, LA, all over the place. I'm his employee, flown in on a private jet specially, to step into your horrid, hell-made life and spy on Ginger. Who, at your command, murdered your sweet wife, Penny."

Clayton wiped at his mouth, his eyes blinking.

"Yup," Gilbert continued. "I've been secretly watching and listening to Ginger's every move. My God, some days I didn't think I'd make it without strangling her, but I kept my cool. I'm not a murderer. That's your department."

"I didn't murder Penny!" Clayton screamed.

Gilbert hit the table. "You planned it. Ginger did it. You're both to blame. Now Ginger's been arrested for trying to murder a witness, and you know who that is too. A fucking *Carrows*, man. She went up against one of the most powerful families in the world, and let me tell you something, they don't mess around. Anything the prosecution needs to get Ginger thrown down a hole forever is coming their way. the Backwoods? Forget about it. One way or another, the Carrows will get it, and they'll throw a match on it and watch it burn to the ground. For the rest of your life, and Ginger's too, they'll do whatever it takes to make your life a living hell."

Clayton twisted in his seat as beads of sweat appeared on his forehead.

"They'll reach right into your prison!" Gilbert challenged. "Your cellmates. *Hey, you need an extra hundred grand? I got a job for you.* I'm telling you, Clayton, the Carrows are merciless. There's Sicilian blood there. And here's the thing. Ginger fucked up yesterday. She tried to kill them, but it didn't work. Her goal to protect you didn't line up with her decision-making skills. *Egodystonic* behavior. She was all over the map, and we got her."

Clayton dropped his head, his hands in his pits, squeezing himself, holding it together.

Gilbert pressed on. "Ginger's down the hall. She's got two counts of premeditated first-degree attempted murder hanging over her head. And the county attorney, anxious as hell to get her to roll over on *you*, will *cut her a deal* to do it."

Clayton's head snapped up. His eyes bulged.

"She's a psychological deviant, Clayton, a narcissist. She has problems sustaining relationships, she has no ability to feel remorse or guilt or empathy. She's *abnormal*. You know it and I know it. I've lived with the bitch, listening to her constant whining over *her* needs. *'When is someone going to take care of me?'* There is no chance in the world she's not going to take care of herself today. She's going to crack, Clayton, and she's going to point her stubby little finger at you."

His eyes closed, Clayton said with a thick tongue. "I need a drink. It's hot in here."

Gilbert sat back and crossed his arms. "Can't do it, Clayton. Not until you tell me the truth. Gavin Stewart, he said first one to crack and tell on the other gets a deal. Only the first one, Clayton. Tick. Tick. Tock. The clock's a tickin'. The walls are closing in. There's no clean air to breathe, you bastard. It's decision time."

Clayton placed his head down on his arms on the table.

Gilbert leaned over and whispered, "Bibbidi Bobbidi Boo, your Ginger came unglued. It's over, dickhead."

Chapter 55

Charlotte and Alex rested their heads on the luxurious leather seats of the private aircraft and listened while Petunia enthusiastically regaled Violet with details about her upcoming life. Violet, experiencing her first flight, alternately looked out the window and at Petunia while she listened too.

"Oh my God, you are just going to love Blue. And Lily! She'll be happy to see you. Let me tell you a little bit about our butler, Havish Khan. He lives with us too. Well, he's really more of a majordomo, but he kinda runs the house. He's sooo nice. You're going to love him too. You can ask him anything. Really. He's very approachable. He may come across as all straight-backed and formal, but underneath it, I'm telling you, he's a marshmallow. Did you ever see that movie with Shirley Temple, *The Little Princess?* He kinda reminds me of that guy, that Indian guy who lived across the attic from her and surprised her with food and clothes. Except Havish doesn't have a beard or wear a turban. So, I'm not sure which bedroom you'll want, but I was thinking the one across the hall from me. It doesn't have a window, but it's got this cool attic-y kind of vibe, really cozy. I'll bet Mom would let you decorate it any way you want."

Alex reached down and picked up her hand. He gave it a squeeze, and she turned her head to smile at him. They were happy, but worried. They knew that Violet was going to have a difficult time. Like a victim with post-traumatic stress, she would most likely suffer through some very dark times. Adjusting to her new life and dealing with her grief would be full-time jobs and a battle not easily won.

They'd stayed in town long enough for Clayton Krueger to break. Gilbert had gotten him to take the deal and give up Ginger. He'd agreed to testify against Ginger at her trial for murdering Penny. For that alone, Ginger would go away for life. Clayton, on the other hand, had agreed to fifteen years. His lawyer didn't need to convince him it was a good deal.

"Do you have a lot of friends?" Violet asked.

"Sure. I can't wait to introduce you to them, and my cousins." Petunia answered. "My grandparents are going to flip. And my Grandma Macchi, you're going to loooovvvve her. We go there every Sunday for dinner. Well, most Sundays, and the whole Macchi family gathers, and we sit at this really long table, and the food. Oh my God, the food! It just keeps coming and coming and coming, and you leave there like soooo full. But my cousins are great. Andria, she's closest to our age, she's like my best friend in the world She's going to love you. Oh my God! I can't wait for you to see Whispering Cliffs. In California, my grandparents live in this big house by the sea. It's so dreamy. Here, let me show you some pictures, and—oh, look, here's a picture I painted for my Grandpa Carrows of Whispering Cliffs, but

I did it when I was younger so it's not as good as the stuff I can do now. Hey? Did you want to go to painting class with me? Do you like to draw or paint? I'm sure they'll have something at the studio that you'll love. You're creative like me."

Petunia stopped to draw a breath and the two girls looked out the window of the plane, talking about the clouds. Then Petunia continued. "I think it was meant to be that we become sisters, Violet. After all, we're both named after flowers. Do you think your mom knew that? She knew somehow that she needed to name you Violet, so we would recognize each other when we met?"

Charlotte squeezed Alex's hand, her eyes watering at the sentiment. She heard Violet respond.

"She always told me that she wanted to name me after something beautiful, and that violets symbolized love."

Charlotte leaned over and made eye contact with Violet, whose eyes were shimmering with tears too. In that moment, Charlotte thought she looked a lot like her mother, Penny. Gazing at the sad, beautiful young girl, she gave her an encouraging smile.

Lying her head once more on the headrest, Charlotte closed her eyes and made a solemn vow to Penny Krueger. *For as long as I live, I'll look after your daughter. Until you're together again.*

Enjoy more of the Carrows Family Chronicles . . .
coming soon! Keep informed by subscribing to
Annabelle's newsletter.

About the Author

Annabelle Lewis is a pseudonym for the author who lives in Minneapolis with her husband, children, and a wild thug of a dog who sleeps beside her. Sign up for her fun, monthly newsletters and giveaways.

https://www. theannabellelewis.com
https://www.goodreads.com/author/show/17868884.Annabelle_Lewis
https://www.amazon.com/author/annabellelewis
https://www.instagram.com/alewisauthor
https://www. twitter.com/alewisauthor
https://www.facebook.com/annabellelewisauthor

Thank you for your reviews and support!